Dream Searchers

The Seekers of the Spirit

First published by O Books, 2009

O Books is an imprint of John Hunt Publishing Ltd., The Bothy, Deershot Lodge, Park Lane, Ropley, Hants, SO24 0BE, UK

office1@o-books.net

www.o-books.net

Distribution in:

UK and Europe
Orca Book Services
orders@orcabookservices.co.uk
Tel: 01202 665432 Fax: 01202 666219
Int. code (44)

USA and Canada
NBN
custserv@nbnbooks.com
Tel: 1 800 462 6420 Fax: 1 800 338 4550

Australia and New Zealand
Brumby Books
sales@brumbybooks.com.au
Tel: 61 3 9761 5535 Fax: 61 3 9761 7095

Far East (offices in Singapore, Thailand, Hong Kong, Taiwan)
Pansing Distribution Pte Ltd
kemal@pansing.com
Tel: 65 6319 9939 Fax: 65 6462 5761

South Africa
Alternative Books
altbook@peterhyde.co.za
Tel: 021 555 4027 Fax: 021 447 1430

Text copyright Andrey Reutov 2008

Design: Stuart Davies

ISBN: 978 1 84694 214 3

A CIP catalogue record for this book is available from the British Library.

Printed by CPI Antony Rowe, Chippenham, UK

O Books operates a distinctive and ethical publishing philosophy in all areas of its business, from its global network of authors to production and worldwide distribution.

This book is produced on FSC certified stock, within ISO14001 standards. The printer plants sufficient trees each year through the Woodland Trust to absorb the level of emitted carbon in its production.

Dream Searchers

The Seekers of the Spirit

Andrey Reutov

BOOKS

Winchester, UK
Washington, USA

CONTENTS

Prologue

A man was walking along a narrow mountain path. It seemed he wasn't in any hurry; it seemed stranger still as dusk was gradually enveloping the world. Even in daylight, these places were dangerous to walk, but to venture out here at night... Raindrops came falling down from the low stormy sky, a sharp gust of wind threatened to throw the lonely traveler off his path into the abyss. He was walking with his head stubbornly bowed, and the raindrops beating against his face evoked nothing but a scornful smile on his face. He was still young, yet the features of his face and his stern gaze spoke of power. The traveler swayed on the edge of a steep hill, then froze at the sound that came from somewhere a bit ahead and above him. A couple of meters away, a rockslide came crashing down the hillside and blocked the mountain path – a few pebbles touched his leg. The traveler only grinned.

"And that's all you can do?" he asked, addressing God knows who. Having passed the boulder laying flat in the middle of the path, he calmly walked on.

It was quickly getting dark and the rare raindrops had gradually turned into a real heavy shower. The traveler's clothes got soaked through, but he seemingly didn't even notice. His face still expressed the same dogged resolve as before.

It was already pitch dark when the traveler reached the peaks of the pass. It was impossible to comprehend how he managed to make out anything at all in this total darkness. There was a big platform on the peaks, open to every passing wind. To the left of the platform was a steep climb leading to a fathomless pit, while to the right, chipped rocky ledges reaching up to the skies. The traveler went out to the middle of the platform and stopped. He turned his face to the wind that had just broken out of a mountain crack, raised his arms and burst out in rolling laughter.

"Well, here I am!" he shouted, his words got instantly caught by the wind and carried away. "You see, there's no one else here, only you and I. Come on, show yourself! You can hear me, I know!"

A bolt of lightning crashed through the air, and the traveler was thrown onto the cliffs. For a few moments, he was lying still, but then he moved. He slowly raised himself a little, ran his hand over his face, wiping off the rain mixed with his blood – there was a lacerated wound on his cheek. Finally, he got up on his legs, looked up and grinned.

"And that's it?" the traveler asked with mockery in his voice. "I expected more of you. Well, come on! Show me what you can do! Come on then!"

New bolts of lightning didn't take long to appear, and it was a real fury of fire. The traveler was standing with his arms spread wide, looking up with a fierce grin; the gusts of fire danced and coiled around him like blue snakes. It seemed an inevitable death awaited the madman, but strangely enough, the deadly discharges passed him by. This continued for more than a minute then the last rush of wind struck his face and everything stopped.

He was standing motionless with his arms still stretched out and with his face under the pouring rain. The roar of thunder was still ringing in his ears. But then he moved, and slowly took his arms down. Once again, a grin distorted the shape of his lips.

"So why didn't you kill me?" the traveler asked mockingly. "You are so powerful! Go on, kill me! Burn me, crush me, grind me into dust! Show your power!"

Again, a deafening lightening rumbled and the electrical discharge pierced a stone by the traveler's feet. He only grinned.

"What? Can't make up your mind? Don't have the guts? And that's all because we both know the truth. You and I. You are almighty – I am worthless. You are immortal – my century is like an instant. It doesn't cost you a thing to kill me – yet not even you are capable of changing me. You cannot make me obey you. And that is the root of your hatred towards me. You robbed me of everything I had. You've killed the people I loved. You've mutilated my body, but my spirit remains free of your power. Now you only have to kill me and thus admit to your loss. And how does that feel, to suffer a defeat? How about it, almighty?" The traveler let out a chuckle. "Never happened to lose to a human before?"

A gush of wind broke out of the abyss and whipped the traveler's face. In that moment another rumble of thunder went through the air. A huge piece of cliff crashed down behind the traveler, missing him by a hair.

The traveler calmly turned around, glanced at the rock lying behind his back. Then he once again stubbornly jerked up his head.

"Not very convincing," he said, grinning. "What's the point in crumbling cliffs if you cannot kill me?" The traveler defiantly spat on the ground.

There was no answer. The rain kept coming down, the wind continued blowing, and yet something had changed.

"Cat got your tongue?" the traveler asked. "That's right. And if you've got nothing to say to that, then just get out of my life, because you have no power over me. Do you understand me?" The traveler clenched his fists and threw his arms in the air. "You've got no power over me!"

~

Part 1
The Spirit Seekers

~

Chapter One

The Mysterious Stranger

The Siberian Fall is always early. Having lived for three years in the South, Maxim was no longer used to such early colds, and that's why every now and then the piercing wind made him shiver and regret that he didn't bring warmer clothes. And even though he bought a knitted cap three days ago, he did not want to spend money on a warmer jacket – he would be home by Sunday anyway.

The clock on the main building of the central station was six in the morning. It was Moscow time, so the local time is plus three, or exactly nine in the morning. Maxim had set his wrist watch on Moscow time already yesterday, as it was more convenient when traveling. Thus, there was more than four hours left until departure of his train...

If it had been a different situation, Maxim would probably not have gone this early to the railway station. But Andrei, Maxim's friend, at whose place Maxim was staying for the last week, couldn't see him to the station. He was working today, and he didn't manage to get permission to leave. Maxim wasn't offended – things like that happen. They said their goodbyes an hour ago, having given each other a friendly hug, and went their separate ways. Andrei went to work, hoping that his boss wouldn't sense the smell of alcohol – they had a good time yesterday – and Maxim went to the railway station, wrapping himself up in his favorite, but oh so thin, jeans jacket.

He got to the station in no time. Having checked the schedule and made sure that his train was still there, he went outside, and that's where he was now standing, thinking about what to do with his spare time. Theoretically, he could even go to the movies, he really had a lot of time on his hands. But they usually show only children's movies at this time of the day.

Maxim never went to the movies. He was strolling along the sidewalk for a while, but then a sign of an internet café caught his eyes. That wasn't a bad idea. Maxim hadn't been online for nine days. Would be nice to check if there's anything new...

And so it happened that Maxim opened the door to this particular establishment on that cold September morning. Moreover, he even turned out to be the very first customer – the café had just opened for the day. Having chatted for a couple of minutes with the female owner of the internet café, a pretty young woman, Maxim paid for an hour online and went to the computer the young woman had pointed out for him...

About half an hour went by. During that time, Maxim checked everything he wanted to check and was now just surfing the internet, trying to find something interesting with the help of search engines. There were more people now, but the café was still half-empty. Maxim was just opening another webpage when he felt a hand on his shoulder.

It was a man about thirty years of age. The first thing Maxim noticed about him was the scar, running across his right cheek, and only later did he notice his piercing grey eyes. Maxim thought he sensed some kind of tension in the appearance of this man.

"Sorry," the stranger said, shamelessly pushing him away from the computer. "I need immediate access to the internet. Take this..." He slipped a hundred ruble bill into Maxim's hand and forced him out of the chair all together.

"But there are plenty of empty places," Maxim said, somewhat taken aback by such impudence. But the man didn't hear him; his fingers were already running across the keyboard. Maxim was standing next to him, confused, squeezing the money in his hand and not knowing what to do, his eyes automatically watching the computer screen. The man opened a webpage and entered a password – Maxim could not catch the quick movements of his fingers, therefore the password remained unknown.

It turned out to be a forum of some kind. The stranger opened one of the topics in a new window, hastily jotted down a few lines in a little window that popped up below then quickly glanced in the direction of the door, above the partition separating the rows of computers. Maxim followed his gaze and saw a couple of people come in – or rather, burst into the salon, – there were at least five of them. They had different clothes, but their actions seemed to be well coordinated. One person remained by the front door, the second went up to the owner of the salon. And the remaining three headed determinedly for the stranger, cutting off all exits.

"Talk of the devil," the man mumbled. He quickly hit the 'Send' button then, having opened the main forum page, hit the 'Block Nickname' button located in the very bottom of the webpage. Then he got up, grabbing Maxim by his jacket in the process, and with a jerk planted him on the chair. All of this happened in mere seconds. What astounded Maxim were the monstrous power of the stranger and the odd smoothness of his movements. In these moments he reminded Maxim of an element of nature coming to life.

Maxim didn't know what was going on. But when one of the people hurrying towards them took out a gun, he realized: all of this is very, very serious. He turned around – the stranger was quickly retreating towards the wall, Maxim caught a strange detachment in his face. It seemed in his mind, this man was in a completely different place. The persecutor was already hugging the trigger, Maxim heard someone's frightened yell – and then something happened that made the skin on his back crawl. The air around the stranger stirred, the man took a step forward and disappeared…

It could not have been real. But it was not a dream either – with a clang, two black long pins punctured the wall where the stranger was standing just a moment ago. There were thin wires attached to the pins. Only now did Maxim realize that the persecutors were not armed with guns, but with some kind of electroshock taser gun.

"He got away," he heard the irritated cry of one of the persecutors. As in a dream Maxim turned to the monitor. A moment later he was drawn out of the chair for the second time. And if the first time it was done insistently, then now Maxim was simply pulled out by his collar and thrown on the floor. One of the persecutors – apparently, the person in charge – grabbed the mouse with his huge paw, opened the window with the stranger's message, which immediately appeared on the forum webpage. Having carefully read the text, he balefully banged his fist on the table.

"Damn it! He gave them a warning." He gave Maxim a gloomy look – all this time Maxim had been obediently lying on the floor – the man turned around and firmly headed for the exit. The members of his team followed. The front door slammed and it got very quiet.

"Did you see that?" a frightened female voice was heard in the silence. "He disappeared." It was a young woman speaking, about seventeen years old. It was her scream Maxim heard earlier.

"Who disappeared?" someone asked.

"That guy. He stepped away to the wall, and then... disappeared."

"I don't know," someone responded. "I didn't notice anything at all. Were they looking for someone?"

"You saw him, didn't you?" The young woman looked at Maxim demandingly. "He did sit in your spot!"

She was obviously on the verge of a breakdown. Having already gotten himself up from the floor, Maxim brushed off his pants, then glanced at the young woman and gave an affirmative nod.

"Yes, I saw him. He walked away to the wall, and then silently made his way to the exit. They didn't notice him."

He didn't know what made him lie. Perhaps, Maxim simply felt sorry for this young woman. Having experienced something like that one could end up in a nuthouse alright.

"But that cannot be!" the woman objected. "I saw him – he disappeared!"

Apparently, apart from Maxim, she was the only one who noticed the disappearance of the stranger.

"He went out the door." Maxim repeated insistently then he sat down in a chair and looked intently into the computer, thereby making it clear that that was the end of discussion.

The young woman didn't say anything. She turned around and quickly left, remembering to slam the door with a bang.

Honestly speaking, Maxim didn't feel any better than the young woman – it is not every day that you witness a miracle. And this miracle was somehow connected to the webpage of an internet forum that was right there, right before his eyes. Now Maxim could read the stranger's message without let or hindrance. It turned out to be one line short:

"The hunt has begun; the catchers are on the field. We are pulling out!!!"

Below was a signature: "Sly."

When Maxim touched the computer mouse, he could feel his arm shaking. Still, Maxim felt curiosity rise in his chest and he couldn't wait to see the other forum messages. There were only two on this page, including that of the stranger. Maxim read the first message – and it didn't make any sense. This is how it went:

"Ilya, you've got it all right. But bear in mind that your actions must follow the course of the flow of power. If you fall out of the flow, the chain won't come together. Therefore, pay careful attention to the series of events, registering events of the right suit; by doing that, you will keep the chain within the limits of the flow."

The current webpage was the eighth. Perhaps, the previous

pages would shed more light. Unfortunately, Maxim was unable to view them: as he attempted to browse the other pages, he was asked to enter a password. Maxim remembered then that the stranger had time to block his nickname – apparently that was what was now stopping Maxim from viewing the other pages.

Maxim didn't know the password. The rest of the time he tried to fathom the secrets of the stranger and his friends, yet all his tricks got him nowhere. Unfortunately, Maxim was a rookie in the computer business and he didn't have the necessary experience for this situation. The only thing left for him to do was to take down the forum link. Maxim was hoping that he could sort all of this out once he got home.

Before leaving – his time online was coming to an end – Maxim erased the link to the interesting forum from the browser history, he didn't want it to catch someone's eye...

It was still windy outside. Maxim put his cap on, so that it covered his ears, threw the strap of his bag across his shoulder and made his way to the central station. He couldn't stop thinking about what he had seen. He could feel a breath of secrecy in everything that had happened. And the key to these secrets - in the form of a link to an Internet forum, written down on a pad - was now in his pocket.

The way home took almost three days. Maxim had time to carefully think about everything that had happened. Now he knew that he really had encountered something supernatural, all Maxim's attempts of finding some reasonable explanation to the stranger's disappearance didn't hold water. True, he was able to calm down that young woman, having said that that strange man simply walked out and his disappearance was just an optical illusion. But Maxim couldn't fool himself: the stranger vanished right before his eyes. And the closer Maxim was getting to home, the stronger was the curiosity rising in him.

Home greeted him with peace and quiet. For more than three years now, Maxim had been renting a one room apartment in a quiet dormitory neighborhood of Rostov. Maxim moved to this southern town right after graduating from the university. Unfortunately, so far he had been unsuccessful in making use of the knowledge he got at his Alma mater. His diploma had been collecting dust in the closet for more than three years now, and the only thing reminding him of his biology degree were the plants on the windowsills. When leaving, Maxim watered them thoroughly, hoping that, being in this half-drowned state, the plants would successfully manage to survive his absence. And that's what happened. Maxim filled a water jug and watered the plants, and only then did he draw a sigh of relief. He was home…

Maxim swapped the unaccomplished career of a scientist for the job of a TV repairman. Fortunately, he had the forethought to complete the necessary courses. Having worked almost a year at one of the town's TV repair shops, Maxim became a free agent – he didn't like being bossed around. It didn't go too well at first, but then business picked up. There were enough orders; Maxim placed his ads in every issue of a popular weekly newspaper. Basically, he could survive, and only when looking at the plants did sadness creep into his heart…

The mysterious vanishing act of the stranger really intrigued him. He had always taken a keen interest in all kinds of other-worldly nonsense, and even though he didn't believe in it much, one couldn't say he didn't believe in it at all. In that sense Maxim was no different to most people who like mysterious tales that make their flesh creep. And here for the first time he got to see a miracle – a real miracle, a miracle that Maxim witnessed himself. It was no longer some old wives' tales – Maxim saw this man disappear with his own eyes. There was a secret, so no wonder that, having taken a bath and quickly finished his dinner, Maxim immediately glued himself to his computer.

Alas, he was in for a harsh disappointment; when trying to access the link written down in his notepad, there was a '404 error' message. And that meant that there was simply no such

Internet resource...

The disappointment was truly great. Maxim spent the entire evening at the computer, using different ways of trying to open the sacred webpage. He changed letters and numbers; he had almost convinced himself that he made a mistake when writing down the address. Unfortunately, no matter what he tried, it was of no help. It was almost midnight when Maxim admitted to his defeat. True, there was still a faint hope that after a while the forum would open after all. And nevertheless, Maxim realized that all his hopes were completely in vain. It was all pretty clear: the stranger had warned his colleagues of danger, and they covered up their trail.

Maxim went to bed in the most depressed mood. And he had a reason to feel this way – the mystery had lured him and disappeared, leaving him feeling empty and despondent.

In the morning, Maxim went to the editorial office of the newspaper and put up his ad for the upcoming week then he dropped into one of the little shops selling parts for foreign brand TV sets. Having bought what he needed, he returned home and once again got in front of the computer. He didn't believe that the ill-fated webpage would open, and indeed, that is what happened. Although, this morning he got another remote possibility – Maxim thought that he should write to Andrey and tell him about what happened. Perhaps he'd be able to find the man with a scar on his cheek. How? That Maxim didn't know. But Andrey had always showed great analytical skill, and Maxim believed he could come up with something. Besides, the stranger had a distinctive mark – a visible scar on his right cheek. That's already something to go by.

Maxim had plenty of time, so he spent more than an hour writing the letter, several times erasing and changing what he had written. Finally, pleased with the end result, he sent the letter by email.

Gloomy days followed. Maxim was impatiently waiting for

Andrey's reply, but there was none. More than a week passed until the long-awaited email finally arrived in Maxim's inbox.

Sadly, Andrey didn't get excited about the suggestion to find the man with the scar. And even though his friend tactfully refrained from doubting the truthfulness of the story, Maxim had the feeling that Andrey didn't believe him. And Maxim understood him very well – perhaps, he would have behaved exactly the same way had Andrey told him something like that. Unfortunately, we no longer believe in miracles…

Time went by. Days turned into weeks, weeks into months. Maxim celebrated the new year of 2002 with new friends, yet he still didn't feel happy. The feeling that he had missed the chance to touch the mystery haunted him…

Spring was early in the new year; by mid-March it was already really warm outside. Maxim was still repairing TV sets, but more often he got to thinking of leaving this business. His heart wasn't in it – and how can you keep doing something that you don't enjoy?

It was a Saturday morning; Maxim was going on a tram to another client. The case with spare parts, a soldering iron, a tester and other necessary junk was in his lap. The melody of a popular song was spinning in his head; Maxim was quietly tapping it out on the cover of the case. Another stop, the next one was his. Maxim cast a lazy glance at those getting on and twitched, as if struck by an electric shock. Standing a few steps away from him was the man with the scar. The very same one…

It came as a real shock to Maxim, like what he would have experienced if he saw an alien. There are no such coincidences – and still there he was, the man with the scar. He was standing, holding onto a handrail and calmly looking through the window. He was about thirty years old, or maybe, even older, with short dark blond hair and a penetrating glance of bottomless grey eyes. He was wearing a black leather jacket and blue jeans; a gold watch gleaming on his left wrist. Maxim was sitting, staring down at his case, and had no clue about what he should do next.

His stop – Maxim stayed seated. A thought was spinning in his consciousness that he should do something, that fate won't gift him another chance. Perhaps that was the reason why Maxim took a deep breath and rose from his seat. Having taken a few steps forward, he got up to the stranger, feeling his heart thumping. In that precise moment the man with the scar turned his head and looked at him – apparently, he sensed the heightened interest to his person. Now it was too late to turn back.

"Hello," said Maxim. "We met last year in Tomsk. Remember, the internet café? You gave me a hundred rubles."

In the eyes of the stranger appeared a strange mix of surprise and curiosity. He spent a few seconds examining Maxim with interest then there was a shadow of a smile.

"Hello. If stars are lit, then, there is someone who needs them. Right?"

"Yeah," Maxim agreed, although he didn't quite understand what this quote had to do with anything.

"Going far?" his companion asked.

"Just taking a ride," Maxim answered. He didn't want to have to admit that he just missed his stop.

"All the better. That's my stop. Shall we take a walk?"

"With pleasure," Maxim agreed, feeling the exultation growing in his chest. This strange man had just invited him for a walk – could Maxim even dream about something like that just an hour ago?!

The tram stopped by the Voroshilov Prospect. The man with the scar was the first one to get off, Maxim followed. The stranger was strolling along the sidewalk, heading towards the park; Maxim caught up to him and walked beside him.

"What's your name?" the man with the scar asked, breaking the silence.

"Maxim."

"I'm Boris. Maybe you've got something to ask me?" A smile slipped across the stranger's lips.

"Yes," Maxim nodded. "That last time you disappeared. And I still do not know if it really happened or if it was some kind of trick – like hypnosis or something."

"You really want to know?" Boris asked.

"I do. I wrote down the web address of the forum where you had posted your message. But I couldn't open it, the forum disappeared. Still, I am not mad, and when a man disappears right before my eyes, I'd like to know how that is possible."

"There is a difference between knowledge and knowledge," Boris sighed. "I believe you noticed that I was being chased back then?"

"I did. One of them was even shooting at you with an electro shocker."

"Then you must understand that knowledge can be dangerous. Do you need that?" Boris slightly raised his eyebrows.

"There are many dangers in life," Maxim shrugged. "You could have a car accident; you could get poisoned by eating mushrooms. But people haven't stopped driving or eating mushrooms." His companion gave a barely noticeable smile.

"Let's sit down," he said, pointing at the closest bench with a nod. There, a couple in love was billing and cooing. Maxim though it would have been better to find a vacant bench, as the couple suddenly got up and leisurely started walking away.

They sat down; Boris gave Maxim a thoughtful look.

"That we've met could hardly be called a coincidence," he said slowly. "And I think I understand why it happened." Boris grew quiet, following with his eyes a man passing by. Maxim noticed that Boris's eyes were a bit squinted. Finally, Boris looked back at him and smiled. "Well, fine… There are paths that we choose. And there are paths that choose us. Let's stop at that for now." Boris fell silent for a few seconds, pondering over something then he asked: "Do you have a phone?"

Instead of an answer, Maxim searched his pocket and silently handed Boris a business card.

"Maxim Vorontsov – fast, quality, cheap TV repairs." Boris read the business card and smiled. "Not a bad profession." He put the business card in his pocket. "Here's what we'll do: I'll call you this week. In the meantime – do some research on the net on this topic…" Having taken out of his pocket a pad and a bullet pen, Boris wrote something down on a piece of paper, then carefully tore it out. "Take this," he said, and with a smile handed Maxim the piece of paper. "I think that will clear up a few things for you. And now I'm sorry, but I must go." Boris clapped him on the shoulder, got up and calmly walked away in the direction of the underground passage. Maxim followed him with his eyes, then looked at the torn out sheet of paper. There, it was written in a small hand: 'Dream Searchers'.

What a strange word combination – confused, Maxim scratched his forehead. Searchers – that's clear. But dream searchers… It's just too weird…

For a few minutes Maxim twirled the piece of paper in his hands, thinking about whether his companion was joking, and if all of this was just a way of getting rid of him. Although, Maxim immediately rejected that thought. Boris couldn't have been fooling him; Maxim's whole impression of that person opposed it.

Having glanced in the direction of the underground passage, Maxim tried to see where Boris would surface. He was looking very carefully, watching all the exits, but he didn't see Boris. He probably missed him while studying the paper.

Only now did Maxim remember that he had to hurry back to his client - they agreed he'd come at ten, and Maxim wasn't used to being late. Having hidden the paper in his pocket and checked that the zipper was tightly closed; he picked up the case and quickly walked away to the bus stop…

That day Maxim had two orders, he got off only at about one in the afternoon. And needless to say, there was joy in his heart.

An incredible, amazing coincidence – to meet the man, he so badly wanted to find, here in Rostov, in his town!

It's not surprising that Maxim was breezing home. However, once at home he didn't rush to the computer, instead, he chose to slightly delay the longed-for minutes by having a quick snack.

But then came the sweet moment of truth. Maxim was sitting at his computer, the torn out piece of paper lying before him. Having opened his favorite search tool, Maxim entered 'Dream Searchers' in the search line and started waiting for the results.

While the search was going on, Maxim was on pins and needles – afraid that the search tool would tell him that there were no hits for the requested material. And even when a long list of links appeared, Maxim still had his doubts – he was sure that he'd simply get a bunch of links to ordinary searcher websites. Indeed, that's what happened; there were plenty of links to searcher sites. But among them, Maxim, with a beating heart, also saw the expression 'Dream Searchers'.

So, Boris wasn't lying. Now all Maxim had to do was to browse through the links, which was exactly what he did…

He continued sitting by the monitor deep into the night, downloading onto his computer all of the necessary information and going through it without hurry this time. The biggest discovery to him was that dream searchers actually existed – and wasn't he the one to know? After all, Maxim spoke with one of them just today – he no longer doubted the fact that Boris was part of the dream searcher group. In addition, the more he got acquainted with the information he found on the net, the more he realized how very fortunate he had been.

Basically, that evening Maxim got the following rough picture.

The group of dream searchers was based in the early nineties of the last century. Maxim only managed to get a very rough idea of what exactly these dream searchers did, and why they called themselves that. Apparently, dream searchers were modern magicians – the fact that Boris slipped away from his persecutors in such a mysterious way confirmed this. Maxim didn't believe in magic much before – turns out, he was wrong. As for the name of the group, it corresponded to the nature of their work and the methods they used. Dream searchers studied the world of dreams, assuming that dreams are something much greater than what we are used to thinking. What's more, they thought dreams to be a protected program of sorts, to which one could apply typical searcher methods – hence the word 'searchers' in the group's name.

Maxim turned off his computer when it was long past midnight. His head was aching from information overload and his eyes were heavy. And yet, Maxim was happy. An amazing world of magic had opened before him – a world that he couldn't even dream of. Now Maxim simply didn't understand how it could have escaped him, why he didn't come across this world before. After all, it was exactly what has been fascinating him - secrets, riddles. That is exactly why he went to study at the university. True, the scientific world didn't accept him – science is dwindling. And now, before him was an example of people that have achieved great success on their own, studying the secrets of the universe. And not just secrets – but secrets, that took your breath away thinking about them…

First thing in the morning, Maxim quickly browsed through the book stores; he needed to find the books by Carlos Castaneda. In the information about dream searchers, Maxim kept stumbling across this name – and that meant that he must read his works. Maxim assumed that Castaneda had written several books, but when he saw an impressive row of thick volumes standing on the book shelf, he felt uneasy – would he really have to read all of this?

But he wasn't going to give up. Having bought all the books by the prolific author, Maxim went home. He was happy that he didn't have a single order today. Usually it would have made him sad – but not today.

Having reached his place, Maxim laid out a pile of new books on the table, wherefrom he retrieved the first volume. Then he made himself comfortable on the sofa and started reading.

The things Castaneda wrote about shocked him. Magic was here, nearby – in order to touch it, you had only to stretch out your hand. Everything Maxim had read or heard about the world of magic now seemed to be terrible nonsense. He tore himself from reading only at four pm, and that was just to get some dinner.

Maxim finished reading the first volume in some six hours then he got in front of the computer and continued reading dream searchers' files until midnight. Then he immediately went to sleep – he felt that he had picked up more than enough information for one day…

And so it came about that Maxim spent all of his spare time reading Castaneda's books and dream searchers' files; it was the fifth day from the day when he met Boris. Maxim was reading another volume by Castaneda, when he heard the phone ring.

"Listening…" Maxim pressed the receiver to his ear, expecting the call to be from one of his clients. And he started when he heard Boris' voice.

"Hi, Maxim," he said. "It's Boris. What's up?"

"I'm reading Castaneda."

"Well done." Boris approved. Maxim sensed a grin in his voice. "How about meeting up?"

"When?" he quickly asked.

"If you are not busy, then we could meet today. Let's say, about half past five on that same bench. Would that be ok?"

"That'd fine," Maxim agreed.

"Then I'll see you later."

Boris hung up. Maxim spent a couple of minutes listening closely to the dial tone. Then he looked at his watch – it was half past four. Then, in an hour he had to be at the Voroshilovsky…

He had a habit of never being late to wherever he was going, for that reason he would come to every meeting in advance. And so this time, when Maxim got off the tram and made his way to the bench, the hand of the watch had barely passed five o'clock in the evening.

Boris hadn't arrived yet, so the remaining half hour Maxim spent simply walking in the park. When it was close to being half past five he started looking closely at the people passing by, yet Boris still appeared unexpectedly.

"Hi," he said, having shaken Maxim's hand. "Well, let's take a walk, shall we?"

"Let's," Maxim agreed and they began to walk slowly down the path.

"Have you found anything on the net?" Boris asked.

"I have," Maxim nodded in confirmation. "Are you really a dream searcher?"

"I am really a dream searcher," Boris smiled. "Only, let's be on familiar terms, ok? It will be easier that way. Among my own, I am known as Sly – if you want, you can call me that; I don't care."

"But there is nothing on the internet about you?" It was not so much of a question, as more of stating a fact. For the last few days Maxim had investigated closely the dream searchers' files, thus he knew almost all searchers and their followers. "I haven't seen that nickname."

"Not everybody knows my name, I rarely appear online. And if I do, I use a different nickname. I don't like being too popular." Boris smiled again. "Many searchers prefer not to advertise their existence at all. It's much safer that way."

"I understand," Maxim nodded. "And those people chasing you, are they from the FSS? I heard they've caused you some problems in the past."

"No, actually those people were from a different office." A grin slipped across Boris' lips. "You see, Maxim, knowledge attracts all kinds of people. Some are researchers of the unknown – we respect people like that, share information with them, accept them into our ranks. But there are also other people – those who need the knowledge of searchers to reach goals of a completely different nature. Knowledge, in this case, is like a weapon, and many are prepared to pay any price in order to get it. And when they find out that knowledge is not for sale…" Boris smiled again, "they take to completely different methods. Starting with discrediting searchers and ending with searcher hunting."

"I can understand that. Although, if one is to talk about knowledge, there is still a lot of things I don't understand. The files I found on the net are all fragmentary and incomplete. Actually, it's all a mess in my head – I don't even understand what your opinion on Castaneda is. Are you for him or against him?"

Boris grinned.

"I can guess which way the wind is blowing," he said. "Echoes of net-wars… You see; if we, say, don't care for certain followers of Castaneda, that doesn't mean that we are against Castaneda himself. Castaneda gave people knowledge – a new, unusual knowledge, and that is his great credit. So I am prepared to take off my hat before papa Carlos, even now." Boris moved his arm, taking off the inexistent hat with a playful gesture. "We don't agree only with those who reject everything that doesn't fit Castaneda's theory. The world is great; there is enough space under the sun for everyone. Then why is it that certain people are so against those with different opinions?" Boris looked at his companion; his eyebrows were raised, prompting an answer.

"I don't know," Maxim shrugged. "Perhaps, they just think they're right?"

"No," Boris shook his head. "These people are simply afraid. Afraid that someone will outstrip them – drive them back to the curb of life. And when someone is making war with searchers, then they care not about the truthfulness of knowledge but about their own wellbeing. Do you remember why Jesus was crucified? Because he was preaching something that was different from what was accepted at the time? By no means – he was crucified because he was bold enough to lead people. They would have forgiven him anything, but this - they could not. And, as in the modern industrial world, there is a war going on for the product market, as there is also a constant struggle in the world of human souls for the flock. Everyone is trying to pull the cover over onto their side."

"And searchers too?" Maxim asked.

Boris looked at him and smiled.

"Well, you see, searchers don't need anything from anybody, we are self-sufficient. As you've pointed out, finding on the net any detailed account of our methods or a more or less clear description of what it is we are actually doing is pretty difficult. And why is that? It's only because dream searchers never made it their goal to propagate their knowledge. "Communication within our circle was quite enough. Even the fact that someone found out about us was a result of a vexing coincidence. That is why, for the time being, we do not strive to 'promote' what we know – we simply leave a loophole for those, who are actually interested in it."

"But why not make your own site where you could, in a sensible and intelligible way, explain everything? I've already spent five days trying to make sense of your files and I still didn't get most of it."

"Five days – that's some time." A grin slipped across Boris's lips. "About the website: I for one do not have any interest in dealing with any website. I haven't yet met any other searcher that would be willing to waste his time doing that either. It's enough that we, from time to time, arrange workshops and upload results of investigations for open access. It's hardly likely that anyone would ask more of us. Well, and when it comes to the mess in your head, I'm ready to help you sort it out." Boris glanced at Maxim, his eyes glistened mockingly. "So you can ask me questions – if you wish."

"All right," Maxim agreed. "Then let's start from the

beginning. First question: who are dream searchers and what do they do?"

"Dream searchers are researchers of the unknown," Boris replied. "We are trying to make sense of the architecture of the universe; attempting to understand its laws. But unlike scientists, we are using a magic description of the world. A scientist operates only with what he is able to touch, measure, describe, stick a pin through and classify. A magician, as opposed to a scientist, introduces something noumenal to the common description of the world. That is, something that you cannot describe, cognize; something that you cannot in any way talk about sensibly. Castaneda calls this unknown the Nagual – a place where power resides. Thanks to the Nagual, the ordinary world becomes a magical world for a magician. And in a magical world everything is possible, starting with little things like controlling the weather and ending with things like immortality. The only existing restriction is the limits of your imagination."

"Could you name, as an example, some specific projects that searchers are working on?" Maxim enquired.

"There are plenty of such projects. Let's say, one of the groups is working on ways of controlling events in a predicted and goal-oriented fashion. They have already unearthed a few things, their methods are working wonderfully. Take a look at that bench over there." Boris stopped and with a nod pointed at a bench on their left. "Would you want for a bird to sit on it right now? Within ten seconds? Start counting. Come on, come on – don't be shy."

Boris was softly smiling, Maxim sensed a catch.

"Are you being serious?" he asked.

"Absolutely. You no longer have to count." Boris pointed back at the bench, Maxim looked at it – and started. Right in front of his eyes a sparrow flew down from a tree branch onto the back of the bench. Having jumped about on the bench for a while, the bird sat still for a few seconds, then took wing and flew away.

"Well, how do you like it?" Boris was looking curiously at

Maxim.

"Yeah, that's interesting," he agreed, and they slowly moved on. "But couldn't it have been just a coincidence?"

"It could. But in this case it was not. Would you like another example?"

"If it's possible."

"All right. In about a minute you will be approached by a man and he'll ask you the time. Will that be a convincing enough of an example?"

"Perhaps." Maxim started thinking, trying to estimate the probability of such an event. True, there's nothing supernatural about someone asking the time. But during the whole time that they were talking, no one came up to them.

"Look, he's already approaching – that guy." With a barely noticeable nod Boris pointed at a man walking down the path.

In Maxim's opinion, the chances of that particular guy asking them the time were nonexistent. Maxim even grinned – he wondered what Boris would say when this guy would walk on by.

Surprisingly enough, he didn't! Having halted a couple of meters away from them, he looked at his watch and quietly cursed – apparently, his watch had stopped.

"Sorry, could you tell me the time?" he asked, having approached Maxim. Boris was standing nearby – as if he wasn't even there.

Maxim silently showed him his watch – he was just speechless.

"Thanks." The guy nodded, and walked on, tampering with his watch.

"What do you think?" Boris looked at Maxim inquisitively.

"That's impressive," Maxim admitted. "But how can that be?"

"I just know how this world works, and I am familiar with the laws governing it. Hence, I can manipulate the reality around us. That is the knowledge of dream searchers."

Maxim was quiet for a couple of minutes, collecting his

thoughts.

"You said that this is what one of the groups does. So, there are more of them?"

"Depends on how you look at it. There are several main groups; they are composed of people who started the searcher movement – the founding-fathers." Boris grinned. "I represent one of these groups. Connected to these groups are several other groups, represented by searchers of the second generation – those, who you could call immediate successors of our tradition. Finally, there are also those who are, so far, just interested in our work, they are familiar with our published investigations. All these people are connected to us in one way or another. In some countries and cities there also are groups, working in the context of our ideas, but they are not connected to us and work independently. So, in general, there are not a whole lot of us out there."

"I see… Then I have another question, about the world of dreams: why have you chosen that particular world for your research? Can it give you anything of practical use?"

"Of course," Boris answered. They had just reached the end of an alley. They turned around and started walking back. "The thing is that the dream world allows you to find the keys to the many secrets of the universe. Usually, people view dreams as something irrelevant. Best case scenario – they try to interpret them somehow – visit any book store, there is a whole assortment of dream books. Searchers adopted a different approach."

"Namely?"

"Let's take a seat." Boris pointed at the bench nearby.

They sat down; Maxim made himself ready to listen, regretting that he didn't have a Dictaphone on him, although he never complained of deficient memory and that was comforting.

"The first thing we did was…" Boris continued, "trying to make sense of the laws at work in the world of dreams. That was a difficult, but fascinating task. So, turns out that in a dream there is always a ban on consciousness. Could you tell me what you were dreaming of today?"

"Today?" Maxim frowned. "I dreamt that I was attending a lecture then I was looking for spare TV parts in a shop. Then someone was chasing me, but I don't really remember now."

"But you knew that you were asleep?"

"No." Maxim shook his head. "I see what you are talking about - Castaneda wrote that you could become aware of yourself in a dream. That is, you would know that you are asleep."

"Exactly," Boris agreed. "In a dream, a normal person is thrown from one plot to another, in that sense he is like a blind string puppet. What do you think? What controls that puppet? What controls you in your dream, making you do things?

"I don't know," Maxim shrugged with an apologetic smile on his face. "I haven't really thought about it."

"That's exactly the point," Boris nodded. "We are so accustomed to dreams that we usually do not even think about why, in dreams, things happen one way, and not any other way. A dream is a dream, why should you give it any more thought? But searchers did start thinking about it, and eventually they discovered something extremely fascinating: each dream we have corresponds to a specific program. The dream changes, the program changes. Imagine that someone is from time to time changing the CDs in a CD player, and just like the disk next in turn would play a recording, you're being thrown a dream plot. And you, being the obedient blind string puppet, conscientiously "voice" – in quotations marks – this recording. That is, you are doing something, fighting someone, running away from somebody or chasing someone – there are tens of plots, and you are the main character in these. At the same time you do not have the opportunity to change the recording; you can only read it – read only, as techies would say. But if your dreams are determined by a certain protected program, then there is the question: can it be cracked?"

"Hence the name of the group – 'Dream Searchers'?" Maxim

asked. He already knew the answer.

"That's right," Boris agreed. "What did Castaneda's teacher tell him to do to become lucid in his dream?"

"To look for his hands," Maxim answered with confidence. "Castaneda had to look at them in his dream."

"Correct. But what does this action represent, why do you need it? What is the point of it?"

"It will help you realize that you are asleep. That's how I understand it so far."

"The whole point is," Boris continued, "to enter your own little program into the dream program; a 'worm' of sorts, which will slowly but surely do its destructive job. Eventually, one day the program will malfunction, and you will become aware of yourself in your dream. Practically speaking, you will wake up in your dream; your consciousness will get out from under the dream program. Your dream will turn into you watching your dream. What do you think, what will happen next?"

"I could do things in my dream. Whatever I want."

"Yes, but not for long. Very soon – perhaps within minutes or even seconds – the dream program would notice the glitch. Consequently, it will attempt to restore the status quo; namely, you either lose your lucidity and go back to the usual dreaming, or you'll simply get kicked out of the dream and wake up. Nevertheless, you will get a grain of experience. With time, if you won't make mistakes, there'll be more and more grains. Eventually, something amazing will happen: the dream program will get sick and tired of messing with you, and it will simply change your status into a higher one. That is, it will fix the current state of events de jure. It's all like in real life." Boris smiled. "The more millions some thief stole, the higher his chances of becoming a State Duma deputy, governor, or even a president. Elections will once and for all secure his new status."

"That I get..." Maxim was also smiling. "...although all this talk about dreams still remains a naked theory to me. But I have already started looking for my hands in my dreams."

"Looking for hands is good, but I would suggest a more efficient way of doing this. Have you ever heard about dream mapping?"

"I have, but I haven't ransacked it yet," Maxim admitted. "I am reading Castaneda."

"Castaneda is good, but when it comes to practical matters you should take up dream mapping; if, of course, all these topics appeal to you."

"They do," Maxim answered. "And how!"

"You just need to be aware of that your life could change dramatically. What's more, you could even die, and I cannot lie to you about that. You are taking a risk, even by simply sitting here with me on this bench. It's not games, Maxim. It's all very serious, and you have to understand that."

"I understand," Maxim replied. "And I regret only one thing: that I didn't find out about searchers earlier."

A shadow of a smile appeared on Boris' face.

"That is, of course, nice to hear," he said, "and yet, be careful. No friends of yours and no one you know should know about what you are doing. And it goes without saying that you shouldn't tell anyone about me. That's not so much for my protection, as for yours. Just trust me on this one."

"I trust you."

"Well and good. Then I'll have to ask you one more thing: as you have probably already realized, there are plenty of different dream forums on the net. On some of them people discuss the techniques of dream searchers. I ask you not to take part in these discussions yet. You can read whatever you want, just don't register on these forums and don't send any messages."

"Is it dangerous?"

"Rather, it could be dangerous. Therefore it's better to be careful."

"Okay, I got it." Maxim started thinking about whether he

should ask Boris the question that he was so interested in. Then he did it nonetheless. "All this time I wanted to ask you – how did you manage to get out of that internet café? What method is that?"

"You could call it teleportation – traveling to another place in this world, – although searchers prefer talking about portals. If you know how to open a portal, then in a dangerous situation you could always simply disappear, having escaped to a safer place."

"Is it hard to learn?"

"It is," Boris nodded. "But it's possible." He looked at his watch then he shifted his gaze back at Maxim. "Well, we've had a good chat. It's time for me to go; I still have some business to attend to. I'll call you."

"See you later, Boris. Good luck."

"You too," Boris smiled, getting up from the bench. "Bye!"

This time Boris didn't head for the underground passage, instead he went up the Bolshaya Sadovaya. Maxim followed him with his eyes until Boris passed out of sight.

This meeting left him with rather contradicting emotions. It seemed to Maxim that Boris was meeting up with him not so much to tell him something, but to once again take a good look at him. The fact that Boris hadn't left his number with Maxim reassured him of this; turns out that he still didn't trust him. That was understandable – how can you trust someone you don't know at all? You have to earn the trust.

Still, Maxim returned home rather pleased with himself. Having eaten a quick supper, he got in front of the computer to work on Boris' assignment.

Chapter Two

The Legion

Only some ten/fifteen years ago this was an ordinary holiday village; a quiet and cozy place with a not too deep and very beautiful little river, in which the local children loved to splash around. However, later that village was discovered by completely different people. They were not interested in potatoes and radishes; they didn't have the burning desire to dig around on vegetable patches. They simply liked this place.

Residential plots were bought up before anyone had much chance to build anything. If someone didn't want to part with his or her six hundred square meters, he or she was first nicely asked to think about it – usually that was enough. Obstinate individuals were dealt with differently. There were plenty of swamps in the area – they say some of them have still not been found.

And so within some ten years, an elite suburban village sprung up in this cozy forest heaven. The most prestigious villas were located on the river bank; it was as if their owners were competing with one another in luxury. Ordinary people were forbidden to enter this place – the road to the village has been cut off with a lifting barrier for some time now. There were always a couple of guards patrolling nearby.

On the outside, this house didn't stand out from the others in any way – the same insane luxury, the same desire to show who is who in this world. Nevertheless, this house was by no means ordinary, and if you'd look closely, you could notice both of the two alarm detection points, and the boxes of TV cameras, controlling access to the house. Along the impressive forged fence, a couple of bull terriers were leisurely strolling about, glowering around. Two guards were posted on the inside by the

31

gate, two more kept watch by the porch. Indeed, the house looked rather 'welcoming'.

On the second floor of the house, in a cozy study decorated with works by most famous masters of painting, three people were leisurely conversing. To all appearances, one of them, the tall and thin gentleman about forty-five years of age, dressed in an expensive robe and soft slippers, was the master of the house. He was sitting in his favorite armchair, slowly puffing on his pipe, from time to time expelling trickles of smoke up to the ceiling. His gaze was distinguished by an amazing calm. What's more, there was a strange heaviness, ruggedness, about it – it seemed this gaze of his was filled with lead. The boss listened to his visitors, deep in thought; sometimes asking short questions when something was unclear.

The other two gentlemen weren't quite of the same impressive appearance. One of them, a still young-looking man of forty years, was twirling a handkerchief and every now and then wiping the drops of sweat off his forehead. The second one, a chubby little man with a puffy face, was trying to avoid the boss' gaze; he was openly afraid of this silent and morose person.

"Well, fine." The boss took the pipe out of his mouth. "Let's say that really is the case and he doesn't come online anymore. But he is not the only one; surely he's got contacts with other searchers or with those who support them. You surprise me, Kramer, - I recall you bragging not that long ago about having excellent specialists. Then why don't you get to work? I need results, not lame excuses. Hack into their inboxes, control their correspondence, trace the phone calls of those who are in one way or another connected to the searchers. It cannot be that Sly disappeared without a trace; he will still reveal himself somehow. And keep in mind, my dear Kramer; I won't forgive you another mistake. You have already caused a great deal of harm."

"But we didn't know then that he'd manage to open the portal!" The man tried to justify himself. "After all, it's not normal.

Ken was trying to convince us that Sly couldn't do it, that you need special conditions for something like that to happen."

"Your Ken is an utter moron," the boss said, having expelled a little smoke cloud up to the ceiling. "All you had to do was to notify me that Sly has been found. Just notify me, and I would have come up with a way of capturing him. But what did you do? You wanted to curry favor with me; you decided to go after Sly on your own. That's foolish, Kramer, and unforgivable. You keep forgetting who you are dealing with. It's not you getting older, is it?"

"But we had to act quickly!" the man disagreed. "We could have lost him again, and that is why I made the decision to capture him. After all, decisions of that kind are part of my competence."

"I decide what part of your competence is and what is not. You take way too much on yourself. Why didn't you tell me about Iris' letter?"

"But there is not a single word about Sly in that letter!"

"Kramer, you surprise me. I am starting to regret that I gave you this assignment. Searchers are obviously a nut you can't crack. If your ability is not enough for you to assess the situation appropriately, then just find a normal and sensible analyst. Why is it that I find out about Elsa's departure two weeks after her return?"

The man was silent, his eyes lowered.

"What if she left to see the searchers? You didn't even bother to learn where she had been." There was a touch of annoyance in boss' voice.

"Elsa is not reckoned to be a searcher," Kramer quietly replied. "We cannot watch everyone that's interested in their methods."

"Why can't you?! What, you don't have enough money? Then tell me, and I'll give you more."

"There is enough money. OK, I'll get more people. We'll watch everyone we can get to."

"I hope so." The boss once again put the pipe in his mouth. "I'm already getting sick and tired of all of this."

"I promise there won't be any more mistakes like this."

"I'm pleased to hear that," the boss answered, looking intently at his companion. "In two days time I expect a full written update on the situation. And keep in mind that another serious slip will prove to be the last one in your career. Now you, Voldemar Vladimirovich." With these words, the little fat man that has been standing silent all along, shuddered. "I recall that you promised me last week some detailed information on the prospective contracts of the Oil Company. I never got it."

"You see, mister Dags, there were a few technical difficulties." The little man nervously rubbed his hands. "Our man at the company is at the present moment on a business trip to Iran, and without him there's no access to the information you're interested in. But, as soon as he returns…"

"Why didn't you take care of it earlier? In a week your information won't be worth a nickel anymore. Or perhaps you think I'm paying you for nothing?"

"Mister Dags, it will all be taken care of. I promise. He'll be back in two days, and already on Monday… no, on Sunday evening all of the information will be on your desk."

"Let's hope so," the boss said wearily, looking at this slimy little man with disgust. "Kramer, now here's a question for you… Just half a year ago you promised to set up a sports club for the young people in the east district. As far as I know, this club still doesn't exist. What's the reason for that – what, you don't have proper trainers?"

"We do, but there is a different problem." Kramer wiped his forehead with the handkerchief. "There is only one suitable venue, in the Palace of Culture, but everything is already taken there."

"So what? Can't you clean up the place?"

"We tried," his companion answered sullenly. "Fist fighters are practising there, you know, the guys from the folklore group. They were on TV not long ago. There's about thirty of them. We tried to have a talk with them, well and…"

"They kicked your ass." Dags finished the sentence for him.

"And what could I have done?" Kramer replied with anger in his voice. "I can't go and just shoot them all now, can I."

"Kramer, you surprise me – is there really no other way? Find out what's going on with their rent, with their heating bills and all the other stuff. Do I really have to spell it out for you? Put some pressure on the manager; let him kick them out on their asses. Promise him a free refurbishment; give him some money if everything else fails."

"Yeah, they've got a lousy manager over there," Kramer replied sullenly. "Some lame dame. She's a philologist herself, and she holds on to this folklore as if it was her panties."

"And still, try to come up with something – say, try to solve this issue through the culture management. We need young personnel." The boss leaned back in his chair and expelled a trickle of smoke up to the ceiling. "On that point, gentlemen, you are free to go. And next time, try to bring me some good news."

Dream mapping turned out to be a pretty interesting thing. As far as Maxim could tell from the research he'd done so far, dream searchers liked using different kinds of cunning in their developments – or tricks, as the searchers themselves preferred to call it. And that's exactly what they did with dream mapping. The main aim was to become aware of yourself in a dream, but instead of Castaneda's example of looking for your hands in a dream, searchers suggested you'd make a map of the dream world. Practically speaking, they replaced the tedious search for hands in your dream with an extremely fascinating business. And there, where there is fascination and interest, there's usually a result.

The first step on the path of dream mapping was to keep a dream journal; there you'd have to write down your dreams on a regular basis. However, main attention was not aimed at the plot, that is, at what was happening in the dream, but at the place where the events unfolded. The plot was outlined very briefly, the place, however, was thoroughly described and sketched. When you had tens of dreams like that, you could start compiling a map, trying to integrate the mosaic of dream landscapes into a comprehensive whole. At the same time, the end result was not as important as your involvement in the process. At first there was a lot of blank spots on the map, many of its bits and pieces just didn't want to come together. But then, if one was to believe the theory, all of these blank spots would gradually get filled up and the dream land would gain certain contours. And here came a very important part: having found yourself in yet another dream, you would suddenly remember that you've already been there before. Your attention prevailed at once, and you 'woke up in your dream' – that is, you became aware of yourself – a simple dream turned into a lucid dream. Maxim couldn't yet be the judge of what a lucid dream was, but he really liked the idea of creating a map of the dream world. No wonder that Maxim enthusiastically got down to business.

Maxim didn't want to wait around until he had enough dreams. Thus, he simply started thinking back, trying to remember what he dreamt of the last couple of days. Strange, but his memory even turned out to hold quite a few dreams he had as a child - of course, Maxim immediately wrote these down. It was a bit worse with place descriptions, so in the end he managed to come up with about ten landscapes – descriptions that he was sure about. Maxim didn't have an appropriately sized piece of paper handy; however, he quickly found a replacement - namely - an old geographical map. The back of the map was perfect for mapping out the dream land.

Just as the theory promised, Maxim was yet unable to join together the bits and pieces of the dream landscapes. But he didn't lose heart – having thrown about the pieces on the map, he waited for new dreams...

He had dreams, but not many. More precisely, many of his dreams simply didn't register in his memory. Sometimes, having awoken in the night, Maxim could remember his dreams to the smallest detail. But when he opened his eyes in the morning, the only thing left from the kaleidoscope of dreams were pitiful fragments of dreams. He had to change his strategy. Now on a bedside table by his bed there was always a piece of paper and a pen. If Maxim woke up in the middle of the night and still remembered the dream he just had, he immediately wrote it down – very briefly, literally in a few words. He didn't even have to turn on the lights; the light from the digital clock on the wall was enough. In the morning Maxim still couldn't remember anything, but it was enough to look at his notes, as images immediately emerged in his consciousness – this string proved to be enough to order and pull out the whole dream. Not surprising that the amount of marked objects on his dream map was quickly increasing.

More than a week had passed since the last meeting with Boris, and there were still no news of him. Bad thoughts started creeping into Maxim's head. He thought perhaps Boris didn't like him, and decided to terminate their contact. Maxim knew these were silly thoughts, but he couldn't get rid of them. Every day he impatiently waited for Boris to call, and still nothing happened...

So far Maxim had no luck becoming aware of himself in a dream, and that really annoyed him. When he was reading dream forums on the net, he got the impression that almost every second participant on the forum was having lucid dreams. And how was he, Maxim, worse, he wondered? Why could they do it and he couldn't?

Almost two weeks passed this way. There was still no news from Boris, and Maxim had already begun to accept that his searcher epic had come to an end, having barely begun.

That night Maxim went to bed very late – he was rereading

one of Castaneda's books. Having turned off the lights, he lay in bed for a long time, thinking about why he couldn't enter the dream land. After all, Maxim knew now that all these wonders were actually possible. And so, with these thoughts he fell asleep…

He was seeing a dream. Maxim was walking along a riverbank; on his left hand side, bones of some ancient animals were looking out from a steep slope. Having gotten a little closer, Maxim tried to find a tooth or a claw of some kind. He thought it would make a pretty nice souvenir.

"Ah, there you are." He heard a voice behind him. Maxim turned around.

Boris was standing in front of him. He wore blue jeans and a dark shirt. Maxim discerned a small dagger on his belt. Weird that he's walking around like that, any policeman would stop him.

"And what are we looking at here?" Boris looked over the bones with interest.

"I think, these are the bones of some kind of pangolin," Maxim replied. "I want to find a claw."

"Bones?" Boris sounded surprised. "Where did you see bones?"

Maxim stared back at the slope in confusion. Indeed, there were no bones. Instead, there were a few old, half-rotten logs – apparently, the slope collapsed and buried a construction of some sort. Maxim bent down and picked up a rusty nail, next to it he discerned a fragment of a horseshoe.

"Perhaps, there was a blacksmith shop here once." Maxim glanced at Boris and handed him the nail.

"There was no blacksmith shop here." Boris smiled a bit ruefully. "Looks like I'll have to help you a little. Give me your hands." He grabbed his wrists.

Suddenly Maxim felt very strange. He had a feeling that he had to do something, but he couldn't remember what exactly. He looked around with agony, and then peered into Boris' shining eyes. They were actually shining; Boris' entire appearance was radiating power. Well, of course. He is a dream searcher...

Dream searcher. Dreams. Dream... A last effort and Maxim looked around, stunned.

"Welcome to the dream land." Boris let go of his arms and smiled. "How are you feeling?"

"Okay." Maxim continued looking around, realizing with a great deal of delight that he was actually asleep. Yet - it wasn't a dream; his consciousness was working just fine – no worse in any way than during the day.

"You are now in a lucid dream," Boris explained, as if reading his mind. "I'm out of town right now. I had to go away for a little while. I'll be back next week – decided to pay you a visit in your dream." Boris smiled. "But you should know that right now you are having a lucid dream at the expense of my energy. You need to learn how to enter dreams yourself.

"Yes, Boris. I understand."

"That's good." Boris was looking at him with a warm smile. "When it comes to the bones or these planks," he kicked one of the logs, "it's just an illusion. Some day you'll learn to see the true nature of what's around you. Oh, they're calling me. Sorry, I've got to run. Got too many things to do!" Boris clapped him on the shoulder. "See you sometime this week. Have fun!" He grinned, turned around and vanished.

Maxim's vision grew dim; it was now hard to maintain focus. A couple more minutes went by, everything went blurry, and Maxim opened his eyes.

He was in his bed; the green numbers of the digital watch on the wall were glowing just the same – four thirty-two am; although, time was of no interest to him now. Maxim was lying in bed, smiling; feeling his heart getting overfilled with joy. A very unusual dream, yet, it wasn't a dream – it was a lucid dream! And not just a lucid dream, but a joint lucid dream. They were both in one dream! On the forums, people spoke of things like that being top notch in the practice of lucid dreaming.

Maxim couldn't fall asleep anymore, he was overflowing with emotions. Now he knew what having a lucid dream was like, and he was fully determined to experience it on his own.

The next meeting with Boris came as a complete surprise. It was a lovely Sunday; he didn't really want to sit at home when it was such beautiful weather outside. First, Maxim went to the radio market then he stopped by a few stores. And that's how, moving from one shop to another, he found himself next to the city park at noon.

He could walk on by. Yet, the desire to stroll along the shady park paths was so strong that Maxim, having thought about it for a second, got onto the main path.

There were quite a lot of people for a Sunday, and that is why Maxim almost immediately turned off the main path onto one of the remote side tracks – he liked walking in the park all by himself. He knew that Boris wasn't there, and that's why he even started, having made out a familiar figure sitting on a bench a bit away from him. That it was Boris, Maxim didn't doubt for a second.

Boris was not alone; sitting beside him was a tall dark-haired young woman. Apparently, Boris had just told her something funny, as the young woman burst out laughing loudly.

Maxim felt uneasy – apparently, this was a bad time. He still had time to turn around and walk away, while he still remained unnoticed. He would have done that very thing. But in that moment Boris turned around, glanced at Maxim and beckoned him to come over. He did it in such a calm and everyday manner, as if he had already long known about Maxim's presence. So Maxim had no other choice but to walk up to them.

"Good day," Maxim said and glanced at the young woman with curiosity. "Hello, Boris. I didn't expect to see you here."

"Hi." Boris shook Maxim's hand. "I'd like you to meet Iris. Have a seat." Maxim sat down next to Boris, all this time the young woman was looking at him with a light smile.

"So that is our whiz kid?" she asked. "So far, I'm not impressed. I expected more."

"You're not being fair," Boris said with a little laugh. "Remember what you were like about five years ago."

"I was strikingly beautiful and charming," the young woman answered. She continued looking at Maxim, the look of her green eyes literally pinned him down to the ground – there was that much power in it. "And now I've become even more beautiful. Isn't that so?" She switched her gaze onto Boris and smiled.

"Well, of course," Boris answered and laughed. Then he looked at Maxim. "Don't pay attention to her jokes. Iris is a stalker, and as a stalker she can be whoever she wants to be. But, for some reason she prefers the image of a bitchy cat."

"It's just that that image makes men melt," Iris explained; a smile once again slipped across her lips. "And I can twist them around my little finger any way I want."

"Not all of them," Boris pointed out.

"I agree. But exceptions only further prove the rule. Ain't that right, baby?"

The question was aimed at him, Maxim involuntarily frowned. No matter what you answer, you'd still look like a fool. To say that he is not a baby would be silly. To answer the question would be to resignedly swallow the 'baby' part, while this girl was of the same age as he, and he could not let her act that offhand.

"The paper said there's been a rich banana harvest this year," he replied. "The monkeys won't go hungry."

Boris and the girl looked at each other and burst out laughing. Boris even clapped his hands; his eyes were glistening with satisfaction. Iris was laughing, throwing back her head; Maxim involuntarily noticed what a beautiful neck she had.

"What did I tell you?" Boris said, turning to the young woman. "Gods are never wrong. Besides, do notice that he arrived here right on time."

"It happens," Iris agreed. She had already stopped laughing and was now staring at Maxim – examining him. Under the gaze of her bottomless green eyes he felt strangely uncomfortable. "All right, boys, I must be going now. I want to drop by the solarium." The young woman gracefully got up from the bench and stretched luxuriously. Maxim simply could not avoid noticing her amazingly slim body. "See you tomorrow, Sly! Well, I guess I'll be seeing you too." She graced Maxim with an utterly heavenly gaze then she threw the small strap of an elegant brown little bag over her shoulder and headed for the park exit.

Her walk seemed to Maxim to be the height of perfection. He followed Iris with his gaze until the young woman passed out of sight.

"She learned to walk that way from cats," Boris explained, returning Maxim to reality. "I hope you didn't get offended?"

"Not really, no." Maxim turned back to Boris. "Is she a dream searcher too?"

"Yes, and she is one of the best. She is part of my group."

"How many of you are there?" Maxim enquired. "In your group?"

"There's about six of us," Boris smiled.

"Your groups are arranged the way Castaneda described it?"

"Not quite. In Castaneda's books each member of the party is allocated a specific role, everything is tied on to the main energy of the groups. We also work in groups, but we have a rather different approach. We proceed from the assumption that man initially is capable of achieving everything on his own, and in that sense his fate cannot depend on the fates of others. And our groups are not just communities of people, related in friendship and similar interests. In certain experiments we may use the general energy of the group, but we do not raise it to a principle."

"I got it… Say, does Iris also live here, in Rostov?"

"No," Boris shook his head. "She's from Belgorod. We're here on business. Watch out though, she's a passionate young woman. If she lays her eye on something, it's as good as lost – she'll get it anyway."

"To lay eyes on something means to want to have that something. But do magicians have desires?" Maxim glanced at his companion inquisitively.

"You see, Castaneda is, of course, saying useful things, but not a single principle should be rendered absolute. After all, giving up desires in your version means to leave this world – to shut yourself off from it. But that is not the answer, and the person who's making a parade of his lack of possessions, only spurs his sense of personal importance. The question is not what you have or what you don't; it's your attitude towards it that matters. I can say that a lot of searchers, including me, are far from being poor. But we treat wealth not as an end in itself, but rather a means that allows us to live the way we want, and not as dictated by the circumstances. At the same time, we consider the ability to ensure a worthy life to be one of the practical exercises in searcher stalking. Well, and when it comes to Iris..." Boris smiled once again, "she is of such a high level stalker that she chooses herself what desires she should have. In so doing she is always impeccable – remember that when trying to judge her actions."

"I'm not judging." Maxim shrugged his shoulders.

"And I'm not accusing you," Boris grinned. "It just seemed appropriate to mention."

"I see... Are there many searchers in Rostov?"

"There are none yet." Boris shook his head; a grin flashed by in his eyes. "Perhaps, you'll be the first one."

"And still, who were those people? Or it's a secret?"

"Not really..." Boris became thoughtful for a couple of seconds. "The problem is that this problem is much more compli-cated than we think. None of us can perceive it in its whole. Usually we use a cut model of the world that's been established in our consciousness. Take a look." Boris moved his hand around.

"The sun, the trees, the blue sky; children are eating ice-cream, birds are singing. It's pure idyll. But this is but a part of a whole. And if there's something you and I do not perceive in this moment, it doesn't mean that it doesn't exist. Tell me, what do we base our impression of any given event on?"

"On what we see and hear," Maxim answered, not under-standing yet what Boris was getting at. "We read newspapers, watch television. Listen to the radio."

"Exactly," Boris agreed. "Bulls eye, and if somewhere, far away from here a war is going on, we only find out about it because television highlights those events; they write about them in the papers. If there was no information, we wouldn't even have a clue that something was going on – agree?"

"Yes," Maxim nodded.

"That's good. Now think about how many events have gone past your attention only because no one has ever mentioned anything about them. These events were happening and are happening for real, but you – as with most people – don't know anything about them. And the most important secrets are those that are left behind the scene. It's possible that crucial events are unfolding this very minute and somewhere close, but we know nothing of them." Boris once again became silent. "In about the year of ninety-six," he continued after a long pause, "We sensed the presence of a very powerful organization. At first we thought it was the FSS, but it soon turned out that these people had nothing to do with the government special agencies. Right at that time we started working on the so-called Akashic Records – the Earth's informational fields. The information gathered there helped us make sense of the situation. When the separate pieces of the puzzle added up into a complete picture, we, frankly speaking, got dismayed. Turns out a powerful organization named the Legion has existed on this Earth for several centuries. In essence, it is an actual World Government – that is, the Supreme Sovereigns of the Legion determine most of what happens in this world. The core of this organization is located in the States. Thousands and thousands of people make up the Legion. Every single country has, in one way or another, got under the influence of the Legion. Some countries are completely under it. Some are still holding on, trying to resist it. While the Soviet Union still existed, its territory remained practically inaccessible to the Legion. Knowing that, the Legion Hierarchs – its Supreme Sovereigns – developed and executed the operation, 'collapse of the Soviet Union'. Everything went brilliantly, the Soviet Empire ceased to exist. Incidentally, there was treason involved. It seemed the Legion had achieved its goal, but that wasn't enough for the rulers of the Legion. Now the Legionaries are striving towards the dissolution of Russia and the emergence of several small states on its territory that they would then control. In the last ten years they have been very active."

"And what do they need that for?" Maxim asked. What Boris was telling him, sounded like another bogeyman-story.

"They are just very well aware of the fact that if they won't manage to conquer Russia now, there might not be another chance. They are afraid of us, Maxim, very afraid. By 'us' I mean the Russian people. We simply don't understand our uniqueness, our strength. It so happened, historically, that not only have the Russian people not lost their spiritual potential during the hundreds of years of its history, but they have even managed to multiply it. Something the Western nations have not been able to do. We live with our Heart, they – with their Mind; God is in our soul, while Dollars are in theirs. They have lost the spirit of the nation in the depths of darkness and hopelessness. They know that perfectly well, but they do not have the power to change anything – it's too late. And everything that's left for them to do is to get the maximum out of what they have, and they are trying to drag us with them into the depths of obscurantism. The sole fact that an independent Christian orthodox Russia exists is, to them, like a red cloth to a bull. That's precisely why incredible forces are now thrown against Russia. All of this has turned into a crusade of sorts, in which even mortal enemies have united against us. There's only one goal – to crush Russia. They'll fight it out among themselves some other time."

"I can believe that Russia is not particularly popular," Maxim said. "But the things you are talking about – it sounds way too fantastic. Enemies, conspiracies…"

"That's why I am saying that, in order to judge the true picture you need to see it. And in reality, it's all even worse than what I'm describing."

"Okay, but what about the police? The FSS? Are they somehow counteracting the Legionaries?"

"It's not that simple. The thing is that in the majority of cases the Legionaries are acting undercover. Some officials or Mafiosos don't even suspect that they are faithfully serving the Legion. Besides, Legionaries use a very good scheme of control takeover. It involves Legionaries pushing one of their men onto a prominent position, following which the entire structure led by this person starts working for the Legion. That's exactly what happened to the many regional offices of internal affairs: they are governed by Legionaries, and that is why hundreds of ordinary policemen, without knowing it themselves, are working for the good of the Legion. I can give you so many examples like that – Legionaries seize courts, prosecutor's offices, revenue services, security businesses. Many mayors and governors are Legionaries. And the only government structure that is actually still capable of resisting the Legion is the FSS. But, they've got their own specificity: a special secret department is dealing with counteracting the Legion, thus the ordinary FSS officers don't know anything about the Legion either."

"Okay, but what does all of that have to do with you?"

"That's a difficult question." Boris rubbed his chin, composing his thoughts. "You see, searchers are first of all researchers of the unknown. And when we found out about the Legion, we unequivocally decided that fighting them is not our business. In short, we decided not to get involved in the fight and concern ourselves only with our explorations. And we would have done just that," Boris softly smiled, "if only the Legion hadn't already noticed us. The Legionaries became interested in our progress and suggested we share our research results with them, making it sound like an ultimatum. Naturally, we said no. That's when the persecutions began, gradually developing into a real hunt. We were put before the choice: to either die, or submit to the Legionaries. We didn't want to die, and working for the Legionaries – even less so. In the end, we chose the third option – namely that of active resistance. Of course," Boris continued after a pause. "We had our way of dealing with this new set of problems. First, we analyzed the situation and discovered something strange: it turned out that some cities are very comfortable to live in, and some, on the contrary, have a very negative effect on people. Searchers tried to find out the reason to this, and they arrived at the following conclusion: the energy of a city is wholly determined by the kind of people that populate it. Seemingly a trivial truth, but behind it were some important technicalities. It turned out that each city had its own aura – its energy. If the energy was good, then it was automatically modifying the aura of the city's inhabitants with its healing vibrations. In a city like that, even a bad person would gradually get rid of his bad habits; it won't let him come down in the world. And, the other way around; if a good nice person winds up in a purely evil city, the chances of his soul turning callous increase significantly. But the most surprising discovery was that the spiritual atmosphere of even a major city could depend on the energy of just one person. We began to study this phenomenon and eventually we arrived at the creation of the Institute of Keepers. A Keeper is a person whose task is to maintain a favorable spiritual atmosphere in a city. Our research showed that women are better fitted for the role of a Keeper, by virtue of the quality of their energy. Each Keeper goes through a special training program, upon completion he moves to a spiritually unfavorable city. Two other searchers move together with him – or rather, her. These three become the core of a future group. Wherever a Keeper shows up, people's lives get better. If we manage to spread this experience onto all regions, the Legionaries will be forced to crawl back under whatever stone they came from – they simply won't have the support from the society." Boris fell silent once again. "Unfortunately," he continued after a long pause, "that ending is still too far away. The Legion has grown very strong, we cannot resist it openly. That's why we've got to be extremely careful."

"Are you cooperating with the FSS?"

"You see, the FSS is a very peculiar organization. These guys have their own take on life, their own view on things. They are government people, and to them the interests of the government are more important than the interests of any given person. Because of that, we've had several arguments. We don't mind helping out occasionally. After all, we live in this country and we cannot distance ourselves from its problems. But we don't like it when we are being used in their games. We are used to an equal partnership; the FSS, however, is always trying to control, direct, tell everyone what to do and how to do it. To us – that's unacceptable. Hence, so far, we don't have a warm, friendly relationship with the FSS. You could say that we're between the devil and the deep sea: on the one side – the FSS, on the other – the Legion."

"Well, okay. You say that the FSS is trying to use you in its games. So do you mean to say that the FSS believes in magic?"

Boris smiled. "You see, Maxim, these guys are convinced pragmatics. There is no faith or unbelief, they only operate with facts. Facts tell us that there is a kernel of good sense in magic. As a result, several closed research institutions were created already back in the Soviet Union dealing with parapsychology problems. Of course, all these institutions were under the special unit of the

FSS. Similar research was also going on in the USA. Eventually, with time, yet another resistance front appeared between the USA and the USSR - the magical one. The States allotted huge funds to this research, while the Soviet Union was spending much less money. As a result, we've lost that war, which in turn led to the collapse of the USSR. I can say that the Russian secret service drew certain conclusions from this defeat. A great deal of attention is now being paid to parapsychology research. And the Russian school of parapsychology – or rather, military parapsychology – is now, once again, coming to the fore, and that has its effect on the present state of the country. That's absolutely unacceptable to the Legion, and that's why now so much power is being thrown against Russia."

"Could you tell me more about the Legion?"

"Certainly, after all, you need to know your enemy by sight." A smile slipped across Boris' lips. "As I've already mentioned, the Legion is more than a hundred years old. It's a powerful structure with a lot of branches. Its main feature is that the ruling top of the Legion is rather directly related to the magical world. In that sense, the Legion is your very real magical order. Of course, that doesn't apply to the regular worker – they are common pawns. At the head of the Legion is the Supreme Hierarch; subordinate to him is the Council of Hierarchs, made out of twelve people. Sovereigns are responsible for each of their own country. On the second, lower level of the hierarchy are the Curators – people responsible for specific branches of their activity. Then there are Deputies; they are in charge of the regional subdivisions of the Legion. Regional subdivisions are now present in almost every major city."

"Is there a Sovereign in Russia as well?"

"Yes, there is. Here Dags is the guy that runs the show. He was appointed Sovereign eight years ago. The former republics of the USSR are part of Dags's area of responsibility."

"Dags? Is that a nickname too?"

"It's more of a magical name. In magic, you don't use real names."

"You said that the Legion is the World Government. But what do the very same European countries think about the existence of such a government? I mean, they've got solid democratic traditions, unlike ours. I doubt the very same France or England would stand someone meddling in their business."

"You're just full of fairy tales about democracy." Boris shook his head with affected condemnation. "What democracy? What are you talking about? It doesn't exist. And if it does, then only in the fevered mind of those, who cannot look further than the tip of their nose. Look at what's happening in the world, don't track separate events, but look at the general flows and you will see that I'm right. The Legionaries have divided this world among themselves long ago. And they didn't split it into spheres of influence, even considering that to be ancient history. Instead, they've divided the world according to the principle of function. And the same Russia is assigned the part of a source for natural resources, nothing more. Just look at how, throughout the last few decades, we've been robbed of allies, pushed out of various regions in the world – only a very naive person could consider it a coincidence. The same sorts of activities are now being planned on the territory of the former USSR. This could result in a series of government coups in the former Soviet republics – here too, the Legionaries want to see rulers that are loyal to them. An attempt will be made to seize control of the main world oil resources. And that means this will definitely spill over into change of power in Iraq. Not even Iran will be left out in the cold – the Legionaries want to get access to the Caspian region and the Caspian oil. And that's only a small part of what we known about the Legionaries' plans."

"The World Government is managed by the United States?"

"It's actually quite the opposite; the World Government is in full control over the United States. And the American people are, in that sense, not any better off than our people. Rather, they are even worse off – they don't have searchers." Boris grinned, his eyes glistened. "While there's something to be gained from the States being strong, they will remain so. The conjuncture will change, and the USA too will have a hard time. The thing with the World Government is that it is supranational, and the interests of one or another people mean absolutely nothing to them."

"And what, there are actually Legionaries here, in Rostov?" Maxim's voice slightly faltered.

"There's no getting away from them." Boris grinned. "There are Legionaries in Rostov, and there are plenty of them."

"And you are not afraid of being here?"

"Not yet." Boris' lips once again moved in a smile. "You see, I am always aware of the approaching danger. It's not like you'll run a red light – you simply know that you could get hit by a car. It's the same with me – if I see a red light, I wait until it turns green."

Maxim was silent then he grinned. Boris noticed it.

"What are we laughing at?" he asked with curiosity.

"Oh nothing." Maxim waved it away. "I just thought about what would have happened if I didn't come here today, then I wouldn't have met Iris and found out so many interesting things."

"I'll make sure to tell Iris that you put her in the first place," Boris answered with a smile. "When it comes to our meeting, believe me, it is far from being a coincidence. You have read Castaneda, haven't you? Remember when his teacher, Don Juan, was waiting for Castaneda at the market, and Castaneda showed up, because he just had to come? It's the same in our case – I wanted to meet you. Iris and I came here, we had a little chat, and then you showed up because you just couldn't escape it, right?" Boris smiled.

"But I ended up here by accident," Maxim disagreed. "I could have decided not to go here at all."

"But you did. That's what magic is about – the ability to manipulate reality. Remember the sparrow and the guy with the watch? You are in that sense not by any means better than them. I hope you won't resent me for saying this."

"I won't. But still it's a bit odd."

"Magic is an odd thing altogether," Boris grinned, getting up from the bench. Maxim too got up hurriedly. "I think we've had a nice little chat. I'll be seeing you." Having winked at Maxim, Boris patted him on the shoulder and started slowly walking away.

Maxim followed him with his eyes, until Boris passed out of sight. Then he looked around – the sun was shining and some sparrows were having an argument in the tree branches. Somewhere nearby, kids were screaming with ringing voices – a picture that was both sweet and habitual to the heart. And how distant and unfounded all this talk about the Legion and the World Government, the Deputies and Sovereigns, seemed to be against its background. All of this really seemed like a dream, an illusion… Maxim slowly started walking towards the park exit, thinking about his meeting with Boris and Iris, and only when he found himself on the Bolshaya Sadovaya, another thought emerged in his consciousness – that the illusion could turn out to be the calm and quiet of this world…

Boris called already on Monday. Maxim had already gotten used to that at least a week passed between their meetings, so Boris' voice was a nice surprise.

"How does your schedule look from about Wednesday onwards?" Boris asked after a short exchange of greetings.

"I'm available," Maxim answered after a short pause. "You've got a suggestion?"

"Yeah. How would you like to fly to Siberia? For about three days?"

"To Siberia?" Maxim drawled, surprised.

"The very same. Don't worry about the expenses, everything is on the firm." One could hear Boris grin.

"Okay, I don't mind," Maxim agreed. "But where exactly are we going and what are we going to do there?"

"Not we, but you," Boris corrected. "You'll go with Dana, she is one of us. Of course, you can still say no if our games are not your cup of tea. I haven't really asked you if you have second thoughts."

"Boris, I've already told you that I'm with you. Let's not talk about it again."

"The words of a husband, not a boy," Boris grinned. "Consider it done. Can we meet in an hour – at the same place, in the park? We'll discuss everything then."

"Yeah, sure." Maxim glanced at his watch; that evening he had one order, but he still had more than enough time. "I'll be there."

"And grab your passport," Boris asked. "We'll need to buy tickets. Can you survive without a passport for a few days?"

"I'll survive, somehow," Maxim shrugged.

"See you then."

Maxim hung up and scratched his head thoughtfully – what do you know... On the one side Boris' offer was slightly frightening with its suddenness – what Siberia, why? At the same time, this piece of news caused ecstatic rapture in his heart – seems like he was actually accepted to the group! And who cares why they are going to Siberia? They're going because they have to..!

Maxim was thinking about the upcoming trip all the way down to the city garden. He was thinking about that he'll meet Dana, yet another representative of dream searchers. What is she like, he wondered? Just as bitchy, as Iris?

He saw Boris right away; he was already waiting for him on the bench.

"Hi." Boris shook Maxim's hand. "Take a seat."

"Hello." Maxim sat down on the bench, then took the passport out of his pocket and handed it to Boris. "My passport."

"Good." Having closely flipped through Maxim's passport, Boris nodded with satisfaction and hid the passport in his pocket.

"Are you not afraid of giving it away? I could take it and that would be the end of that."

"No, I'm not afraid," Maxim replied. "If something would happen, I'll tell them it was stolen. And I'll go to the police and describe your defining features."

"Then it's ok." Boris gave a ghost of a smile. "I'm waiting for your questions. It cannot be that you have none."

"I have always more than enough questions. For example, where are we going, and what are we going to do there?"

"Well, first you are going to Svetlomorsk – have you ever heard about that city?"

Maxim thought about it. He had never heard about a city like that in Siberia.

"Don't strain your brain," Boris smiled. "There is no such city on the map. As a safety precaution we've simply renamed the cities where searchers live. It's very convenient – even if someone accidentally finds out that some searcher lives in Svetlomorsk, it won't tell him anything. It's simple, but efficient. Svetlomorsk is Novosibirsk."

"And why Svetlomorsk exactly?" Maxim raised his eyebrows in surprise. "There is no sea there, only a reservoir."

"We try to choose city names so that no one would ever be able to figure them out. We've got Yuzhnogorsk, Sibirsk, Klyonovsk, Gus'-gorod and many others. But you'll never figure out where any of these cities are by their names only."

"Gus'-gorod?" Maxim even started laughing. "Is that Moscow by any chance?"

"No." Boris shook his head. "Gus'- gorod is Odessa. Karina came up with that name – she is one of the new ones, living in Odessa. We call Moscow – Borisovsk."

"Is that after you?" Maxim asked.

"Actually, yes," Boris agreed, to Maxim's surprise. "A rather good name, doesn't tell anyone anything. And you wouldn't think that it's Moscow."

"Got it," Maxim nodded. "So what are we going to do in this Svetlomorsk?"

"You'll get to the coach station and get on a bus." Once again a smile slipped across Boris' lips. "A couple of hours, and you are in Klyonovsk, there we've got one of our three main residences. Dana is bringing certain materials from the St. Petersburg group. These materials are very valuable, and we cannot trust them to the internet or the regular mail. Your task is to remember the route, and you'll meet a few people too. In the future you'll have to make several trips like that on your own. The role of a courier is not the most difficult, but it is a necessary and critical one. Plus you'll learn a few things in terms of magic, your job will get more complicated, and there'll be more responsibility. I think you won't mind such a prospect?"

"Not really," Maxim replied. "And what is this city Klyonovsk?"

Boris barely noticeably grinned.

"You'll find that out on the spot – after all, I have to make it just a little bit intriguing for you. This is what we'll do: you'll meet with Dana on Wednesday morning at the airport. Bring a bag with you with a minimum of things; a passenger with no luggage looks suspicious. And we should not be attracting any attention to ourselves. At half past six am, sharp, you should get up to the airport entrance – not later, not sooner. Dana will meet you."

"And how do I recognize her?" Maxim asked.

"She'll come up to you herself," Boris answered. "With the time difference, you'll arrive in Novosibirsk at two in the afternoon. Your task is to remember the route, so that you won't go wandering off, in case you'll have to fly next time yourself. And of course, do whatever Dana tells you to do. She is, by the way, a Keeper. She's just passing by Rostov."

"Can any searcher become a Keeper?" Maxim asked.

"I'd say rather no, than yes. You see, to be a Keeper means to develop very specific talents. It's like with musicians – say, a violinist and a pianist are equally good at reading sheet music; if they would want to, the violinist could learn how to play the piano and the pianist – how to play the violin. But is there a point in doing that? Everyone has to do his own thing. And it is better to be a good pianist, than an average violinist, and the other way around. Once again, nothing stops various musicians from playing in the same orchestra." Boris smiled. "And that's what we are doing, putting our groups together. In each group there's usually one Keeper – more precisely, a female Keeper – and a few traditional searchers. Have you got more questions?"

"Yes," Maxim nodded. "You say that Legionaries are your enemies; that they are after the searchers. But what do you do with Legionaries?"

"It's a difficult question." Boris thought about it for a few seconds. "It happened that our enemies died, but it was always in self-defense. No one has the right to make an attempt on your life or freedom, and within the limits of this right you can defend yourself by any means available to you. In all other cases, we prefer avoiding direct confrontation – we just think that the Path of Knowledge is incompatible with violence. Meanwhile, for some time now all searchers have been undertaking very serious combat training, it helps you handle difficult situations. You too will have to familiarize yourself with that side of knowledge." Boris sighed then demonstratively looked at his watch. "I think the quiz is over." He got up from the bench, Maxim rose too.

"Don't be late for the flight. And dress warm – it's still a bit chilly in Siberia." Boris shook Maxim's hand, clapped him on the shoulder and calmly headed off.

The audience was over. Maxim followed Boris with his eyes and then slowly started walking down the path leading further into the park, he was thinking about the upcoming trip. And the more he thought about it, the more captivating it seemed to him. He had already met Boris and Iris, this Wednesday he would meet

Dana – that meeting was of most interest to him. And then he'd get to meet other searchers. All of this made his head spin…

Maxim spent half an hour walking around in the city garden, then he remembered that that evening he still had a job to do, and went home.

That Wednesday Maxim woke up at half past four in the morning. He had a quick breakfast, grabbed the bag he'd prepared the day before and, precisely at five o'clock in the morning, went outside.

He reached the airport building a bit earlier than he thought he would, and spent the whole remaining time walking around, not too far away from the entrance. Precisely at six twenty-nine Maxim headed for the entrance doors, trying to make out Dana from all the passengers buzzing around. What about that girl over there in a short little skirt and a light-colored blouse? Or this one in jeans and a light fashionable jacket? Probably this one – she is obviously waiting for someone…

The young woman wasn't waiting for him – having slipped her lazy gaze across Maxim, she once again started looking for someone in the flow of arriving passengers – a bus had just arrived at the bus stop. Maxim was already by the doors, when someone softly called his name:

"Maxim!"

Maxim turned around, and saw a woman about fifty years of age. Neatly dressed, with a brown leather purse in her hands, she was looking at Maxim and softly smiling.

"Hello, Maxim. I'm Dana."

"Hello," Maxim greeted her, feeling a little lost. He expected to meet an attractive young woman, but instead… No, this woman was rather nice as well, she was even good-looking, and still this meeting threw him out of gear. Maxim even felt a little fooled.

"Your passport and your ticket." The woman handed Maxim his passport with a ticket inside.

"Thank you." Maxim took the passport, still feeling a bit uneasy.

"They are already checking in," Dana smiled. "It's time…"

Dana didn't let him know in any way that she had noticed his confusion. Nevertheless, Maxim felt very uneasy. He understood that she had probably realized the reason for his agitation.

However, already in a couple of minutes Maxim forgot about his awkwardness. Dana turned out to be a very nice woman; her soft voice was strangely soothing. They made small talk while they were checking in, and by the time Maxim finally took his seat on the airplane, he had already clearly taken a liking to Dana. True, she was not young, but so what? As one of the great ones rightly noticed, youth is a flaw that passes very quickly…

When the plane had landed in Novosibirsk, Maxim set his watch to local time – it was easier that way. He didn't sleep well that night, and he didn't get much sleep on the plane, so Maxim was yawning now and then, covering his mouth with his palm. As for Dana, she looked rather rested; her brown eyes seemed strangely bright. Moreover, sometimes strange power flashed across her eyes – although, it was instantly replaced by the softness and sweetness that Maxim had already grown accustomed to.

It was raining outside; Maxim regretted that he didn't take an umbrella with him. In compliance with Dana's request, Maxim got a cab; a bright yellow car of foreign make successfully got them to the coach terminal. They got there just in time – as Dana said, the next bus was in one and a half hour. A couple more minutes went by, and the bus gently steered out of the coach terminal area.

Chapter Three

The Death of the Courier

Low clouds hanged just above the ground, a dreary rain has been drizzling since early morning. A Lada car, that had seen better days, was standing by the roadside; its passengers looked seriously bored. A fair-haired, middle aged man was sitting behind the wheel; quietly smoking through the slightly opened car window, he cast an occasional glance at the highway, shiny from the rain. His companion, a young woman about twenty-five years old, was carelessly going through a pile of audio tapes, quietly cursing their owner for having terrible taste.

Two sturdy young men were sitting in the back seat of the car. By the way they looked you could easily tell that they hardly made their living with their heads. The one that was a bit taller was called Kim, the other – Venya. Kim was dressed in a dark long leather jacket; Venya was attired in a green weatherproof jacket. Right now, they were obviously not doing their jobs, bored stiff, they were working a magazine crossword puzzle. Listening to their strained attempts to try to guess anything at all, the woman was now and then smiling to herself.

"A freshwater fish," Kim slowly continued reading. "Six letters, the second is 'u'."

"Mermaid," Venya answered and laughed.

"Oh, come on." Kim got offended. "I'm serious."

"Read on."

"Stairs on a vessel – six letters. I know this one – ladder."

"Next one."

"A Zodiac sign – five letters, the second is 'i'." Kim thought to himself, the young woman once again smiled arrogantly.

"We've got Leo, Scorpio… What else?" Venya was already

59

pleased that he was able to name at least these two signs. However, he didn't have the time to fully show the buds of his expertise.

"It's coming," the driver said quickly and started the engine.

"Everyone get ready," the young woman commanded; turned out she had a surprisingly firm voice.

A red 'Ikaros' bus appeared in the distance. It passed the open spot without much hurry and once again disappeared from view, concealed by a thick forest wall. A few more minutes shall pass, and the bus will turn up from around the corner – there was now no time to lose. The passengers of the Lada immediately transformed; Kim threw aside the magazine, got out of the car and opened the trunk. He quickly pulled out a spare wheel and threw it on the ground, next to the car. Venya threw back the seat cushion and fished out a couple of Kalashnikovs.

Having made sure that the spare wheel was clearly visible from the road – an ordinary minor repair – Kim took the AK, clicked the safety catch and released the handle, then he hid the weapon under his jacket, covering it with the long flap of the jacket and keeping it in place with his hand. Venya got back into the car and put the AK in his lap, having softly closed the door behind him. Everything was ready to go. A minute passed, then another. At last they heard an even rumbling of the engine in the distance.

'Ikaros' was quickly approaching.

Lulled to sleep by the even hum of the engine and the monotonous rocking, Maxim was quietly drowsing, leaned back into the seat. Dana was silently looking through the misted up window, it was obvious that her mind was occupied by something completely different than the scenery, sweeping past the window. 'Ikaros' hit a pothole, and shook violently. Maxim opened his eyes and lazily glanced at his watch – half past three. It would be another hour until Klyonovsk, a strange name of a well-known city made Maxim smile for the nth time. He opened the bag at his feet and took out a newspaper he bought back in Rostov. Maxim yawned and briefly glanced at Dana – she was still looking out the window, a soft smile frozen on her lips. Maxim opened the newspaper and thought to himself that Dana was probably very beautiful when she was young – at least because she was still looking good. They hadn't spoken since the coach terminal, Dana asked him not to. According to her, these were dangerous places, and it was better to stay on your guard. No one should know they were travelling together.

Maxim had time to finish a small news story, when the bus started slowing down. Having folded the newspaper, Maxim glanced through the windscreen of the bus, being methodically cleaned by wipers.

A weather-beaten Lada car was parked on the roadside; a spare wheel was lying next to it. A man in a black leather jacket was briskly waving his hand, asking for the bus to stop, beside him was a young woman, obviously cold, wrapping herself up in a light overcoat. The bus stopped.

"What have you got there?" the bus driver asked the man that had run up to the bus.

"We've got this," he replied, having drawn the AK from under the flap and aimed it at the driver. "If you wanna live, sit, don't move and do as I say. Got it?"

The driver was silent.

"Open the door!" the terrorist commanded. The driver obeyed just as silently.

A man in a green waterproof jacket, armed with an AK, promptly jumped onto the bus through the open door, the woman in the trench coat got up right after him.

"Everyone stay in your seats. This is a robbery," the man in the waterproof jacket said and grinned. "Who wants a bullet in the head, raise a hand!"

Maxim was looking at this man not really with fear – more

with surprise, all that had happened was to him totally unexpected. He was desperately trying to come up with what he could do in this situation, and immediately felt Dana's hand on his.

"Sit tight," she whispered. Maxim gave a hardly perceptible nod.

The bus turned very quiet, only somewhere in the back someone gave out a cry and immediately grew quiet with fear.

In the meantime, the first terrorist had time to get on the bus and was now, once again, aiming at the driver.

"Now follow the Lada, and don't you try anything," he commanded.

The Lada revved up and drove onto the highway, the bus slowly followed behind. After a few kilometers, the car turned to a worn-down gravel road, and the 'Ikaros', wobbling heavily over pits and bumps, slowly followed. After a while there was another turn onto a forest road overgrown with grass.

"I won't go there, it's too wet and narrow," the driver of the 'Ikaros' said.

"You'll go," the man in the leather jacket assured him, pushing the tip of the barrel into his ribs.

Tree branches whipped against the windows, and the engine roared and strained. The Lada loomed ahead, covered in mud. The bus passengers were quiet, controlled by the joker with the AK. Meanwhile, the woman in the trench coat was slowly surveying the passengers; she was clearly looking for someone.

Finally, the car stopped.

"Stop! Stop the engine. Now get up and go to an empty seat."

The driver silently did as he was told.

"Where have you taken us?" one passenger asked in a voice that reflected indignation rather than wonderment.

"To Never-Never land," the terrorist in the waterproof jacket replied. "What, you're our first candidate? Shut your mouth and be quiet, before I blow your brains out."

The bus passengers were quiet, now and then whispering among each other, the old woman in the front seat, with her face turned to the window, was secretly making the sign of the cross.

"Don't be afraid, we won't harm anyone, it's not you that we need," the woman in the trench coat finally uttered. "We only need the courier, and he should come out on his own."

Everyone was quiet; a tense silence was hanging in the bus. Maxim was silent too, realizing with horror that these people were not looking for someone, but for Dana and him; or rather Dana, because she was the one carrying the searchers' files. That meant that the information about this trip somehow had reached the Legionaries. Though, at this point something else was on Maxim's mind – he was trying to find a way out of this pickle. He was looking for it, and he couldn't find it. And what could he do against armed gangsters?

The woman in the trench coat was calmly walking along the cabin, carefully examining the passengers' faces.

Slowly walking along the cabin, Yana was taking a good look at the passengers' faces, trying to figure out the courier:

This old man? Hardly, your ordinary hick. The two men in the back of the cabin? One has gone grey with fear, the other clearly with a hangover – searchers won't even let the likes of these two close to them. This guy? He's got a watchful gaze, got himself all steeled. No, no way it's him – he's still green and completely empty, there's no power in him. Then who?

"Sit, you scum!" Yana suddenly heard Kim's angry and shrill voice, she turned around.

A man in a worn leather jacket, sitting in the front of the cabin, was quietly fingering on something in the bag that was lying in his lap. Having noticed this, Kim jabbed him in the ribs with the barrel of the AK.

"Check what he's got there," he commanded Venya, who came running.

Having grabbed the bag, Venya ransacked it and gave a whistle of surprise, as he pulled out a large adjustable wrench.

"Wow!" Kim was amazed. "And you, you son of a bitch, wanted to hit me with this?"

"Maybe this is who we're looking for?" He turned to Yana.

Yana went up to them, looked at the man that had turned pale by now. What do you know – a grey mouse, trash, a nobody. And still, he's grabbing a wrench. And what if it really is him? Yana stared at him intensively; the man couldn't take it and looked away.

"Take him to the car," Yana commanded. "And this one." She pointed at a burly guy in a tie. He was the one who asked, not long before, where the gangsters had taken them.

"What have I got to do with anything?" the man objected, but Venya silently punched him in the guts with the AK and under Kim's supervision threw him outside, where the man immediately found himself in the safe hands of Gor.

"And these two, just to be safe." Yana pointed at the drunk and the man with a grey face. "As for the rest of you – stay in your seats, and no funny business! The swamps are deep in this place, there's room for everyone." With a stern look she surveyed the quiet passengers and got out of the bus. In the meantime, Venya got himself comfortable by the front door, threw the Kalashnikov into his left hand and started nibbling on pine nuts. All this time he kept looking at the passengers with his big blue eyes.

"Well, what's with the gloomy faces?" he said, spitting the shell on the floor. "We're just gonna straighten out a few things with these losers, and you'll wheel out of here in no time. Don't worry; it's only five minutes left of business."

Maxim listened to his pushy speech without any emotions what so ever, then he turned away to the window, trying to see where they had taken the prisoners.

They didn't take them far; Maxim looked closely and saw them right away. All four of them were already with their faces on the

ground, and the two fighters were working them rather profes-
sionally – you could hear the dull impact sounds.

However, that wasn't what attracted his attention. Having
quickly thrown a glance at the guard, Dana inconspicuously took
a small black cosmetics bag out of her purse.

"Hide it," she whispered barely audibly, having touched
Maxim's hand. "Save it at all costs. If worst comes to the worst –
destroy it. Remember the address: Komsomolskaya, twenty-four.
Take it there, they'll help you. And don't interfere, no matter what
happens. It's an order – do you understand?"

There was something about Dana's voice that made Maxim not
dare to disobey her. Having obediently taken the cosmetics bag,
he carefully hid it in the side pocket of his jacket.

Dana stayed seated another minute, as if gathering her
thoughts, then she barely noticeably smiled and got up from her
seat.

"Young man, let me through," she loudly asked Maxim,
whose heart sank – what was she up to? He wanted to force her
down back into her seat, but he stumbled across the whip of her
steel look and obediently got up, making way.

"Hey, where the hell do you think you're going?" Venya's
voice sounded through the bus, he got up and aimed the AK at
the woman.

"Fetch Yana. Tell her, the courier is calling." Dana's voice
suddenly became incredibly pure and melodic.

Venya looked at her in surprise. Then he peered out of the bus
door and gave a whistle. Kim came up to him.

"The courier is here. Tell Yana."

However, Yana was already there.

"We've got the courier!" Venya cheerfully declared, getting
out of the bus. "Get out," he said to Dana...

Once the courier was outside, Yana lifted her brows in
surprise. The courier is a woman? Since when?

"Hello, Yana." The courier's voice was cold, her eyes were

watching calmly and relaxed. "You really don't recognize me, do you?"

Yana was silent, intently looking at the face of the stranger.

"And how about now?" The woman took a few pins out of her hairdo, took off the wig with a few motions and shook her head, revealing shortly cut thick chestnut hair. "Hi, girlfriend..."

Maxim, watching the whole thing through the window, was taken aback – now he was looking at a thirty year old woman. The whole old woman thing turned out to be a fake!

His pulse was throbbing; Maxim didn't know what to do. He desperately wanted to get to her – to help her, protect her, but Dana's strict order kept him seated. With his hands clutching the armrest of the seat, Maxim was listening closely to what was being said, trying not to miss a single word.

"Dana?"

"Well finally. Did you put up this show just for me?"

"I didn't expect to see you." Yana's voice became hoarse; she took a few steps back, as if Dana's gaze had burnt her. "Get the drop on her, this bitch is dangerous," she commanded, without taking her eyes off Dana. Both fighters took out the AKs, a gun appeared in Gor's hands.

"Oh really?" Dana gifted them a frosty smile.

"You'll come with us." Yana licked her dry lips. "Gor, cuff her."

The driver took the 'bracelets' out of his pocket and moved in Dana's direction, but he immediately stopped, as if he had stumbled on her cold gaze.

"The best you can do now is to get into the car and drive away." Dana was looking intently at the enemies, and there was something in her gaze that made the two fighters and the driver back away involuntarily. Sweat drops started crawling on Yana's face; her eyes were glued to the eyes of the courier.

"Stop it, Dana. Stop it and get into the car, and I promise... I won't kill you."

"And Dags will do that later?" There was sarcasm in the young woman's voice. "No, Yana, we're going different ways. We've been going different ways for a very long time now."

"You don't leave me any choice." Yana made a step forward, silently snatched the AK from Kim's hands and aimed at Dana's chest. "Either you get into the car, or else..." She didn't finish – a soundless ringing hung in midair, some unknown weight filled the space and the AK in Yana's hands suddenly became incredibly heavy. Kim, gasping for air, dropped down to the ground and slowly started backing away without taking his eyes off the courier. Beside him, having dropped to his knees and with his hands on his head, Venya was moaning quietly and terribly, his AK was lying next to him. Gor hurriedly stepped aside and pressed against a tree. There was a mixture of fear and hate in his eyes. The courier's figure was shaking in the sight; Gor made an effort to pull the trigger, but his fingers didn't obey him.

In an attempt to drive away the haze that had come over her, Yana was quietly whispering spells, but the courier's power suppressed her mind, stopping her from concentrating, not allowing her to feel the right rhythm. There was a throbbing pain, pulsating with a fiery trickle somewhere deep in her head, its glowing light was ready to blow any second now. And still, little by little, Yana was making her way up to the surface, feeling the ring of illusion that had been squeezing her, slowly releasing – even Dana couldn't hold four people at the same time.

Sensing her powers being nearly exhausted, Dana dashed towards the AK lying on the moist grass. And, in that moment, there was a dry bang that threw her on her back; a crimson stain slowly emerged on her chest. Supporting herself on the right hand, Dana pressed her wound together with her left hand and turned to Gor. Under her incinerating gaze, Gor dropped the smoking gun and squealed. His faltering shriek covered everything around him. Suddenly the shrieking stopped, Gor looked at Dana with a glassy glare and came falling with his face down onto the moist grass. Having gotten up to her knees, Dana tried to stand up, but in that second the AK briefly rattled in Yana's hands, and gloomy silence once again fell over the woods...

Yana was silently standing over Dana's body, squeezing the weapon in her hands; her breathing was hoarse and heavy. Kim came up to her, his face had swollen beyond recognition and blood drops had appeared on his bitten-through lip. Venya was sitting on the ground, slowly rocking from side to side; his vacant stare was aimed at something in the distance.

"Put everyone on the bus." Yana finally broke the silence that was frightening her then she bent down and picked up Dana's purse. Kim silently nodded and walked over to the perplexed men sitting in the wet grass – they too came under the wave, now they were slowly coming around. 'Encouraging' them with kicks, Kim quickly drove everyone back into the 'Ikaros'.

"What are we going to do with them?" he asked, nodding at the bus.

"Make a few holes in their tires, and let's go." Yana looked at the bus with a tired gaze then walked over to Gor, who was lying under a tree. "And don't forget Venya."

Kim threw up the AK and ran two bursts of fire through the wheels. The bus swayed and sank heavily onto the side; one could hear the screams of frightened passengers inside. Having thrown the AK on his back, Kim turned around, got up to Venya, took him by the collar and, without looking back, dragged him to the car...

When there was a shot and Dana fell to the ground, Maxim jumped up. His first impulse was to rush out and help her. Somewhere on the outside a scream was heard then it suddenly stopped. A moment later he heard gun shots. Maxim looked through the window at Dana lying in the grass and, drained of power, dropped into the seat. He was too late...

His heart was overflowing with despair – chaos reigned in his mind. How could it have happened? How could Dana die? How could he let it happen? And what will he tell Boris and the other searchers now? How will he explain all of this? How will he be able to look into the eyes of these people? He, a man, had survived – but this young woman was dead…

One couldn't even imagine anything worse than that. For Maxim, there was only one way out – to share Dana's lot. Living on with this burden was simply impossible.

Outside, another crackle of gunfire was heard. There was the clank of the rebound bullets and a hissing sound of air escaping the tires from under the bus. 'Ikaros' swayed and sunk on its side, and the cabin filled with screams of frightened passengers. Maxim involuntarily grasped the armchair, and immediately felt something hard in his pocket. Dana's cosmetics bag…

Save it at all costs – that's what Dana said. And that meant he didn't even have the right to die. He had to deliver the cosmetics bag as intended. That was the last and only thing he could do for them. If only he and the other passengers wouldn't get killed too.

They didn't get killed. A couple more minutes went by, and the engine of the Lada, with the fighters, revved up. The car turned around and slowly crawled away…

Maxim was standing next to the bus, silently watching the driver and a few volunteers tinker with it. The passengers had poured outside and were now quietly discussing what had happened. Some gave sidelong glances to the blood stain that has started running under the rain – the body of the dead woman had already been placed in the backseat of the bus. But, despite such a tragic finale, everyone had a hard time covering up their feeling of relief. The first versions explaining what happened were made up and the theme of a mafia shoot-out was the most popular among these.

Maxim didn't take part in this fuss, even Dana's body was taken to the bus without him. Something made him feel that it would be better this way; that this is how it had to be. No one must know that they were together.

Now, once the fighters had left, in his bitterness Maxim was going over and over again what had happened. As many others on the bus, he clearly felt the tough intoxicating wave that came over the clearing at the moment of the fight. Dana died; the terrorists too had their losses. Maxim clearly remembered how they loaded the body of their driver into the car and, how they dragged the fighter by his arms, the one in the green waterproof jacket that lost his mind. But are the lives of these bastards worth Dana's life? Now Maxim realized full well what Boris meant by necessary self-defense. Clearly, magic was involved, but even magic couldn't save Dana from the bullets of the AK. Last time Boris escaped his persecutors by simply disappearing. Why didn't Dana do the same thing? Couldn't or wouldn't? Or she was simply distracting them – from him and the information hidden in the cosmetics bag?

Maxim's hand instinctively touched the pocket – it was still there all right. Having taken a breath, he slowly went to the bus, completely unaware that, all this time, someone had been watching him intently with a vigilant eye.

It took almost two hours to fix the bus. They couldn't call for help either – cell phones didn't work in this little valley. Apparently, the gangsters took that into account as well when picking out the spot. When the bus finally had its engine roaring and with difficulty started turning around on the glade soaking with rain, a sigh of relief rolled across the cabin – finally...

Maxim didn't reach the city. He didn't want to meet the police, who would most definitely start investigating the causes of the young woman's death. Despite the objections of some of the passengers, he got off already in the suburbs, before the first police control, and he took the public bus to reach the city. Leaving Dana was very unsettling for him, even when she was dead, but the latest developments had greatly changed Maxim. Perhaps he only now realized how serious this all was. And if it was a war, then you had to play by its rules. The Legionaries have probably got their own people at the police – if he were to stay on the bus, things would perhaps get even worse...

Maxim didn't know the city, but that didn't stop him. Having caught a cab, he simply named the address and already, in twenty minutes, he was walking down the right street.

Komsomolskaya Street was located in the outskirts. The rain had finally stopped, but the sullen sky indicated that it wouldn't last for long. The Private sector was located in this area. Maxim was slowly walking down a narrow little street, looking closely at the house numbers. Twenty-eight, twenty-six... And the number twenty-four – that was the address Dana gave him. Already thinking about what he'd tell the masters of the house, Maxim suddenly remembered Dana's warning; who knows – perhaps he was being watched? That is why he passed by the house without stopping, only casting a quick glance inside the front yard and at the windows of the house. Having reached the first lane, he stopped, took off his shoe and carefully looked around, at the same time shaking out the non-existent pebble. No one was watching him, the street was empty. Maxim quietly cursed, quickly put on his shoe and without a moment's thought went up to the twenty-fourth house.

The doorbell was fixed by the garden gate. Maxim pushed the black little button a couple of times. He didn't hear the bell ring, but he'd already been noticed. The door on the porch slowly opened and an old slender woman in a thin white headscarf came out on the porch, supporting herself on a crutch. Having noticed Maxim, she gave a faint wave with her hand, as if asking him to wait. She put her feet into shiny black galoshes, carefully came down the stairs and slowly walked up to the gate, limping on her right foot as she walked.

"What did you want, son?" she asked, kindly looking at Maxim and brushing a lock of grey hair off her face with her hand.

Maxim had a very hard time telling her what his business here actually was; finding the right words in his situation was unbearably difficult.

"Hello… I was asked to deliver this to your address…" Maxim took the cosmetics bag out of the pocket of his jacket and handed it to the old woman, who carefully took it.

"Deliver to whom, son?" The woman looked closely at Maxim, he felt very ill at ease.

"I was going together with Dana," he said. "The bus was attacked – Dana died."

The woman stood still for a second, her kind eyes grew dim at once.

"Get in," she said in an unexpectedly simple and everyday manner, having quickly opened the gate before Maxim.

Maxim entered, the mistress of the house quietly slipped after him. Maxim wasn't even surprised by the fact that she had stopped limping. Obeying her nod, he took off his shoes on the porch and went into the house.

"Wait in the living room for a minute, I'll be right back."

Maxim silently went into the room. One could hear the quiet peep of the telephone coming from the room next door – the woman was calling someone. Maxim tried to make out the words, but he heard only indistinct mumbling.

When the mistress came in, Maxim was sitting in a chair, calmly examining the room. The interior of the room wasn't that of a wealthy home, but it was tidy – walls white as milk, an icon in a simple framework, a white cloth on an antique table with carved legs and photos on the walls. The big screen TV of foreign make, with its remote control lying on the table, was the only thing that stood out.

"Tell me everything that happened." The woman's voice was quiet and sad. She sat down on the edge of the sofa and was now looking through the window with a vacant gaze. Outside, the rain was drizzling again.

Maxim told her what had happened that morning, trying not to omit any details. Not once was he interrupted, and only one time did he notice the woman's shoulders move – when he said that the assault was directed by a young woman named Yana. When Maxim had finished telling his story, there was a gloomy silence in the room.

"Where is Dana now?" the woman finally asked after a long pause.

"I don't know." Maxim lowered his head. "Dana ordered me to deliver the cosmetics bag to you at all costs. I didn't want to deal with the police, that's why I got off before town."

"You weren't being watched?"

"I don't think so. The bad guys drove off in the car – no one was left."

"It's not about them. They most probably had one of their men on the bus, an observer, and he could have noticed you – you were the one sitting next to Dana, and it's you she could have given something to. Do you remember, when you got off, did anyone else leave the bus with you?"

The word 'no' was already about to escape his lips, as he stopped short. He was not the only one to leave the bus, there was actually a woman getting off after him. Maxim couldn't describe her; he only remembered a grey trench coat and a string bag with some packages in her hand. And where she went, what she did, having left the bus, he didn't know either – his thoughts, at that time, were some place completely different.

"That's bad. If she has tracked you down, then they already know about this house. But I doubt that they'll risk an immediate attack, revealing our connections – the whole chain from the beginning to the end – is more important to them."

Maxim frowned. Turns out, he had made yet another mistake.

"I'm sorry," he said quietly. "I didn't know it would turn out this way."

"Don't think about it," the woman replied. "There'll be time to analyze mistakes later. Our task is now not to make new ones."

"Can I be of any help at all?" Maxim asked.

The woman thought about it for a few seconds.

"This is what we're going to do," she finally said. "Roman should arrive any second now, and you'll stay with him for a while. Then we'll see."

There was a sound of a car approaching.

"Here comes Roman. Stay here; I'll be back in a minute." The mistress left to open the gates.

Having gotten up from the chair, Maxim walked up to the window and looked out on the street through the curtain lace. The mistress had already opened the gates; a white hatchback covered in mud drove into the front yard. The driver silenced the engine and quickly dived under the porch roof. It was really pouring down outside. Maxim got himself back into the chair and started to wait.

The mistress and the guest accompanying her showed up ten minutes later. What they were talking about all this time, Maxim couldn't hear. The guest turned out to be a sturdy thin man about thirty five years of age, fit and dark haired.

"Roman," he introduced himself, stretching out his hand to Maxim.

"Maxim," he said, having gotten himself in front of the visitor.

"As I understand it, things are not too good. Dana has died." The man said these words with apparent bitterness. "The house has been exposed. But we can't bring Dana back, and we have to get out of here and take over the initiative. If we are being watched, then we have to turn all of this to our advantage. Now, Maxim, we'll load a few things into the car, you'll help me. And we'll discuss everything tonight – ok?"

"Ok," Maxim said and went out of the room, following Roman.

The rain was not subsiding. Having opened the back door, Roman loaded a few boxes and a couple of suitcases into the car – Maxim had the self-restraint to not ask questions about their contents.

"Get in." Roman pointed at the front seat.

"But what about the mistress?" Maxim asked, settling in next to the driver.

"Don't worry about her, all attention will now be glued on us."

The mistress of the house opened the gates; the car's engine softly began to spin.

"Well, baby, don't let me down," Roman said quietly, nodded to the mistress of the house and gently drove out of the yard.

"Buckle up," Roman ordered, closely looking in the rear-view mirror. Maxim silently obeyed.

The white hatchback drove about on the wet city roads for about twenty minutes, and only then could Roman trace their persecutors – that's how professional they were. Taking turns, at least four cars were closely following them, and that's only the cars Roman had managed to notice. Two Toyotas – a white and a blue one; a beige BMW and a small blue Opel.

"Time to let them know that we've noticed them," Roman said and accelerated. The BMW following them in the next lane didn't react in any way, but after about a minute the Opel turned up from a side street and confidently placed itself a little bit behind them.

"Very good. Now hold on tight." Roman gave a cold smile, switched on the right turn indicator and, without slowing down, suddenly turned to the left, right before the hood of a Moskvich car. Tires squeaked and Maxim gasped – that's how inevitable a collision seemed to be.

But the hatchback's engine only revved up even more; Maxim was pressed into the back of the seat. A moment later the Moskvich, with a frightened driver behind the wheel, was left far behind.

Maxim glanced back – the blue Opel was nowhere to be seen, it was hopelessly left behind at the intersection, letting through a line of cars. Roman slowed down – Maxim looked at him in surprise.

"They mustn't lose us. Yet the chase should not be too easy for them either. We've got to have a sense of proportion. Let them think that we are serious players."

However, they didn't have to wait for the Opel to show up; on the next intersection they were already expected by a familiar white Toyota.

"Still," Roman shook his head. "They're doing a good job."

He looked at his watch – it was about seven o'clock.

"A couple more minutes, and we'll get out of the city." Roman was closely watching the car with the persecutors looming behind them. Its windows were tinted, and it was impossible to make out the number of people sitting in the cabin.

Now Roman was no longer giving in – squeezing everything he could out of the car. It must have been some great driver behind the wheel of the car following them. Tires squeaking; the cars were tearing along the city streets in a frenzied chase. Fortunately, there were not too many other cars out on the streets this rainy evening. At one of the intersections Maxim had time to notice the dumbfounded face of a young policeman on duty, but that was about it – the cars rushed by in such hurry that the guy simply didn't have the time to do anything about it. So he continued standing there for quite a while, looking in confusion at the quickly escaping cars.

Tiny pine trees flashed by, then a thin ribbon of river; the car shook when driving off a bridge – the city remained behind, now Roman was confidently driving the car towards Novosibirsk. Maxim had already been there today, the surroundings were familiar to him. The white Toyota was relentlessly 'hanging' about a hundred meters behind. Even further away, the Opel flickered now and then with its blue color.

"They won't get us?" Maxim asked, anxiously looking at the car pursuing them. "It's a car of foreign make, after all."

"Hardly." Roman shook his head. "They've done a good job on this baby, and it's not that easy catching up to it."

"Where are we going?"

"We're almost there," Roman calmly answered, all his

attention was aimed at controlling the car – the slippery wet highway demanded pretty good driving skills. The windshield wipers were monotonously squeaking and the rain puddles were exploding with a soft rustling sound under the wheels.

"Now we're going to wrap this up. This road leads to summer cottages that belonged to the Communist Party. That's where they are going to wait for us."

"In a cottage?" Maxim asked.

"No," his companion grinned. "On the way to the cottages; we'll lure our 'colleagues' into a trap." Roman nodded at the cars pursuing them. "And thereby we'll take over the initiative. There is nothing more pleasant than shooting the hunter tracking you down."

The wet highway loop went off the thick pine woods and receded with a straight string into the distance. Two men in green spotted camouflage cloaks had settled underneath a branchy pine crown, hiding from the rain. Sparse shrubbery concealed them from accidental gazes, and it's doubtful anyone could see them at such a late hour. Only once did a black luxurious limo sweep past them on the highway, heading towards the summer cottages of former party members, but the quietly talking fighters underneath the tree crown didn't even notice it.

"But there were three of us. So, we're sitting, and suddenly this guy – the tall one – comes up to us, and calls Denis; you know, 'let's step aside, have a chat, 'cuz of his broad, you know, Denis danced with her a little.' 'Well, if he wanted to chat, no problem.' They went outside, and we even had a laugh: 'watch out, Denis-boy, we're going to a wedding tomorrow, make sure you don't get shiners all over your face.' He came back a couple of minutes later, laughing a little, but he didn't want to tell us what happened, 'later,' he says. So, we keep sitting around, listening to the music, and swilling beer. And all of the sudden that tall guy comes flying in again. He's all wet – turns out Denis smacked him in the face a couple of times and put the guy's mug into a fountain – to freshen him up. So, the guy jumps in, and behind him there are five more guys, all dressed up – leather jackets, tattoos, the backs of their heads shaved – a freak show, all in all. The tall guy jumps up to Denis, grabs him by the collar, lifts him off the chair, and immediately gives out a moan and falls down. Denis hooked him under with the knee. And then we all had to get up – and it took off... These five guys were the local gang or something, they ganged up on us, but they don't know any moves. They've got pretty swelled heads but they arms don't reach. So we knocked them down pretty good and left; the barman ran to call the cops, but we don't need any exposure, right? Well, whatever. Then about a week later, Denis and I were walking one night – and suddenly, 'there's that tall dude and his broad coming towards us.' The broad saw us, started smiling, but this guy almost turned white, and all of the sudden he slaps her in the face. Like, what's up with the grin? Denis, of course, couldn't stand it, nailed that ass down to the pavement pretty good. And that broad gave Denis a lot of trouble later – she stuck to him like glue. Finally, he got her a job in a town nearby, and so she stayed there. But listen to this. I ran into Denis one day, and he asks me: 'Remember that tall guy?' 'Of course,' I say. Turns out that guy found Denis and was almost down on his knees, begging Denis to give him that broad's address. And you know Denis, he doesn't bear grudges. He felt sorry for that nitwit, took his address and sent it to that chick. And what do you think – in about a month they got married. And this broad and the tall goon even invited us to their wedding, can you imagine?"

"And you went?"

"Nope, we had some pressing business to attend to. And on top of that, Denis messed up his arm the day before. He had to wear a cast for two weeks. This tall guy is now in Yurga, working in a service center, I see him sometimes – turned out to be a good repairman."

"I too had an incident with the broads. We were working for a businessman then – he was a cool guy, but too pushy. And so he stole the march on us – in short, we couldn't stand it any longer. We warned him nicely one time, a second time – he just doesn't get it. And we really didn't want to take him out – he had a real nice wife, and a cute little daughter – shame to leave her without a dad. What are you gonna do? I bugged his car. And so he is going down a highway at about hundred and fifty, and we're behind him, about a kilometer away. I was working together with Roman back then. And so Roman calls him up in his car and explains to him very nicely that this is the last warning, and that in exactly ten seconds there'll be only pieces left of his Mercedes. 'You see where I'm going with this?' he says. That guy, though a businessman, quickly got the message. The car was already on the roadside, and both of them – him and his bodyguard – were running away like deer. Roman pushes the button, and in a second there is only a pile of rubbish left from his Mercedes. It was beautiful! This go-getter calmed down and was quiet for about a month. Surrounded himself with bodyguards, they wouldn't leave his car unattended even for a minute. But in about a month he made another mistake – he couldn't resist throwing sand in our wheels, that son of a bitch. He thought everything will be hush-hush. But we poked around a little, and one guy let the cat out of the bag – showed us where the stench came from. We followed it – and what do you know, it led us right to the tough guy.

"So, we sent him a message. He found out he was doomed, and took to his heels. He just knew very well that once you're doomed – then you are already a dead guy, even though you are still walking. Fear is an excellent weapon. That's the reason why we sent those little notes, although it seriously complicated our work later on. So, he grabbed his family and ran off, away from us, but he left a small trace. That became his ruin. We figured out the town he ran off to, and left him alone for half a year – let him calm down, cool down. And that's what happened. Barely a couple of months went but, as he had already set up his business on the new spot. And the local Legionaries helped him, of course. But then he really got out of hand; he even transferred money from his old accounts into the new region. In other words, he started living in grand style; he even wanted to run for mayor." The storyteller stopped for a few seconds, glanced at his watch, then continued. "And then one day he got a little cottage by the sea, nothing his wife knew about, of course – it was one fancy cottage, I must say! We liked the sauna in particular – Russian style, with a steam room. This sauna was right in his yard, next to the pool. He usually went there on Saturdays, without any bodyguards and every time with some broad. And so, on a Friday night I got to the sauna, put up our business card on the ceiling, hid the explosive below, left a few 'bugs' and left the place. But it was clearly not our day that day, and everything went haywire... It all began with him arriving with two broads. They had quite a lot to drink – they were really wasted, and then he dragged them to the sauna. That was our first washout – usually he'd go for a steam all by himself and then have a good time with the ladies. And it was already evening, getting dark and all. We are sitting nearby and thinking what to do – we can't go ahead and blow him up together with these hookers. Roman was already lamenting – we shouldn't have been showing off, we should've just put a bullet in his brain from the nearby little forest and got it over with. And so, we're sitting there, listening to what they're doing. You could hear everything. And suddenly I hear our client getting scalded with boiling water. He gave out a strange cry then started moaning and groaning. We've realized that he probably lay down on the sweating shelf and noticed our business card. But the funny thing is that he began to suspect his broads. He thought they were responsible. He decided that they've slipped him these broads on purpose, to finish him off. But the broads don't understand what's going on – why did the guy suddenly change color, grow languid?

And they are trying to help him, idiots, thinking that he's not feeling well. And he starts yelling, 'don't get any closer, bitches.' Grabs a scoop of boiling water and scalds them once, twice… They start yelling too, there's screaming on air, cutting our ears. The sauna door opens, and our ladies jump out of there buck naked. It's funny now, but it wasn't at all funny back then – we had a job to do. And the broads are whimpering; he got them pretty good. And they'd be happy to leave, but they've got nothing to wear and nowhere to go – it's forty-six kilometers to town. And their clothes are all inside, but they're scared of going in there again – that idiot is probably going to scald them again. They are cursing him, yelling 'give us our clothes back, you degenerate!' And he does the exact opposite. He locks himself inside afraid of going outside. It would have been nice to blow him to pieces right then, but the broads were standing nearby. 'We can't blow them up too,' Roman curses through his teeth, then grabs me by the shoulder. 'Come on,' he says. We jump over the fence, run for the sauna. The broads notice us and start screaming. You cannot imagine the scene: naked broads, we're dressed in camouflage and masks, and that idiot in the sauna, he has quieted down by now – doesn't understand what's going on. And the chicks are screaming! Roman snaps at them, cursing, so they'd shut up. We grab them and drag them out to the street. Our client is still in the sauna – I had an earphone in my ear, could still hear his heavy breathing. We run off to the forest, we had a car there; parked on a dirt road. Push the girls in. Roman presses the button – boom; there's a glow across half the sky. The broads are sitting, all quiet with fear; don't know what's going on. We made sure that our client was toast, and headed home. While we were driving, we had to run the situation down for our female companions – that is, they hadn't seen or heard anything, they haven't ever even been close to that cottage. They got it all very quickly, and it ended with us giving them a ride home – we couldn't just leave them naked in the middle of the road. Thank goodness we didn't meet a single traffic cop; we were driving with our masks on – couldn't take them off in front of the broads. Fortunately, it was already dark. Basically, we dropped them off and only then drew a sigh of relief. Although later at the debriefing we got such a dressing-down for that operation... But it's ok, the whole thing got settled."

"Not bad. We too had an incident in Moscow last year. Believe me; I've never been so scared in my life. It was in November, it had already been snowing..."

A soft ringing signal was heard from the big canvas bag, standing under the cedar pine. The fighter, who had just started telling his story, quickly took the portable radio transmitter out of the bag, pressed it against his ear and spent about a minute carefully listening to instructions. Finally, he put the radio transmitter aside and looked at his partner.

"They're coming. They'll be here in about five minutes – they've passed the first station. Our guys are in a white hatchback; behind them are two engines – a white Toyota and a blue Opel. The Toyota is on their tail, the Opel is lagging behind, dragging on about a kilometer away. The Toyota is ours, and we'll see about the Opel."

"Well, it's time to do some work." The second fighter got up and stretched himself with pleasure. "You'll start?"

"Yeah," his partner nodded in agreement. "Cover me, if anything happens –you'll add some more." With these words he undid the zipper on the big bag and took out two one-shot grenade launchers.

It was getting dark. Roman was driving in silence; Maxim was also quiet, from time to time glancing back at the car pursuing them. For the last couple of minutes the Toyota had made two attempts to get closer, but Roman still managed to keep a safe distance.

"We're almost there," Roman finally said. "They're waiting for us behind the next turn."

"They'll shoot?"

"Something like that," Roman said.

They got up to the meeting point when the pursuers made another attempt to reach them. Roman slowed down before making the turn, and right away the white Toyota got dangerously close to them. The window from its right side had already been lowered; an AK appeared from the open car window.

"They're about to shoot," Maxim said, alarmed, looking back at the car looming behind them.

"They won't make it," Roman replied, accelerating. "The hatchback had already finished turning and was now regaining the nearly lost distance."

Maxim peered ahead into the quickly gathering dusk, trying to make out those who were supposed to meet them, and suddenly, by instinct, he drew in his head close to his shoulders, deafened by the sudden crash. He quickly turned around, in time to make out a breathtaking spectacle – the car that has been pursuing them had suddenly turned into a ball of fire and was now slowly falling apart, while moving along the highway.

"What's that?" Maxim quietly asked, shocked by this terrible sight.

"That's a 'bumblebee'," Roman replied in short.

Maxim looked blank.

"A grenade launcher," Roman explained, slowing down and pressing against the roadside. "Well, actually it's a flame-thrower. I told you, they'll meet us, and we have nothing to worry about. Now we can calmly go back."

"And what about the other car?"

"They are not stupid," Roman answered. "You can see the explosion from afar, and they won't come here now. But that's not important anymore; the important thing is that we beat them." Roman slowed down, then carefully turned around and stopped on the roadside. Now the burning car debris that had slid down into a ditch was clearly visible.

"You see, Maxim," Roman nodded at the flaming pile of metal. "We were in a trap, but we managed to get out and even made a retaliatory move."

"I was the one to bring them to you." Maxim's voice was quiet and sad. "And all of this," he pointed at the burning car, "is because of me."

"Don't blame yourself. You did what Dana told you to do, and that says it all. You can't change what happened, but we'll get back at them for Dana."

A man in a green camouflage cloak appeared on the roadside and waved his hand – the road was free.

"That's it, we can go now." Roman drove onto the road, and soon the smoking Toyota debris passed out of sight behind the bend.

They drove back in silence, only once did Maxim turn around, having noticed that a jeep was following them.

"That's our guys," Roman calmed him down. "Our escort, they'll follow us to town. Their orders are to deliver us safe and sound."

It was dark. Roman turned on the headlights. While looking on the highway, shiny from the rain, Maxim suddenly felt extremely tired – so many things have happened in one day. And even now he didn't have a clue about where they were going – where they were taking him. He felt strangely empty at heart and didn't want to think about anything at all.

They arrived in town already after dark. Their escort disappeared just as discreetly as it appeared. Maxim tried to orient himself, but with no luck. Roman kept dodging around the night alleys for several minutes, trying to put off track any potential pursuers, whereupon Maxim lost any idea of their location. Finally, the car stopped in front of a big two-story tall house, surrounded by a thick brick wall. The massive metal gates silently opened and the car drove into the front yard. With involuntary wonder, Maxim saw two guards armed with short machine guns of unknown make.

"Home sweet home. You'll rest, and then we'll figure out what to do." Roman silenced the engine and turned off the headlights.

Maxim got out of the car and, with pleasure, inhaled the pure night air – after the rain, everything was breathing primordial freshness. A lock quietly clanked behind them – the gates closed. Roman had a few words with the guards. Then the front door softly creaked, and a young woman in jeans and a thin light sweater came out onto the porch. She greeted Roman with a slight nod, then she came up to Maxim.

"Let's make our acquaintance. I am Oxana." The young woman was looking at Maxim with a warm and friendly gaze; everything in her – from the funny snub-nose to thick blonde hair – breathed some unworldly charm. Maxim involuntarily smiled in response to her disarming smile.

"Maxim," he introduced himself, and immediately got embarrassed: it's not every day he got to meet such a beautiful young woman.

"Let's go inside, Maxim, I'll show you your room." They went inside the house; Oxana explained where everything was as they were walking.

"Here's the guards' room," she said, pointing to the left. "And there's the sports hall. Down this hall you'll find the kitchen and the dining room. Let's go upstairs."

They went up the tracery stairs to the second floor, the young woman again looked at Maxim.

"This is your room," she said and opened one of the doors. "On that side is the balcony, next to it is the bathroom and the toilet. You can take a shower. Come down in about half an hour, we'll have supper. We're waiting for you."

"Yes, got it. Thanks." Maxim went inside. Oxana softly closed the door behind him.

He turned on some cold water and was enjoying the shower –

the hard water jets washed away his weariness and chased away the worries of the day that had passed. On the background of cheerfully purling water, the morning terrorists and Dana's death, the long chase and the ball of fire seemed extremely remote and unreal. Having changed into comfortable clothes – he brought them just for an occasion like this – Maxim put his feet into his slippers and went downstairs, following the voices coming from the dining room and the soft sizzling of the nearly boiling kettle.

Roman and Oxana were in the dining room. They were sitting at a small table, covered with a white cloth, softly talking about something. Roman saw Maxim and pointed at the chair next to him.

"Take a seat, Maxim," Oxana instructed.

The young woman gave a vague nod, went through to the kitchen and started putting out food on the table.

Maxim sat down, feeling somewhat awkward; he simply didn't know how to behave around these people. Roman looked at him thoughtfully, rubbing his chin with his palm.

"Tell me, Maxim, did you get a good look at the people shooting at Dana?"

"Yes." Maxim stopped short for a second. "The man was the first one to shoot – tall, about forty, fair haired. He was their driver. Dana fell to the ground, then that woman shot at her, the one that was together with the bad guys – Yana. I think she was in charge of it all."

"How did they find Dana?"

"They were looking for the courier – started beating up passengers. That's when Dana got out, after she'd given me the cosmetics bag. They wanted Dana to go with them, she said no." Maxim lowered his head, talking about what had happened was upsetting for him. "Then... Then something odd happened; there was a ringing, my head got heavy, then they started shooting. That guy with the gun died – I saw them drag him into the car. Also, something happened to another guy's head, they put him into the car as well and drove away."

"How many were there all together?"

"Four – three men and that young woman."

"Describe her," Roman asked.

"Tall, beautiful... Black hair at shoulder-length..."

"Did she have a birthmark on her face?"

"Yes, she did," Maxim remembered. "Right here, on the left side, just above the lip."

Roman barely noticeably shivered.

"That's her."

Oxana quickly cut some bread and put some forks and plates on the table.

"Eat, Maxim." Roman took a fork and started poking half-heartedly at a mouthwatering burger. It was clear that his mind was busy with something completely different.

They ate in silence. Maxim didn't ask anything; the hosts were quiet too. Having finished drinking a cup of aromatic tea, Maxim got up.

"Oxana, thank you... I'll go up to my room?"

"Yes, of course." Roman put his fork aside, pushed away the plate with the unfinished burger and looked up at Maxim. "Have a rest. It's been a hard day."

The sunrise had only started painting the sky gold, when Maxim woke up. He realized right away what made him wake up – soft music was playing in the room. Maxim yawned, and looked around with sleepy eyes. Only now did he notice two stereo speakers attached to the wall. But he didn't see any music player, the speaker wires stretched into another room. Maxim glanced at his watch – it was six in the morning. He stayed in bed a couple more minutes, then got dressed and made his bed. The music was playing for about five minutes then it gradually died away, just as softly as it had started. Having washed his face, Maxim examined himself in the mirror, brushed his hair and headed downstairs.

Once downstairs and in the hall, he bumped into a plump woman about forty years old, there was some kind of charm in her entire appearance. The woman glanced at Maxim; her round face was radiating hospitality.

"And here is our new guest," she said. "I'm Galina. Or rather, Galina Andreevna, but it'd better if you'd just call me Galina. I am the housekeeper; just like in that cartoon *Kid and Carlson*." The woman smiled even more. "Breakfast is ready, go through to the kitchen."

"Thank you. By the way, I'm Maxim."

"I know," Galina smiled again.

"And where is everybody?" Maxim asked.

"They left already. They've got a lot to do today." Galina suddenly grew sad – tears glistened in her eyes. "And how could this happen to poor little Dana? I feel so sorry for her... You go ahead, or everything will get cold."

While Maxim was eating breakfast, Galina was chatting away – although, she did ask, whether she was a bother or not. And if she was, she could be quiet. And actually, talkativeness was her main characteristic. But she chatters only about things you can chatter about, she never chatters about the things that you cannot chatter about.

While he was eating breakfast, Maxim found out quite a few things about this woman. Galina told him that she used to live in the neighboring village, in a small private house, which burned down to the ground in a fire. According to her, the house burned down because of her neighbor – the drunk – so many times has she told him to be more careful, and all in vain. He gets drunk as a skunk and doesn't give a damn – God, rest his soul...

Left without a house, Galina moved to the big city. She tried to find a job and got one as a storekeeper at some warehouse. The warehouse was robbed, and she was blamed for everything. And if it wasn't for Roman and the boys, she'd be in jail now... But now, here she is, keeping herself busy – making food, looking after the house and praying to God that everything will be ok with the boys and the girls...

If, at first, Maxim was actually somewhat annoyed by Galina's endless chattering, then towards the end of the breakfast he got quite used to it. More than that, he started liking her; she was a very kind and simple woman. God didn't give her a family and children, and now she gave all her unspent love to the residents of this house.

After breakfast Maxim went up to his room. He had things to think about – sitting in an armchair or lying on the bed, he agonized over what had happened. Dana's death haunted him. Was he to blame for her death? Maxim believed he was.

He dined in the presence of Galina and two guards; they turned out to be pretty cool guys. They treated Maxim with obvious respect, thinking that he was a searcher. That made Maxim feel uneasy – some searcher he was! Yet, he quickly got along with the guards.

The actual searchers arrived only in the evening. Roman was still as gloomy as before, Oxana wasn't smiling either. Galina had made supper, Roman apologized to Maxim that they'd left him alone; according to the searcher, they had too much on their hands today. They had to find out where they'd taken Dana's body and find some people to organize the funeral. All of this had to be done so that the Legionaries wouldn't use Dana's funeral to pursue their goals and so that they wouldn't be able to find the searchers.

"Dana will be buried without us," Roman said. "Time will pass, and we'll bury her in a different place. We'll get back at them for Dana, I promise that. But we have to live on."

Yet another day announced its presence with quiet music. Having dressed, Maxim washed his face and went downstairs.

He found the hosts by the dull clang of metal coming from the left wing of the house. Going towards this strange sound, Maxim carefully opened the massive door and found himself in the sports hall.

Firmly holding in her hands a predatory glimmering sword, Oxana was delivering Roman a hail of blows, which he, however, parried without further effort.

"Stop!" For a second the tip of Roman's sword touched the young woman's belly, then he quickly blocked the blade descending upon him from above. "Here you made a mistake. Look – you had to either hold my sword, or break the distance and only then launch a new attack. And what did you do? Like a proper fool, you lifted the sword up, opened up – and that's it, you're out."

Having noticed that Maxim entered the room, Roman waved.

"Come on in, Maxim. That's our morning warm up. Everyone is trying to impart good manners to this damsel, but she is an extremely untalented student…" Roman didn't finish and slipped aside; another second, and the glaring blade would have cut his head. A subtle movement with the blade, and Oxana's sword flew aside with a clang. "And besides, I am already tired of telling her: don't get angry, one day your anger will bring you to your grave. You could lose your fingers that way."

Oxana was softly smiling, rubbing her hurt palm.

"Animal," she said, looking at Maxim. "He's a real animal."

"Take a sword." Roman pointed at the blade lying on the wooden floor. "Ever had an interest in weapons?"

"Not really, I didn't really have any reason to." Maxim carefully picked up the sword.

The blade was neatly rounded; it turned out to be a training sword. "But now people don't use swords to fight anymore, so what is the point of this?"

"No, they don't use them. But sometimes even a sword can be of use. Besides, working with a sword helps you fine-tune your moves; it cultivates plenty of useful skills, and in that sense a sword is simply indispensable."

"Is this a Japanese sword?"

"Yes, it's a Katana, although we work with different weapons. Give it a try."

Maxim made a few strokes with the sword. Even in his amateur opinion it came out rather clumsy.

"There are a few main rules." Roman was closely watching Maxim's maneuvers. "Most importantly – feel the sword, become one with the sword. Don't wave it around like a club. You deliver the stroke with your body; the sword only focuses your energy. And don't squeeze the handle too hard. You shouldn't have too much tension in your hands. Hold the sword, like a bird: too hard – you'll strangle it, too weak – it'll fly away. From what I can tell, you've never had an interest in martial arts?"

"No," Maxim answered, somewhat embarrassed.

"Cheer up, it has its advantages – at least, I won't have to retrain you." Roman smiled. "Ok, give the sword back to this feisty chick." He looked at Oxana satirically, "And let's go and have breakfast."

Galina hadn't been there since morning; she went to the market to pick up some groceries, accompanied by one of the guards. Oxana was making a simple breakfast. Maxim was sitting at the table, still feeling rather uneasy. Nearby, on the stove, a kettle was making a quiet noise, coming to boil. Having noticed his embarrassment, Roman smiled.

"You know, Max, there is one important rule – the rule of situation conformity. In other words, when you are fighting – fight, but when you are drinking tea, then just drink tea and don't think about anything else. Think that the last events remain in the past; you are not to blame for them. You need to live the present – in the name of the future. Don't waste your power on empty regrets."

Oxana smiled, her smile was full of warmth and gentleness.

"That's what Roman is all about," she said. "You'll see, for everything in this world he has some sort of an important rule.

He would have become a great teacher, if it wasn't for his appalling teaching style."

"What are you calling an appalling teaching style?" Roman looked at her, pretending to be upset.

"You are just too fond of having fun. And don't think that I've forgotten all about your pranks. I remember everything, and one fine day I'll return it a hundredfold."

"And that's after all that I've done for her! Black ingratitude, I can't call it anything else. Maxim, don't trust her and don't do her any favors – she is completely incapable of appreciating kindness. And in spite of all this she's looking to become a Keeper!"

Listening to this playful squabble, Maxim relaxed a little and discovered, to his very surprise, that he felt good in the presence of these strange people.

"And I didn't ask for it, it's all your fault. If it wasn't for you people, I would be on my third year of undergraduate studies." Oxana adjusted some flyaway hair with her hand; this simple movement performed by her came out as utterly charming.

"The tea is ready, Keeper," Roman grinned, watching the young woman jump up. While arguing with Roman she completely forgot about the tea and didn't notice the rattling of the teapot cover.

"And that's after two years of teaching!" Roman shook his head, full of regret. "Now it's blatantly obvious that all my efforts were in vain."

Oxana took the teapot off the stove, poured the boiling water into a smaller teapot for brewing, a delicate pleasant smell spread in the room.

"Currant leaves," Maxim said, drawing in the smell with his nose. "And something else."

"Exactly, currant leaves," Oxana smiled. "And some wild strawberries, plus a little Indian tea for the color."

"Be careful, she's a witch," Roman put in. "Before you know it, she'll have you drink some potion."

"If anyone, I'll someday have you drink something. I can't stand watching your crooked grin any more."

Roman grinned, his smile did actually come out a bit crooked, then he burst out laughing.

"They say everything in this world is changing. And still, I would never have thought that in two years time one could turn such a charming student into a hard-hearted, ungrateful, soulless creature."

"You better be quiet. Don't forget that I have a pot of boiling water in my hands." Having poured tea in the cups, Oxana sat down on a chair and buttered a cut-off slice of fresh bun. Then she looked at Maxim.

"There are buns, butter, sugar, jam. Help yourself – don't be shy."

"Thank you." Maxim poured some sugar into his tea, stirred it around, then buttered a mouthwatering piece of bun, and with great pleasure started drinking the aromatic tea that smelled of forest.

Everyone was quiet for a few minutes, savoring the forest aromas. All of this time, Maxim kept glancing at Oxana from the corner of his eye. There was something exciting about her; something that made his spirit stir. Roman mentioned that she was looking to become a Keeper – then that means you cannot become a Keeper just like that, it too requires a certain level of maturity. Maxim glanced at Oxana once again and started from the sound of a creaking door. He quickly turned around and sighed with relief. Boris had stepped into the kitchen...

Chapter Four

First Lessons

He really didn't want to go into Dags'. Standing in front of the office door, Kramer wiped off the drops of sweat that stood out on his forehead with a handkerchief. Alas, nothing good could come out of this meeting. And even though Kramer could not personally be blamed for what had happened, he was still afraid – whichever way you look at it – Yana was directly under his command. And that meant he would be the one responsible. And they did mess up with that punk – Kramer frowned. Having sighed once again, he quietly made a cross-sign and carefully knocked on the door.

"Come in," Dags's soft voice came from the office.

Kramer entered, carefully closing the heavy door behind him. He glanced at the boss – he was sitting in an armchair, puffing on his favorite pipe.

"It's time you got rid of the filthy habit of standing outside my door," Dags said, having taken the pipe out of his mouth. "If you cannot bring yourself to enter at once, then gather your courage someplace else. Although," Dags grinned, "my advice might prove unnecessary now."

Kramer grew pale; he caught the hidden meaning in the Sovereign's voice. He got up to Dags and stopped, not daring to lift his eyes.

"I'm waiting," Dags reminded, looking at Kramer with a grave smile. "I'm even curious – how will you explain your failure this time?"

"Sovereign, forgive me." Kramer finally had the courage to look up at Dags. "It just happened this way... How could we have known that that bitch would be there? We were expecting an ordinary courier – just as our source has told us."

"My dear Kramer, we are no longer talking about Dana. Although even her, your charges handled rather poorly. Why didn't you tell me about the boy?"

"But I simply didn't have time, the boy led us straight to their base – and I saw fit to act on my authority."

"And as a result of which you've lost your best people." Dags grinned. "Looks like, you're still under the influence of your former successes, and that gets to your head. If you would have told me about the boy right away, and refrained from engaging in unauthorized activity, it all could have ended quite differently."

"I promise, there won't be more mistakes like that."

"You've already promised me that last time!" Dags's voice turned heavy. "Understand, Kramer, I'm sick and tired of your failures. You're smart, if that wouldn't have been the case, I would have grinded you to dust long time ago. And I understand that you have to resist a very serious enemy. But even that cannot justify your endless failures. I need results, Kramer – results! If a horse keeps losing the race time after time, it's not worth a dime. Perhaps, I've made the wrong choice?"

"I'll find them!" Kramer once again gathered the courage to look at the boss. "Now we are going through the passenger lists, trying to find out what flight Dana and her companion were on and where they came from. It won't take too long, we've got Dana's passport. Then we'll know where they came from. Perhaps we'll be able to find something on the boy too. It's a substantial lead, it may give results."

Kramer became silent, and so did Dags, puffing on his pipe deep in thought. Finally, he took the pipe out of his mouth and lazily opened his lips.

"Fine, I'll give you one more chance," he said, thoughtfully looking at his company. "But know this, my dear Kramer; you won't survive another mistake."

Maxim perceived Boris' appearance with mixed feelings of relief and shame. He was pleased to see a familiar face, and at the same time, he felt he was to blame for Dana's death. He had no excuses...

He had to retell the story of what had happened. Boris was listening silently, sometimes asking specific questions. Oxana and Roman didn't break into the conversation.

"Yana again," Boris sighed, when Maxim had finished telling his story. "And this time she has crossed the line."

Maxim had questions. Yet, he remained quiet – he simply didn't know whether he had the right to ask them now. He thought that after what happened, Boris won't even want to speak to him.

It became very quiet, only the damped jingling of the spoon could be heard in this silence – Roman was stirring sugar in a cup of tea.

"We need to get to the bottom of this," Boris said. "Yana knew there would be a courier on the bus. So the question is: where was the leak? Who knew about Dana's arrival?"

"That's something we'd have to find out," Roman agreed. "Dana told us about her arrival on Saturday. We used our regular inbox – having read her message, I destroyed it at once. It remained in the inbox no more than two hours. Apart from me, Oxana was the only one who knew Dana was coming. There was nothing about Maxim in her message.

"I didn't tell anyone anything." Oxana shrugged her shoulders. "Not a word."

"I'm clean too, I'm sure of that," Boris said. "I spoke to Dana one on one; there couldn't have been a leak. I suggested she'd take Maxim – she agreed. Maxim didn't know any details about the trip, but he knew he was going with Dana. If the Legionaries had gotten the information from him, they would have been looking for Dana on the bus. But they were expecting a regular courier." Boris glanced at Maxim

"No offence, Maxim, but such are our rules – we have to find the leak. No one is accusing anyone of anything; we are simply examining all possibilities."

"I understand," Maxim answered.

"If the information leaked from Maxim, Sly would have gotten locked up long ago," Oxana put in. "Kramer wouldn't have wasted such an opportunity."

"I agree," Roman nodded. "I think the most likely leak is the mailbox. That means either Dana's mailbox or ours. We just have to figure out who knew about these mailboxes."

"What email address did she use to send you the message?" Boris asked.

"Her regular one." Roman shrugged his shoulders.

"I have passwords to her mailboxes…" Boris became thoughtful. "I'll check who Dana's been talking to lately. By the way, in her email, did Dana specify the time of her arrival?"

"She said she'll be in Svetlomorsk on Wednesday, at about two o'clock in the afternoon and that she'd be at our place at five," Roman answered. "She asked us not to meet her. She said she'll take the bus; it would be safer that way. She used the nickname 'Hamlet' – even having read the email; no one could guess it was her."

"If Legionaries have read her email, they could have figured out what bus she'd take," Boris said slowly. "But only if they know about Svetlomorsk."

"I didn't tell anyone anything," Maxim put in. "Not a word."

"I know Maxim," Boris said. "Svetlomorsk is already a couple of years old, and if Legionaries have been monitoring our correspondence at some point, they could have figured out both Svetlomorsk and Klyonovsk. Then they only had to check the bus timetable to find the right one. I'll check who Dana has been talking to the last few days. Then we'll be able to make some kind of a conclusion. But we'll have to change our inboxes in any case."

It became quiet, everyone was silent. Then Boris spoke once

again:

"Let's say we've sorted this out. Now we need to solve another issue: what to do with Maxim?"

Maxim lowered his head. That's right, the fault for Dana's death still lied with him.

"You misunderstand me," Boris corrected himself. "Dana's passport got into the hands of the Legionaries. The passport is in another person's name, but they'll still find out where she was flying from. Besides, they'll be looking for you. You were sitting next to Dana on the plane – that means they've got all the necessary information. I won't be surprised if this very moment they are already searching through your apartment."

"And that means you don't have a flat anymore," Roman added. "You can't go back there."

That was very bad news. Maxim didn't even think about such a turn of events.

"It's not my apartment, I was renting it," he said. "But I've got documents there – my diploma, my military ID."

"You'll have to forget about those," Oxana said and smiled. "Look at me; I've been using someone else's documents for almost two years now. And I'm not complaining."

"That's our world," Boris added. "Come on, let's talk in private." He got up from the chair and patted Maxim on the shoulder.

Boris had his own room in this house; that was obvious as Boris was completely at home in that room.

"Make yourself comfortable," he suggested and pointed at the armchair, while he got himself seated in the other. "I believe we actually do have something to discuss."

Maxim sat down and glanced at Boris with uncertainty.

"I know I am to blame for Dana's death," he said. "And I don't want to make excuses."

Boris sighed.

"Maxim, I know how difficult it must be for you now. And,

trust me; it is not easier for us either. Dana was a wonderful young woman and a true friend. Yes, you were unable to save her, but it's not your fault. The only thing you could have done was to complete her assignment. You've done that. The rest is the work of the devil. If you think that you have to draw some conclusions from what happened, do it. But you need to look ahead, as moaning and torturing yourself won't help anything. Now you see how serious the things that we are doing are. The world of dream searchers is full of wonders, but it also hides a lot of dangers. And now I'd like to give you yet another opportunity to leave this world. Just don't get offended." Boris stretch out his hand, instantly brushing away Maxim's attempt to object. "This is not a place for hurt feelings. We are grown ups, and our conversation must be that of adults. You've got two options. First one – to stay with us. What danger it will put you in, you already know. And the second option is this: we buy you a flat of your choice in any Russian city, we make a complete package of new documents – any, even diplomas. Plus, we throw in a certain sum of money as a compensation for your moral costs. Then we part forever. You live your life, we live ours. You've got a couple of hours to make your decision."

"Yesterday I got new enemies," Maxim answered. "So I've already made my choice and I don't want to change it. I will stay with you – unless you don't want me to."

Boris barely noticeably smiled.

"Your sense of personal importance is blown up to the limit," he said. "But it's okay; we'll tackle this shortcoming of yours somehow. When it comes to enemies, your attitude is wrong too."

"What do you mean?" Maxim quickly glanced at Boris.

"You cannot divide the world up into friends and enemies. Rather, you can leave your friends there, but you'd have to forget all about your enemies. That is one of the laws of the real world. The more you think about enemies – the more people you consider as such – the more enemies will appear around you."

"That's natural," Maxim agreed. "If I name ten people to be my enemies, then there'll be ten. And if I'd gather a hundred – then, I'd have a hundred enemies."

"I'm talking about something slightly different. Imagine that you don't like certain people – it doesn't matter who exactly; Communists, democrats, Jews, black people – whoever. The point is that the more you hate these people, the more of them will there be around you. Not because you'll start noticing them more often. There will actually be more of those people in your surroundings. Would you like me to reveal the greatest secret of the universe?" Boris softly smiled.

"Of course." Maxim smiled too, sensing a load of anxiety falling off his mind.

"The most important secret of the universe," Boris began, "is that there are a great number of all kinds of different flows operating in this world. And what is happening to you depends in many respects on your involvement in one flow or another. I'll give you a classic example: there was once a boy. He smoked, cursed, wrote bad words on the walls. Then one day he found an ancient coin on the road. He took it home and cleaned it; he really liked this coin. He showed it to his mom – she noticed her son's interest and went through the trouble to buy an album for his coins. Eventually, our boy stopped smoking and cursing, he stopped writing bad words on the walls. He got a new circle of friends, who shared his new interest. Thus, our cursing boy was relegated to oblivion, and in his place there was now a 'sweet and cuddly' numismatist boy. His interest in coins made him finish school with top grades and go study at the School of History. Eventually, he became a respected man – a university professor. It's a good story, don't you think?"

"Yes," Maxim agreed, not really understanding what Boris was getting at. "Educational."

"And now imagine that the boy didn't find the coin," Boris continued. "He would have continued smoking, cursing and hanging around little morons just like him. With time he'd have taken to drugs and started stealing, in order to get the money for another dose. Perhaps he would have become a member of some gang. Eventually, he would have been killed in a drunken fight or he'd get his brains blown out during a gang showdown. As you see, I've described two ways in which this situation could have developed. What's the difference between these two? The difference is that we are looking at two alternatives of involvement in two different flows. In the first case, the found coin was the transit; transferring the lad from one flow to another. The boy's mother secured his choice by buying him an album for his coins. That's it. The former flow remained behind, and the boy was now carried by a new one. In that sense a flow is like a river, but the most important thing is that each flow also has its own attributes. Having left the former flow, the attributes of which were cursing, stealing, drugs and other rubbish, the boy entered a new flow and gained the attributes of that flow. One could say that the world around him remained the same, but it got recreated for the boy – its configuration had changed. Certain attributes left, their place was taken by other attributes. If you'll give these conceptions some closer thought, you'll see what I'm talking about. And considering that we've started with enemies, I'm ready to maintain that if you will continue thinking of some people as your enemies, then you'll face a world where the number of these enemies will always keep growing. Basically, the world will simply respond to your requests."

"But the very same Legionaries exist, and trying to convince yourself that they don't is just stupid." Maxim didn't agree.

"And I am not saying that you should convince yourself," Boris replied. "Just stop seeing these people as your enemies, as something that's important in your life. Let's say you are walking down a street and suddenly stumble on an unnoticed step on the sidewalk; is it worth getting angry at it? Is it worth seeing it as an enemy? You simply have to accept the fact of its existence and try to avoid stumbling on it next time. It's just that if you'll constantly keep thinking about how not to slip, stumble or fall, you'll keep stumbling and falling. The world around us is created by our thoughts – if you remember that, you'll be able to escape a great deal of unpleasant problems."

"You have a point," Maxim admitted. Boris only grinned in response.

"It's not just that I have a point; that is actually one of the main points determining our fate. Just remember how you got here. Where did it all start? It all began with you seeing me in an internet café. This event became the transit to you, transferring your thoughts, and then your whole life onto a different plane. You thought about what happened, you tried to make sense of it, you tried to reach our forum. You had the intention to meet me, and we met. Practically, it was the power of your intention that brought you into the flow of the dream searchers' tradition. And the fact that you managed to do that is already saying a lot."

"Yes, it all fits," Maxim admitted. "I'll think about it."

"You do that," Boris got up and patted Maxim on the shoulder. "And don't mourn the past. From this day on you are starting a completely new life."

That chap going with Dana turned out to be Maxim Vorontsov. They obtained this information, after browsing through the passenger lists, having figured out who was sitting next to Dana on the bus.

It took more than twenty-four hours to find out where he lived. Turned out he was renting a flat, but they couldn't find any information about it. The flat was found, once they'd checked the database of the mobile network users. There was both the phone number and the address at which Vorontsov was registered.

The flat was checked immediately. They didn't manage to find anything worthwhile, yet they did discover some information from the internet forums dedicated to dream searchers. That convinced Kramer that they had picked up the right scent.

Of course, they immediately tried to figure out where Vorontsov was now, by tracking his cell phone. Unfortunately, the user was unavailable. All attempts, trying to reveal Vorontsov's relatives in Rostov, were unsuccessful. Everyone they found with the same last name turned out to be unrelated. Hope remained that Vorontsov would come back, but Kramer didn't believe that anymore. Searchers always knew how to cover their tracks.

Vorontsov's university diploma, which they found in the closet, proved to be of some interest. The diploma was awarded in Tomsk, and Sly spent some time living in that very same city. Then the connection between Vorontsov and Sly could have been established back then. Having thought about it for a while, Kramer ordered his people to check all Vorontsov's connections in Tomsk – friends, university professors, potential relatives. Dags was expecting good news, and Kramer really didn't want to disappoint his boss. He just knew all too well what the Sovereign's wrath would turn into for him.

The talk with Boris brought relief to Maxim. The most surprising thing was that neither Boris, Roman or Oxana actually thought him to be responsible for Dana's death – Maxim just felt that. They couldn't be acting against their conscience, deceiving and just pretending like nothing happened. True, they were upset by Dana's death; however, that didn't throw them off track. And they were no longer thinking about yesterday's tragedy, but about how to live on.

After breakfast everyone went to work – unfortunately, there was plenty of things to do. To begin with Maxim was introduced to a couple more guards as a searcher, a new member of their team. Maxim even got a bit embarrassed – he was no searcher yet, he was just called that. Still, from that moment onwards, the guards, and there were six of them in the house, treated Maxim with marked respect. Right after that, Roman left, having said that while he was at it he'll also try to find out about Maxim's new documents. Boris went upstairs, to the Communication Room – to take a look at Dana's inbox. He had to find out where the information leak came from and to understand why it happened. Was it a result of trivial carelessness, or was Dana betrayed by someone she was in contact with?

The Communication Room astounded Maxim with an abundance of equipment. There was everything, starting with ordinary computers and other office equipment and ending with radio and short-wave transmitters. Boris confidently got in front of one of the computers, Maxim got up next to him, not knowing whether he should leave and not to disturb him – or stay.

"Can't Legionaries establish where you live, by tracking the connection?" Maxim inquired, simply wishing to break the silence.

"Theoretically they can," Boris agreed. "But it is practically impossible. Here we're working directly through a satellite, and we also use special software."

"And where is the satellite dish?" Maxim asked. "I haven't seen it."

"It's under the roof," Boris answered. "The roof is radioparent. But you can't see anything from the outside; it's just your average house. By the way, Oxana has probably got tired of waiting for you. She's going to town; I suggested she'd take you with her. Would you like to take a ride?"

"Got it. I'm going and leaving you in peace," Maxim answered. Boris grinned and turned away to the computer.

Maxim found Oxana in the front yard; she had just taken out, from the underground garage, a green nimble Renault. Upon seeing Maxim, she invited him into the car with a smile.

"Get in," she said, and Maxim took the passenger seat with caution. He was feeling a little uneasy about the fact that a woman was going to drive the car – such a young woman too; in Maxim's opinion she didn't even look twenty. He'd be happy to take the driver's seat, but he didn't dare to offer himself – he was afraid of hurting the girl's feelings.

The entrance gate opened automatically. Followed by the guards' glances, Oxana, rather skillfully, got the car out on the street. Maxim turned around and saw the heavy metallic gate close behind them. Now he could properly appreciate the searchers' residence, and, needless to say, it looked pretty impressive.

"And where are we going?" he asked, having glanced at the girl.

Oxana smiled.

"We've got enough to do," she answered. "First, we'll go to one computer firm, Boris asked us to find a couple of programs. Then we're going to pay a visit to a certain somebody. He's tracking the phone calls of various bad guys at our request. Well, and finally we'll go to the library, we need to study the newspapers for the last year and find out a few things."

"And how long ago did you join the searchers?" he glanced at the girl and asked.

"It's been almost three years already," Oxana shrugged, guiding the car out onto the highway with exceptional skill. "And I'm not complaining yet." Again, a smile slipped across her lips.

The Renault was confidently making its way through the stream of cars. Amazed and outright envious, Maxim was watching Oxana drive the car.

"Where did you learn how to do this?" he looked at the young woman and asked.

"You mean to drive? Wait 'til Roman gets to you, he'll make a racing driver out of you in a month. After his classes I was, at first, afraid of even getting close to the car." Oxana smiled again. "But then it was ok, I got used to it. Now it all happens on its own – I'm just driving, and that's all." She skillfully switched over to another lane.

"Are you from around here?"

"Not really. There is a village about sixty kilometers from here, that's where I'm from. My parents still think I'm studying to become a teacher."

"Do you visit often?"

"About once a month." Oxana shrugged.

"By car?"

"Nope, by bus. Where does a poor student get a car from?"

"Don't your parents visit you?"

"It happens," Oxana grinned. "I have to make up all kinds of stories for their sake. They think that I'm renting a room at Granny Katya's house. It's that woman, whose house you've been to. She's helping us. Now I'll have to come up with a completely different story, look for another room."

"And is granny Katya all right?" Only now did it occur to Maxim that that woman could actually be in danger.

"Of course. As soon as Roman and yourself whirled away the Legionaries – they actually thought you were taking something valuable out of town – Granny Katya escaped through the back way, and our people picked her up."

Maxim didn't catch some of the details of what the young woman had just said.

"Tell me, what was in those boxes?"

Oxana laughed.

"And you really thought it was something valuable? Roman was loading all that garbage in front of the Legionaries so that they'd go after you."

"Turns out we were just bait?"

"Exactly. At first Roman wanted to leave you with Granny Katya, but then he changed his mind and took you with him. I'll be honest with you; he likes you."

Maxim chuckled with distrust.

"No, really." Oxana's lips moved in a smile. "Even though you didn't actually do anything. But you did a good job not doing anything. Roman appreciated that. Trust me when I tell you that one has to earn his praise. So Boris wasn't wrong about you. Just remember, I didn't tell you any of this."

For some time they were driving in silence; Maxim was looking at the new city with interest. Then he glanced back at the young woman.

"I've been meaning to ask you – are you actually a dreamer?"

"Did Boris tell you that?" Oxana quickly glanced at Maxim and then turned her gaze back onto the road. "I'm just good at it. You know how it is – everyone has got some kind of talent. I'm good at lucid dreaming. Roman is a stalker. Everyone ought to do his thing." She smiled once again.

Maxim smiled too – he liked Oxana. In some sense she was a positive copy of Iris. These girls shared some kind of an imperceptible resemblance.

"And who taught you how to have lucid dreams?"

"Rada. It's a name," Oxana specified. "She too is a searcher, one of the best. Perhaps you know her?" Oxana quickly glanced at Maxim.

"No," Maxim shook his head. "I've only been with the searchers for a very short time."

"You'll like her," the young woman said, convinced. "They are the best people I know." She changed lanes, slowed down and smoothly made a turn into a pass. She stopped the car by a building with a sign of the computer firm, then looked at Maxim and smiled.

"Wait here, ok?"

"I'll wait," Maxim agreed.

They got back to the searchers' residence around noon. Boris met them. Oxana immediately went out to the kitchen to help Galina, while Boris invited Maxim up to his room.

"Take a seat," he said, making himself comfortable in the opposite armchair. He was quiet for a couple of seconds, thoughtfully looking at Maxim then he continued:

"The leak was indeed Dana's fault. And that, once again, confirms how careful we must be."

"Someone hacked into her inbox?" Maxim guessed.

"Yes. She was corresponding with one of our followers; information about his email is available on the net. There's nothing strange about that, but Dana made a mistake through lack of attention – she once sent him a letter from her closed email account. An unfortunate blunder, but it cost Dana her life. Legionaries track the correspondence of our followers, so the information about Dana's closed email account got into their hands. Well, hacking into someone's inbox is not that hard. Any defense can be broken. Now we'll have to change all of our inboxes and find out what else the Legionaries could have learned."

It became quiet. Boris was silent, and so was Maxim, thinking about whether now was a good time to ask questions that interested him. He finally made up his mind:

"I've been meaning to ask you; if I cannot go back to Rostov, I'll need to somehow settle here. I'll need something to do; a job – way of making money."

"I understand," Boris nodded. "However, we're organized in a slightly different way. First off, having joined searchers, you've entered a rather large organization that has considerable financial resources. Thus, from this day onward you get the opportunity to use these resources. In the next couple of days Roman will give you a credit card. This is how it works: you may use this money anyway you wish; however, you must be reasonably economical. You may think of it as a salary of sorts, which every searcher has a right to have." Boris grinned. "But it's, once again, just one side of the coin. We too don't get money out of thin air, we earn it. Each searcher must strive towards replenishing our accounts to his best ability. After all, if everyone will just spend the money, then soon there will be nothing left to spend. So, each and every one of us has some kind of a job that generates an income. Do you remember, I've already told you about this – that searchers see the ability to secure a worthy life for oneself as one of the stalking exercises? In a couple of days you'll have new papers, meanwhile you have some time to decide what you want to do."

"And what are you doing?" Maxim inquired.

"I own a few firms," Boris answered, "two Russian ones and one in England. I can say that not all searchers are doing business - there are painters, writers, doctors among us. And on the whole it doesn't really matter what you are doing, only one thing is important – that you like your work, enjoy it."

"So what you're saying is that you like doing business?" Maxim looked at Boris distrustfully. "I've always considered business to be a rather troublesome endeavor."

"Yes, but that is entirely your opinion. To me business is a puzzle of sorts – an intellectual game with lots of unknown variables. And trust me, when you realize some intricate combination you get real pleasure out of it."

"Fine, I can understand that, but you mentioned doctors. Seems to me that it's rather difficult for a doctor to make a good living in our days."

"The problem is that you continue to apply an ordinary yardstick to the searchers," Boris answered. "And you do not take into account that searchers plan their lives themselves, letting it enter the right channel. Remember the flows I've told you about. And if a doctor in an ordinary hospital makes very little money, then why can't he transfer to some elite clinic?"

"But everyone can't work in elite clinics?"

"I'm not talking about everyone." Boris looked closely at Maxim. "Understand that searchers are not benefactors; they do not strive towards changing the world around them. They change their place in this world. Just find something to do that you really like doing, and do it. Take for example Oxana – she's got the talent of an artist, but she had never thought of painting for a living – making it her profession. She was studying to become a teacher. Yet it wasn't her choice, but that of her parents. And only thanks to having met us was she able to reveal her true calling. Now her paintings are spread all over the world. And the most important thing, Oxana is doing what she likes – something that she really loves doing. That's the whole point – find your thing, find out where your heart lies. The rest is already a matter of technicality. Use our methods, and you'll definitely achieve success."

"Namely? What methods are you talking about?"

"There are quite a few different methods," Boris shrugged. "But you get best results only when you combine them all. There is a certain effect of accumulation, when one method comple-ments the other. It could be likened to fighter training: even if a fighter has learned one punch very well, it won't guarantee his unconditional victory in a fight. But once he's mastered a technique involving several moves, he'll actually get somewhere. The same thing here – each technique in isolation will probably not get you to the level of a magician, but in combination with other techniques it will give the right effect. That's, by the way, the reason why our techniques are sometimes criticized – some people say they don't work. People just don't understand that you can't get it all overnight. But that's actually a good thing – random people drop out, only those remain that are stubborn enough and who have a craving for knowledge."

"That makes sense," Maxim agreed. "And still, what would you recommend I start with? It's just that I feel a bit weird – the guards treat me as if I was a searcher, but in practice I don't know anything at all."

"Skills are something that come with time. When it comes to your start, according to our tradition, people usually start with the Patience of Medici – ever read about it?"

"Only in very general terms," Maxim admitted. "I didn't really manage to find a proper explanation."

"Then you were looking in the wrong places," Boris smiled.

"Let's do it this way: I explain the basic idea to you, and then you'll read about it in our archives and sort out all the details. Ok?"

"Ok," Maxim agreed. "You may begin."

"Then I'll begin." Boris made himself comfortable in the armchair. "I'll start with that there's been a bit of a mix up with the name of the solitaire. It's called the Patience of Medici in honor of the French queen, Maria Medici. But it would be more correct to call it the Patience of the Scottish queen, Mary Stuart. John Dee taught the queen how to spread the cards; he was a famous mystic at the time, her court astrologist. The first mention of the solitaire is connected to Mary Stuart; however, it surfaces later as The Patience of Medici. It could be explained by a human mistake, and also by the fact that Maria Medici was as well familiar with this solitaire. From the point of view of historical justice it would be more correct to call it 'The Patience of Mary Stuart'. Still, the name, The Patience of Medici, has become such a firm custom that changing it now would be pointless. So just take into account this small inaccuracy." Boris was looking at Maxim with a soft smile. "It doesn't change its meaning for that matter. And the point with The Patience of Medici, or, shortly, the PM, boils down to the following..." Boris became thoughtful for a few seconds. "Let's start with that everything that happens in the world is determined by a set of laws. An apple falls down; a helium balloon flies up; water expands when freezing; electric currents, when moving through a tungsten spiral, make it burning hot. There is a myriad of such laws, but they all have one thing in common: the invariability of their execution. That is, water, when freezing, always turns to ice, and not to gasoline or cream or wheat. When you pull the switch, the lamp either lights up, or not, but it doesn't turn into a parrot or a water tap. That is, the course of processes determined by such laws is invariable. Paying their tribute to Castaneda, searchers call these laws the laws of the Eagle – that indescribable, incomprehensible something which is above everything in existence and which determines our being. You could call these laws the laws of God, the laws of the universe – it won't change their meaning. Searchers got attracted by the invariability of the execution of these laws. If the law of the Eagle starts realizing, then it will be executed, no matter what. The only limitation is related to the fact that some laws of the Eagle may influence the activity of others. Let's say that if you jump out of a plane, you'll get smashed up. But if you have a parachute, you'll live. In this situation one law of the Eagle doesn't let the other law – the law of gravity – realize itself to the fullest. We must be aware of these limitations." Boris went quiet for a couple of minutes, collecting his thoughts then continued. "While examining how the laws of the Eagle get realized, searchers asked themselves: can't we use the invariability of their execution to our benefit? At that time we were interested in controlling events. We tried to understand why events of the world around us are shaped in one way or another. What defines this shaping? That was the time when we encountered infor-mation about John Dee and his solitaire in our dreams. And to our surprise, we found out that the Patience of Medici allows us to program the manifestation of desired events. This is how it happens: the Patience of Medici is laid out with a regular pack of thirty six cards. It has a certain composition algorithm related to the suit and the value of a card. Each card in the solitaire is assigned a particular event in real life. And the rest is very simple: when sorting the solitaire, we introduce the goal unit – that is, we pick out a card that will represent our wish. The created solitaire is a law of the Eagle, and that means, it always comes true. Having sorted the solitaire, we start carrying it out IRL – that is, we consciously start realizing certain actions that correspond to the suit and value of the cards. And that's where real magic begins: the law of the Eagle starts operating, and the chain of events starts developing in accordance with the preselected scenario. Everything happens surprisingly on time. Each new event is determined by the card next in turn in the solitaire. The solitaire becomes a template of sorts, which defines the course of real events. At some point the chain of events reaches the goal card and realizes our wish. That's it. The goal has been reached. And why? Well, because the chain of events, created by the law of the Eagle, is given priority in comparison to other chains of events. Or if, for example..." Boris grinned, "...you use the Patience of Medici to win the lottery, you will be the one to win the prize, and not somebody else."

"And it really works?" There was a tone of disbelief in Maxim's voice.

"Try to find that out by putting it to practice," Boris suggested. "Magic is strictly an applied science. There's no room for naked theory in magic."

"And the queen?" Maxim remembered. "Did it work for her?"

"It did," Boris nodded. "Although not every time. The thing is that we've got a very big advantage: we've got computer programs to sort the solitaire. To successfully sort a solitaire by hand is rather difficult – especially, if you are creating a chain of goals to achieve a specific result. According to the legend, Maria Stuart was imprisoned and she was to be executed in the morning by the order of her cousin, Elizabeth I. She didn't have a computer, but she had a pack of cards and some input data – namely, the guard outside the door, her friends that were going to help her escape, and time until the morning. She had to weave together a solitaire chain that would include and consider the elements she had at her disposal. She was working at the solitaire until morning. But it had been too long since her last classes with John Dee – the queen had forgotten a lot. As the legend goes, when the guards came for her in the morning, she gathered the cards from the table, smiled and said, 'What a pity. I almost got it'."

"She was executed?"

"Yes. And that tells us that magic doesn't stand a breezy

attitude." An ironic smile flashed by in Boris' eyes. "I think you'll sort out all of the details with the PM on your own; you'll find everything described more than clearly in our archive. Well, and if you have any questions, ask." Boris looked in the direction of the window. "Roman's here. Let's go see what's new with him."

The main news concerned the upcoming mayor elections. Legionaries wanted to leave the current boss of Klyonovsk on that post – one of their guys. Searchers tried to stop them, having brought into play forces opposing the mayor. Maxim didn't know much about these issues yet; still, he tried with interest to get the details of the conversation. And then the discussion touched on him, there was talk about his new documents.

"You'll have them in three days time," Roman promised. "But I'll have to take a few pictures of you and send them away. Let's do it right now."

Maxim was led to a small room, obviously intended for photography. Behind the folding screen, in the right part of the room, was a real treasure of all kinds of clothes, for men and for women. Boris made Maxim put on a dark shirt, a suit and a tie, then he put him on a stool. Roman turned on a couple of flood-light projectors, and a digital camera appeared in the hands of the searcher. Having made a few shots; he finished them off on the computer and seemed to be rather pleased with the result. After that, they once again changed Maxim's clothes. This time he was dressed in a sweater. As it was explained to Maxim, the second photo was for the military ID. Then they made a third photo – for the driver's license. Roman saved the completed photos on a disc and then got up from the chair.

"That's it," he said. "I'll go upstairs and send it."

"And what's my last name going to be?" Maxim inquired.

"I have no idea," Roman shrugged. "It all depends." He went out of the room, and Maxim looked at Boris.

"And do you have to make new papers often?"

"Not really," Boris replied. "Maybe once in a few years; each of us has several sets of papers, and this makes it easy for us to disappear when necessary."

"But how do you do business, if you have to always be on the run?"

"You just had bad luck, and came to us at a wrong time," Boris explained. "And the running about is rather an exception than a rule. Regarding my business, it's all very simple: I have one set of documents for business, which I do not expose anywhere else. I've got a villa in England, and, as a businessman, that's my official place of residence. As for the actual firm management, there are managers to do that."

"But if you've got a villa in England, what were you doing in Rostov?" There was surprise in Maxim's voice.

"I met you there," Boris answered, a smile slipped across his lips. "Seriously though, I came to Rostov on business; Iris and I were checking up some interesting information."

"Mind telling me about it?" Maxim inquired. "Unless it's a secret."

"It is a secret, but I can tell you about it. In one of the articles Iris found a record of underground monasteries located by the river Don. There was even a mention of the approximate spot – about a hundred kilometers away from Rostov. That interested us. We came there, talked to the locals, and one of them actually showed us the entrance into the underground monastery. It wasn't even an entrance, rather more of a burrow in a bank overgrown with bushes. We squeezed through and found ourselves in a huge cave. Once, it really was a monastery, we found crucifixes and plenty of very strange writings carved right on the walls of the cave. We copied these down, and one of the searchers from the St. Petersburg group is now trying to decipher them. He had no luck so far; these writings are nothing like we've ever seen. But since a searcher took on this task, he'll definitely see it through. As for Iris, she'll soon finish up in Rostov and come back to Belgorod."

"But isn't it dangerous for her to stay in Rostov?"

"Not for her. She is a real witch, in all senses of the word." A grin slipped across Boris' lips. "I don't envy those Legionaries who are trying to give her a hard time. She's not one to be trifled with. Perhaps she'll move to Rostov all together – she likes the place."

"And what does she do? What's her profession?"

"She enjoys life," Boris answered and grinned once again. "It's just that Iris has so many things going on that it is difficult to name them all. She is the owner of a prestigious Moscow dental clinic; she owns a pleasure boat. She's got stocks in several major industrial companies to the total of about three million dollars. She also acts in movies – both as an actress, and as a stuntwoman – where you need to film all kind of cool scenes. She loves diving, and now she's planning on learning skydiving. And she'll do it – I have no doubts about that. So when you meet her, try not to anger or annoy her – she's got a really bad temper, and a heavy hand." Boris looked Maxim in the eyes and burst out laughing. Maxim smiled too.

"Can she open portals?" he inquired.

"Iris can open anything," Boris answered. "Starting with portals and ending with bank vaults." He grinned again.

"The vault thing – you're joking, right?" Maxim asked.

"Not at all," Boris answered with a smile. "You see, Iris had never been a good girl. And in her time, she actually did rob the office of a very well-known commercial firm together with a friend. She was, by the way, not even seventeen years old at the time."

"Are you serious?" Maxim didn't believe him. Somehow what his friend was telling him didn't accord with the image of dream searchers.

"Dead serious," Boris assured him. "They chose New Year's Eve; the night from the thirty first of December to the first of January. When the clock struck midnight and there were fireworks going off with loud bangs, Iris blasted the vault door. Incidentally, she made the explosives herself. She had always liked Chemistry – just the applied part of it, to be more specific. They even entered the office in an original way: turned out that what once was an integrated building was twenty years ago divided in two, by bricking up the door. The businessmen working in that building didn't know that, but Iris somehow found out about it. A library was located in the other part of the building. Iris and her friend had no problem getting in there. They took apart the brick wall before midnight and entered the office. And exactly at midnight they blasted the vault. There was about forty thousand dollars. Although, Iris's friend turned out to be an idiot and was soon caught, immediately giving up his girlfriend. When Iris was asked in court, why she did it, she said she had very large expenses." Boris started laughing again.

"She was put in jail?"

"She got away with a suspended sentence. Her dad is a very influential official," Boris explained. "And right after that incident she joined us."

"And you accepted her?" Maxim couldn't believe it.

"What do you mean, 'accepted'? She came on her own. Had we only tried not to accept her."

Boris's eyes were shining. He was looking at Maxim, obviously enjoying his confusion.

"It just doesn't really tie in with the image of dream searchers," Maxim said. "Still, studying the secrets of the universe and breaking vaults open are somewhat different things."

"I think it's the same thing." Boris couldn't contain himself and started laughing again. Having finished laughing, he looked at Maxim. "You're just too rigid. It's like in Soviet films about the revolution: all 'red' ones are good and honest, all 'white' ones are bastards and scum. That doesn't happen in real life. Learn to look at things from a wider perspective. Don't divide everything up in black and white. Accept people the way they are, with all their virtues and imperfections. When it comes to Iris, I can assure you: she doesn't blow up vaults anymore. Not because she is a good girl now, but because she doesn't need it anymore. And I wouldn't have told you the story about the vault if Iris had tried to hide it in any way. I think she's actually proud of it. That was one of the very first adventures in her life."

"I don't know," Maxim shrugged. "Still, I considered searchers to be more 'proper'."

"We are 'proper'," Boris grinned. "The problem is that you and I have a different idea of the notion 'proper'. You are set on observing laws, norms – the social moral, while searchers have only got one law – the law of the Spirit. If a person is hollow, then no matter how proper he is, he's of no interest to us – he will never amount to anything. And the other way around, if a person's got Spirit, then all the worldly dirt sticking to him doesn't mean a thing. You can clean off the dirt, but you can't fill the void."

"What do you understand by the Spirit?" Maxim inquired.

"You've read Castaneda, right? Remember, when his teacher, Don Juan, told him about the Spirit. The Spirit cannot be described, explained, identified – it's something abstract, elusive – and, at the same time, it's so apparent. The minimum for magicians is to see the Spirit in everything around them, and they express the Spirit through their actions."

"The Spirit is God?"

"That's one way of putting it," Boris agreed. "The problem is that it's only a way of talking – an attempt to turn the unknown into forms that our mind is more or less used to. Someday you'll understand what the Spirit is, yet when someone will ask you what it is, you'll just shrug your shoulders with a smile."

"But Castaneda says that you can use the Spirit. Can you really use God?"

"That's why I am saying that words can mislead you, and you cannot grasp the essence of the Spirit with your mind. How can we use the infinity surrounding us? The actual thought sounds blasphemous. But when you realize that you are a tiny part of this infinity, understanding will come on its own. Not on the level of your mind but on the level of your body. And having realized that you are a part of this immenseness, you suddenly understand that you can also control it – only because you have merged with it into a whole..."

There was a knock, then the door opened and Maxim saw Oxana.

"You're still enlightening?" the young woman asked, looking at Boris with a smile. Then she added: "Lunch is ready. You can chat later..."

It was beet soup for lunch – delicious, Ukrainian borsch. Maxim's parents lived in Ukraine, so Maxim knew his borsch and prized Galina's cooking talent. While they were eating, the searchers started discussing Maxim's fate.

"Let him stay here for a while," Roman suggested. "He'll live here a month or two – get used to the place, have a look round. He'll have a chance to come up with something do to. And then we'll see."

"I'll teach him lucid dreaming," Oxana added. "And Roman and Denis will teach him how to kick ass." The young woman looked at Maxim with a smile.

Maxim shrugged his shoulders and looked at Boris, expecting his opinion.

"It wouldn't be too bad for a start," Boris agreed. "Things will have time to settle down a little, and then we might even go back to Rostov. It's a good town, and if we won't be there, the Legionaries will run wild. We can take Oxana with us. What do you say, Keeper?"

"Rostov?" Oxana shook her head thoughtfully. "I could go to Rostov. We haven't got any of our guys there yet, right?"

"Only Iris, and she is only there occasionally," Boris answered. "Although we wouldn't want to re-unite you two, or else there'll be another natural disaster." He looked at Maxim and explained: "Last year they cooked up a storm here. It took three days to get the blown down maples off the streets and set up new cable work. At least no one died, thank God."

"It was an accident," Oxana answered with an emphasis. "Iris was teaching me how to twist ascending currents. We overdid it a little bit."

"Right," Boris nodded, having taken another spoonful of borsch, "and then half the city was left without electricity for two days."

"But it was some current they managed to create," Roman added and everyone softly laughed. Maxim too smiled tactfully, although he didn't really understand what they were talking about.

"Then that's settled." Boris glanced at Maxim. "You'll live here for a while, learn a little, and then we'll make a decision about what to do next."

"Ok," Maxim agreed. "I don't mind."

After lunch Boris helped take one of the computers to Maxim's room and connect it to the internal LAN. Then he brought two CDs.

"Study these," he said and handed Maxim the discs. "On one of them you'll find everything about mapping, and there's information about the Patience of Medici on the other. It's the most detailed description to date. About the internet: we have unlimited traffic, so you can browse the net as much as you like. But only on one condition: no messaging and no emails. I'll ask Oxana to show you how to get online, she'll explain you all the safety procedures as well. As for me, I'm going to Moscow for a week or two; I've got some business to take care of." Boris glanced at his watch. "That's it, Maxim. I have to go now; must catch the evening flight to Moscow. And don't be shy – it's your home now." Boris shook Maxim's hand, clapped him on the shoulder and left the room.

Of course, Maxim immediately got himself in front of the computer to examine the contents of the CDs. There was more than plenty of information; however, now and then Maxim caught himself thinking about Oxana rather than searcher techniques. He was already aware of that he really liked this girl in a way that he had never liked anyone in his life. He was drawn to her, and Maxim couldn't do anything about it. Right now Oxana was working in her studio. Maxim didn't know whether it would be appropriate to pay her a visit, but finally he decided to give it a go. And the purpose of his visit was quite decent – to familiarize himself with her art.

To his knocking on the door of the studio, Maxim heard a soft permission to enter.

"Hi," Maxim said, having entered the studio and gently closed the door behind him. "I wanted to see what you are painting. You don't mind?"

"No, I don't," Oxana smiled. She was standing by the easel; Maxim noticed that the tip of Oxana's nose was stained with green paint. It looked very funny. "What are you laughing at?" Oxana asked, having noticed Maxim's smile.

"You've got paint on your nose," Maxim answered.

"It always gets stained." Oxana took a cloth and wiped her nose. "Is it ok now?"

"Yeah!"

"It's just when I am thinking about a painting, I sometimes rub the tip of my nose. And I've got paint all over my fingers, so that's how my nose gets stained," Oxana smiled.

Maxim didn't answer; he was already looking at Oxana's paintings. There were five of them, some unfinished. One painting, already finished, was standing by the wall; it depicted a huge soaring eagle. Oxana painted with rather large heavy strokes, but the effect was still amazing. Looking at the eagle, Maxim was involuntarily astonished by its power, pride and calm. It seemed incredible that Oxana managed to pass these feelings onto the painting.

"So, what do you think?" Oxana asked.

"Amazing!" Maxim answered sincerely. "Like a live one – even better than a live one. Did you learn this from somebody?"

"I just walked around museums," Oxana answered.

Another painting, unfinished, portrayed the autumn breath. The yellow leaves were already falling off the trees and grey gloomy sky was reflected in the rain puddles. Yet the painting didn't appear solemn. Rather, it conveyed a feeling of calm; nature was resting after a long hot summer.

Other paintings were like these two – even the unfinished ones; they attracted one's gaze. There was Life – the Spirit – in them. When looking at Oxana's work, Maxim involuntarily compared them to other paintings – those he'd seen in museums, at art exhibitions. True, there too he'd seen some good works. But, there were more dead paintings. Everything appeared to be beautiful – smooth, tidy, according to all the pictorial canons. But there was no soul in them…

"You're always doing several paintings at a time?" he inquired.

"Yes," Oxana nodded. "It's easier for me that way. Sometimes something doesn't come out the way I want it to. Then I simply put the painting aside and start working on another. The painting has to lie for a while then when you catch the thread again, every-thing comes out wonderfully."

"What thread?" Maxim didn't get it.

"The Thread of the Spirit." Oxana smiled. "The Spirit is what's responsible for creativity in us. Without the Spirit we can't do a thing."

Maxim didn't answer. For some time he remained, looking closely at the paintings then he looked up at Oxana and smiled.

"I like them very much," he admitted. "You are a true painter. I'm gonna go, I won't be in your way."

"You can stop by whenever you like," Oxana said.

"Ok," Maxim agreed and went out of the studio.

Chapter Five

The Secrets of Magic

The first couple of days, Maxim didn't feel entirely comfortable at the new place. However, soon he began to feel at home. Yet, he had to accept some of the traditions of the house; for example, the morning warm-up in the sports hall. At first Maxim was not too enthusiastic about the whole thing, but already on the third day he felt he was starting to like these sessions. The warm-up took place before breakfast; more serious exercise was left for the evening hours.

The exercises were all very different – from purely physical training to working with cold steel arms and hand-to-hand combat. Denis, the local security manager, was the one to start educating Maxim in the art of combat. Roman assigned him to coach the new guy.

Maxim had never before had anything to do with martial arts, and many things became a real eye-opener to him. Moreover, the training turned out to be completely different from what Maxim first imagined it to be. Having critically examined Maxim upon their first meeting, and having heard that he had never done anything like this, Denis only grinned and declared that in a month's time he'll make Steven Seagal out of him. Maxim got ready for hardcore training, but there was nothing of the kind or even close to it. There were no traditional kimonos; he was dressed in ordinary jeans and a dark short sleeved shirt with ordinary sneakers on his feet. As Denis explained it, you've got to work in the clothes you usually wear. Worst case scenario, all of this would be nothing more than ordinary sport, which is quite removed from real life situations. Denis didn't force Maxim to fine-tune some standard punches or combinations until he dropped. Everything in his system was based on spontaneity, on natural human reactions, for that reason it contained no combat holds what so ever.

"Don't see everything I show you as rigid schemes," Denis told Maxim. "The important thing for a fighter is to have a movement culture, to teach your body how to work spontaneously, based on a specific situation. Never study holds as such, there are simply no such things; use principles – general movement forms. When fighting, you never know what you'll do next – your body decides that, and the important thing is not to be in its way. Never think about what you are doing, your body must work spontaneously – only then will you get somewhere."

Denis was slightly past thirty and, according to him; he'd been practicing martial arts not more than seven years. But it was very hard to believe, especially when looking at all the things he did in a fight. Denis' body reminded him of a bundle of mercury – that's how plastic all his movements appeared to be.

"Try grabbing me," Denis offered his new student during their first class. "Come on, don't be shy."

Maxim tried – at first rather timidly, then after the first few unsuccessful attempts, he got really carried away. But he still didn't manage to grab hold of Denis; in some incomprehensible way he kept slipping away, easily extricating himself from any embrace, tearing through any holds with barely perceptible movements. He was here, he wasn't running away, and still grabbing hold of him turned out to be impossible. What's more, Maxim kept falling down. Every time, when Denis was almost in his arms, he did an imperceptible – almost unnoticeable – movement, and Maxim, having lost his footing, fell on the floor. On top of everything, Denis even had the time to catch him.

Hot and heavily breathing, Maxim was standing and puffing wearily. Denis looked at him with an ironic smile.

"Ok, I'll allow you to beat me," he said. "Attack me. Hit me with your arms, legs – in other words, do whatever you want."

Anger was growing in Maxim's chest. "Well, if you say so..." and he flew at Denis with new strength.

He chased him around the hall for about five minutes, and the result was practically the same, only with the difference that Maxim was now falling down even more frequently. Using indiscernible, blurred movements, Denis reduced any of Maxim's actions to absurdity – no matter what he did, everything was turned against him. It seemed there was an enchanted area of space around Denis that was completely impenetrable to any external impact...

'God!' Maxim thought, getting himself up from the floor for the nth time. 'What will happen if he starts fighting?'

This was the first demonstration lesson, then it was time teach Maxim the actual technique. Denis treated Maxim's training very seriously, as he did with any other task.

"No, that's not right," Denis explained to Maxim during another training session. His voice was very calm; there was no impatience or irritation in it. "Don't run away from a blow. You don't need to dodge it – that's your mistake. On the contrary, you should get up close to your enemy – cling to him. And the way you're rolling your blow is wrong too. I'm going to show you one more time. Hit me."

Maxim took a step forward, towards Denis and slowly – that way it was easier to understand the nature of the movements – delivered a blow.

"Look," Denis continued just as calmly. "I meet your right hand with my left wrist, catching it from underneath then I raise my elbow; notice that my elbow is now higher than my wrist. Got it? And now, I simply follow your arm, controlling it with my forearm, my head goes a little bit to the side – it's as if you are trying to wave away the blow. You see? The whole point is in the naturalness of this movement – in its reflex nature; you get it once, and it will work all your life. One more time."

Maxim repeated the blow, closely watching Denis'

movements.

"So, I meet with my wrist; make a circular motion – notice that my torso gets slightly twisted... And now – I take a step towards you with my left leg, and upon untwisting my torso, I knee you in the crotch... Although there could be many different continuations – to hit you in your crotch with my hand, put an elbow in your face and so on." Denis demonstrated on Maxim, like on a dummy, the possible continuations of a counterattack. "Now try it yourself."

Of course, martial arts were not the only part of his new life. Training sessions in the sports hall took about two hours a day, all of the remaining time Maxim dedicated to magic. Following Boris' directions, he focused mainly on two topics: dream mapping and the Patience of Medici. He had to start over on the mapping. All his notes and drawings were left in Rostov. However, now Maxim had access to detailed instructions, describing the tiniest nuances, instead of the scant information from the internet forums.

It turned out that the general understanding of the structure of the world of dreams takes up an important place in mapping. When falling asleep, a person doesn't simply get into a dream, but he finds himself in a sphere of perception. The sphere of perception is a little piece of virtual dream space. It's a peculiar little sphere, inside of which a certain dream scenario is played for us. In an ordinary dream, man is not aware of the limits of this space, so he takes it all in good faith. Searchers managed to find out about the illusory nature of these worlds. To see it for yourself, it's enough to, in any of your dreams, walk straight ahead for some time without turning aside. During the process, every now and then, attempts will be made to distract the lucid dreamer from the set goal – all kinds of obstacles will appear on his way. But if he will remain determined, he will actually reach the end of the dream sphere of perception. He'll be literally pressing against a barrier of some kind, a curtain of the world of sorts – the border of the dream bubble. Something of the kind can be observed in the cinema; seemingly, you are watching a scenario unfold in front of your eyes, but if you try to get up close, you'll definitely be pressing against the screen...

Information about dream spheres of perception really fascinated Maxim. It was strange, realizing that a dream has limits of some kind and that these limits could be reached in a lucid dream. Maxim decided to test it himself as soon as possible. For the time being, he tried to grasp the theory's ABCs, discovering more new subtleties.

As Maxim understood it, each sphere of perception had a corresponding scenario. There are good dream spheres and sometimes you come across very bad dream spheres – these are the ones responsible for nightmares. Transfers between the spheres of perception are determined by a complex web of transits – dream portals of sorts. If one were to pay attention to the transfer moments, when moving from one dream into another, one would notice that almost every time it has something to do with an element of a dream sphere. Practically any object could be an element; it simply draws the dreamer over into another sphere of perception. The knowledge about the system of transits allows you to enter any sphere of perception.

And that's where mapping emerged. While compiling the map of dream landscapes, searchers introduced an element of order to the dream world, creating certain reference points. The spheres of perception, previously uncoordinated, gradually started merging – this happened when some pieces of landscape on the dream map were put together. The most interesting part was that, in some strange way, the elements of all kinds of cities could be combined together, and some street in Moscow could, for example, lead to another street in Kiev. Basically, the dream map joined together the elements of all cities in which the dreaming person had been before. And not only cities – there was place for villages and rural areas; fields and forests; rivers and seas. Hundreds and hundreds of previously scattered/separate spheres of perception were brought together into one strange, but quite coherent picture.

Maxim had some difficulties with the unusual method of orienting the dream map. On the assumption that the dream world mirrors the real world, searchers introduced a few changes to the coordinate system. And if west and east were in place, north and south had swapped places. As it turned out, searchers were not the first ones to apply this system of orientation – that had already been done by Taoists and Northern shamans before them. Having thought about this scheme, Maxim chose the Solomonic solution; namely, he noted the directions as up, down, to the left side and to the right. It was much easier that way.

A very special place on the dream map was allocated to the, so called, bordering limits. These were usually seas, deserts, mountains and forests. Getting beyond the bordering limits was considered to be either impossible, or very difficult.

As far as Maxim could remember, he sometimes dreamt of a forest and a few times of the sea. Did he reach the bordering limits in these dreams? All of these things he had to find out.

Somewhere in the middle of a dreamer's map was his home. The peculiarity of this place was that it was in the transmutation zone and, unlike other areas of the dream map, it was constantly changing. If the dreamer often changed his place of living, then that became even more apparent every time his home acquired new features. Searchers believed that you had to treat it calmly; after all, the point with mapping was not creating the map as such, but in the actual work done in applying some kind of order to the dream world. Because the map in this case is a trick, it allows you to achieve some rather specific goals. Namely, becoming aware of yourself in a dream and making your dream memory 'explode'. In the first stage, a person would start recognizing familiar places in his dream and at some point he'd realize that he was sleeping, and so his dream turned into a lucid dream. With time, changes would take place in the dream memory as well; the dreamer started remembering his old dreams more and more often. At first these were isolated dreams then their stream increased dramatically, turning into a real avalanche. Basically, you'd eventually remember all the dreams you've ever had, at that point you could draw a very detailed version of your dream map. This process was the main point of mapping. Searchers believed that only once an explosion of dream memory had taken place, you'd start having real lucid dreams.

To grasp the entire mapping in one go proved to be simply impossible. The more Maxim studied searchers' explanations, the more he understood how broad this topic was. Finally, having realized that he wouldn't even manage to get through the theory in one day, Maxim decided to take things one at a time. He decided to start with compiling the map, taking his time in making sense of the subtleties of this method. Following Oxana's advice, he spent at least an hour a day doing mapping, not only working with present dreams, but with all the old ones he had managed to remember.

Given that Maxim had more or less figured out the mapping, The Patience of Medici turned out to be a rather tricky thing. To Maxim's surprise, Oxana refused to help him with that, having said that the PM is purely a stalker technique and she had barely done it at all.

"It's just that the Keepers have their own methods of training," she explained with a smile. "I'll be happy to help you with your lucid dreaming, but stalking is not my element. You better turn to Boris or Roman, they know much more about it than I do."

So that's how it came about that Maxim had to get his head around the PM on his own. At first, he was just reading the materials on the CD, then having realized that a lot of things slipped through his fingers, he got a notebook and started writing down all of the interesting details of this particular method.

It turned out there were quite a few of them. As far as Maxim had understood, the patience was based on the concepts of attraction and valence. Attraction was a certain unconscious strive of the similar towards the similar; more specifically, cards of one suit attracted cards of the same suit. Valence determined the size, the number and the measure of something. In cards, it corresponded to their nominal value, and cards of the same value also attracted each other.

At first, each card was given a certain meaning. One of the standard schemes looked something like this:

Ace – power. Any external event that happens by a will that is not our own and which often forces us to act in one way or another.

King – law. The necessity to obey certain rules, act one way and not another – everything that somehow constrains us.

Queen – a persona. Any living being, from a human to a mosquito.

Jack – the courier of power. In this case, our desires and ambitions.

Ten – result or expectation.

Nine – an action.

Eight – communication – socializing with other people.

Seven – intake.

Six – movement.

Suits too had their own meaning:

Spades – manifestations of force and will-power.

Diamonds – everything that has to do with money, and interest in its broad sense.

Hearts – the realm of feelings. Love, friendship, hatred – in other words, any manifestation of emotion.

Clubs – everyday life, work, routine.

There were examples provided to get a better grasp of this system. Let's say the Ace could be your boss that wants to have a talk with you. If your boss had called you up to give you a hard time, then it's clearly the Ace of Spades – 'AS'. If he's told you that you are going to get a raise, that's the Ace of Diamonds – 'AD'. If he just had a talk with you about your current work – that's the Ace of Clubs – 'AC'. Finally, if your boss is not indifferent to you, then that's the Ace of Hearts – 'AH'. Aces could also be a car that covered you in mud, a broken computer, a light that went out, etc. They could also be an unexpected, pleasant event – winning the lottery, or any fortunate coincidence.

Kings represented the law. For example, you stopped at the red light – the King of Clubs – 'KC'. You need to pay for something – the 'KD'. You don't want to go to work, but you have to, so you must force yourself – the 'KS'. It's someone's birthday, you have to bring a gift – the 'KH'. Or the 'KD', if you are more worried about the money that you'll have to spend on the gift.

Anybody could be the Queen – the persona. You met a friend – the 'QH'. A dog barked at you – the 'QS'. A cashier – the 'QD'. A bus driver – the 'QC'. What was special about personas was that you didn't have to interact with them; you could simply note them in your environment.

Jacks represented our desires. You have a firm intention of attaining something – the 'JS'. You want to make a lot of money – the 'JD'. You want to meet someone – the JH'. You want to do your job better – the 'JC'.

Tens marked expectation or result. Completing a project – the '10C'. Happy that everything is over – the '10H'. A bad outcome – the '10S'. The result has to do with money – the '10D'.

Any action on our part was assigned to the nines. Brushed your hair – the '9C'. Bought something – the '9D'. Punched someone in the eye – the '9S'. Or the '9H' – if you enjoyed it.

Eights – communication. Any talks with the beings around us. You had an argument with someone – the '8S'. You're talking to a shop assistant – the '8D'. You are discussing business problems – the '8C'. You are chatting with someone you like – the '8H'.

Sevens – intake. This included both trivial intake of food, as well as intake of information. For example, you found out something unpleasant – the '7S'. The other way around, you've heard a good piece of news – the '7H'. You're eating breakfast – the '7C'. You've counted the money in your wallet – the '7D'.

Sixes – movement. That's our movement as well as moving something or someone from one place to another. You're going to work in the morning – the '6C'. You're going to a shop – the '6D'. You're going on a date – the '6H'. You're going to beat someone up – the '6S'.

It was crucial to understand that any event could be described with a card of practically any suit or value. Everything depended on the person's attitude towards this event. Let's say you drank a glass of juice with great pleasure – the '7H'. I don't want to, but I am drinking – the '7S'. I'm drinking, thinking that it costs money – the '7D'. I'm just drinking – the '7C'. That is, the scheme was not a fixed one; every person could change it at his will or discretion. What's more, you were advised to adjust the standard scheme, make it convenient, so that it would fit you personally. Everything was allowed – you could change the meaning of the cards, expand the interpretations. There were no limitations. Basically, any searcher made his own, unique language of communicating with the Universe.

After familiarizing oneself with the program language, one had to learn the technique of dealing the patience. Despite the fact that searchers had computer programs for sorting the patience, one had to learn how to sort it by hand.

The patience was sorted the following way. First, any three cards were put in a row, from left to right, face down. Then you started analyzing these cards by their suit and value. The 'sorting' happened only when the middle card of the three was in between the cards of the same suit or value. For example, in the group of three cards, 'JD', '8S' and 'JH', the eight of spades was situated between two jacks. Hence, the 'JD' and 'JH' were drawn towards each other because of their equal value; at the same time, the eight was 'pushed out' to the top and covered the 'JH'. So, there was now a chain of two cards: '8S' and 'JH'. Then another card was dealt; let's say it was the '9S'. Then the chain looked like this; '8S', 'JH' and '9S'. The Jack was now between the two cards of spades – the cards agreed in suit, so the 'JH' covered the '8S'. The chain took the following form 'JH', '9S', then a new card was taken. If the new card didn't bring about an agreement, then another card was pulled out, until there was another agreement. For example, it could happen this way:

'JH', '9S', 'QD', '7C', '10S', 'QC'

In this chain there was no agreement up to the 'QC'. Bringing out the 'QC' meant that you could fold according to suit between the cards the '7C' and the 'QC'. Consequently, the '10S' covered the '7C', and the chain took on the following shape:

'JH', '9S', 'QD', '10S', 'QC'

Now you had to examine the chain looking for possible folds. There were two of them in the chain above – between the '9S' and the '10S' and between the two queens. And here you had to remember a very important rule: if in the process of putting together the chain there were several possible folding alternatives, then you first folded the one at the very left – in this case it's the fold between the nine and the ten of spades. Having folded these, you get the chain 'JH', 'QD', '10S' 'QC'. Now you can do the queens – you get the chain 'JH', '10S', 'QC'. After that, the chain doesn't fold anymore, so you may take out new cards.

The rest of the cards were dealt in much the same fashion. If you managed to sort the whole patience, then you'd have a pile of cards on the left and one card – the last one – on the right. A patience sorted this way corresponded to the Law of the Eagle, and that meant that it was imbued with qualities of priority before other chains. Having sorted the patience, you had to put it into practice – doing things or noticing things going on around you that would correspond to specific cards. For example, the chain could have the following appearance:

<JD 8S JH> <9S> <QD 7C 10S QC> <AH 9C> <6C KD 7S 9D> <AS> <AC QH JC> <7H> <JS> <KH> <10C 10D KC> <QS AD 10H

8C KS 7D 6H 8D> <8H> <6D> <9H> <6S>

The brackets represented the borders of the rhythm, or folds. The goal card in this chain was the 'AD', so it could be used to get a money result – for example, to play the lottery.

For convenience's sake, the patience was recorded in a notebook then you had to put down the timing – that is, the approximate time allocated to realize each card. There were a couple of timing schemes; in the simplest one, you could set your own rhythm that's the most convenient to you – for example, ten minutes a card. And if the 'JD' – the diamond wish – was made at 9.00 am, then the '8S' must be realized at about 9.10 am. The third card, the 'JH', was realized at 9.20 am, and so on, until the whole chain had been carried out. And roughly after the fifth-seventh card, the chain entered automatic mode. That meant that the law of the Eagle had come into effect, and the chain would continue developing until its logical end, having realized the requested result in the meantime. You had to focus your attention on each action, otherwise it didn't get included in the chain, and the course of the chain got disrupted. Again, once the chain had entered automatic mode and events started happening on their own, it was recommended to pay close attention to the progression of the chain of events, so that you wouldn't lose the chain or note a similar event instead of the one that was part of your chain. According to searchers, such mishaps happened to beginners all the time; however, with practice the number of these failures dropped.

You should also accurately choose the moment of initiating the chain, using the famous principle: 'Yesterday was early, tomorrow will be too late'. The start time for carrying out the chain was determined by, so called, Signs of Power. For example, if you have decided to carry out a diamond chain, then you'd have to start on it after having received some kind of sign from the world around you that mentioned money. It could be someone's conversation, a phrase from a TV-show, a coin you found. In many cases, searchers used a more progressive method: you had to, in your mind, ask the Power – that is, the Spirit, the Universe – a question about the start of the chain, and if everything fit, the real world replied at once. It could be a bird that flew by, a falling leaf or the sun coming out of the clouds. It was claimed that a magician never misinterpreted the sings and he always felt when the world was answering his request, and when it was silent. If there was no answer from the world, then you'd have to postpone the chain until a more favorable moment; this could be ten minutes, or an entire day.

All of these explanations greatly intrigued Maxim. Turns out we can actually order things we want to happen, simply by having included them into a chain of The Patience of Medici. No wonder Maxim wanted to try it out...

It was the twelfth day of his stay at the Siberian searcher residence. Maxim had just returned from the sports hall – Denis had another training session with him – his hands were slightly shaking. Maxim was studying the computer program for creating chains of Patience of Medici and so he was sitting in front of the computer when Roman entered the room.

"Here you go," he said with a smile and handed Maxim a crisp new passport and a military ID. "From this moment on, you are Igor Novoselov. And the military ID is fine too, you've even been registered. You can unregister when you leave town. I'll have your driver's license ready in a couple of days. And this is some pocket money." Roman put an envelope on the table. "That's ten thousand dollars. Later you'll get access to one of the main accounts."

"Thanks." Maxim picked up the envelope with hesitation. "I'll give it back to you as soon as I can."

"You will," Roman agreed, "by contributing to the piggy bank of human spirit." Roman winked at Maxim and left the room.

His hands still shaking, Maxim carefully opened the passport. Igor Novoselov – it was a stranger's name and a stranger's surname. But it was his face. He took a look at his military ID, closely examined the small photo. Yes, that was him alright...

Having closely examined the papers, Maxim opened the envelope. It contained a plastic card, directions on how to use it and pin-code information. Ten thousand dollars – quite an impressive sum. Maxim never had that kind of money on him prior to that day. The only thing that made him uneasy was that it was someone else's money. And even though Roman said something about making a contribution to the piggy bank of human spirit, Maxim decided right away that he'd return the money as soon as possible. He felt better that way.

He returned to the Patience of Medici forty minutes later, happy that he now had new papers, which meant that he could go outside and not worry about the police controls. The old passport was lying on the table nearby, looking at it made him sad. Maxim still hoped that maybe someday he could become himself again.

He put together his first chain to win the lottery – not because he wanted to return the money at once, but simply because this exercise was suggested as one of the first ones. The chain, including a few subtleties, came out like this:

<JD 9S AD> <QC KC JH 9C> <KH> <7S 6S QD KS> <QS> <AS> <7C 7D 10S 9H AC 9D> <8S 10H 6D 10D> <AH 6H 10C 7H> <KD JC 8D> <6C> <QH 8C> <JS 8H>

In this chain the first unit – 'JD', '9S', 'AD' – was considered to be the unit of the Spirit's greeting. It was carried out as a whole, without any timing. At first you silently expressed your wish – the 'JD'. The next card, the '9S' in this configuration. was considered to be a flag card. Flags in the PM were actions aimed at the Spirit. It was recommended to choose actions that would seem inconspicuous to other people. A flag action could be to adjust your collar, to comb your hair, to undo or do up a button on your shirt – the range of possible actions was only limited by your imagination. Maxim went with the collar option. The third card – the 'AD' – was the Spirit's answer. If the Spirit gave you an answer, the chain continued. If there was no answer, you had to wait for some time and then start over.

Maxim paid special attention to the appearance of the goal unit. It started with the '9D' – to give money to a clerk in a lottery booth. The flag – the '8S' - immediately followed; Maxim had to realize it before obtaining the lottery ticket. Once he got the ticket – the result of the purchase – the '10S' – he had to go – the '6D' – to someplace where he would learn about his win. The ten of diamonds symbolized the actual win. Then there was joy – the 'AH', going back to the booth – the '6H', collecting the money – the '10C'. All other cards Maxim left at the Spirit's discretion.

Maxim carefully noted down the chain he had put together. He didn't include any timing, having decided that he'd rely on his intuition, that option was also available. He decided he'd start with the chain in the morning, so he put aside his notebook somewhat regretting that he wouldn't start right away...

In the morning, he could barely wait until breakfast. When Maxim told the searchers that he was going outside to carry out the chain of the PM, they smiled with restraint.

"You shouldn't overrate this method," Roman said. "But you shouldn't underestimate it either. The Patience of Medici is not a magic wand, but a master key to the doors of the Spirit. Iris even calls the PM the ABC book for first graders. The ABC will never replace serious literature, yet you can't do without it either. Someday you'll laugh, thinking back on your current experiments. But without them you won't be able to move on. So do what you have to do, and don't forget the most important thing: you are not off to get some dough, instead you are going to learn about Intention, about interacting with the Spirit."

"I understand that," Maxim answered.

"Then good luck to you," Roman instructed him. Oxana, who had been listening to their conversation all of this time, only smiled mysteriously.

And so, everything was ready. Feeling incredibly upbeat,

Maxim went outside the mansion area, and the guard closed the gate behind him. Having stepped aside a little, Maxim looked around to see if someone was watching him, then he took out a pad and a pen. He drew a deep sigh and then silently expressed his wish to win the lottery. Then he put a mark in his pad that the first card has been realized. Then he did the flag action – he adjusted his collar and ticked off the second card. He started waiting for the world's reply, and even twitched – a small pod of sparrows flew by with their wings rustling right in front of him. That was so well-timed that Maxim didn't have any more doubts – that was the Spirit's reply! Having marked the third card, Maxim headed for the park, thinking about whether the appearance of the sparrows was just a coincidence. True, it's just sparrows, there's nothing unusual about them. But their timing was perfect!

The fourth card was the queen of clubs. Maxim was walking along the sidewalk, trying to figure out whom he should take for the queen and if one of the chance passersby was perhaps the queen, when he saw the mailwoman with a bag thrown across her shoulder. The young woman was walking along with a smile on her face. Maxim thought she was very pretty. And at the same moment he went hot – that's the queen of clubs! He felt it with his whole body, as if something just clicked. The young woman passed him by. Maxim quickly pulled out his pad and marked the fourth card…

After that things went just as smoothly. The cards Maxim remembered the most were the king of clubs – the need to stop by the crosswalk and let a car through, the queen of spades – a hard-faced looking woman with a leather folder in her hands. The ace of spades realized itself in the form of a sullen elderly Caucasian gentleman sweeping the sidewalk; that it was the ace of spades, Maxim didn't doubt for a second – the Caucasian man gave him a heavy look, Maxim quickened his steps in order to get out of there and not be in the way of the working man. The coincidences didn't just amaze him, they bewildered him. How could this happen?

What connected all these externally unrelated things? Or are these actually ordinary coincidences? Out of the thousands of events happening around us, can we always find a suitable event that fits the chain?

However, Maxim chose to leave all of these questions for now – ahead of him appeared the precious lottery booth. Maxim noticed it already when he was in town with Oxana. That he was approaching the booth in time with the goal unit about to commence was also quite impressive. The ace of clubs became the queue consisting of three people – like it or not, he had to wait. An external event independent of our will – a typical ace...

Finally, it was his turn, Maxim handed the salesperson a five ruble coin, and silently noted the '9C'.

"One ticket, please." He asked.

The salesperson was a woman about fifty years of age – very amiable. While she was looking for the right tickets, Maxim brushed his hair with his palm – a flag action – the '8S'. A gesture aimed at the Spirit. Meanwhile, the saleswoman found the tickets and handed them to him.

"Thank you." Having chosen a ticket, Maxim stepped aside. So, the ticket was now in his hands. According to the cards it's...? Maxim took out his pad and checked against his notes. According to the cards it's the '10H'. Having noted in the pad the last few events, he slowly walked towards the bench located about a hundred meters away from the booth. Yes, and not to forget to note the path leading to it – the '6C'.

And here's the bench. Maxim sat down, and with a palpitating heart opened the ticket and carefully unfolded it. The sign inside said: 'Ten rubles'.

He had actually won. Having realized that, Maxim felt great joy. And he immediately noted in the pad – joy, the 'AH'. Yes, ten rubles, it is peanuts – a price that's not even worth mentioning. But money wasn't the important bit in this exercise. What's important is that it actually worked!

Maxim got up and headed back to the booth – the '6H'. There was no one by the window. He gave the unfolded ticket to the saleswoman; she took it and gave it a look.

"You're going to take some more?" she asked, having handed Maxim a pack of tickets.

The temptation was great. Yet, Maxim declined. He didn't want to ruin the impression from the chain. What if he won't win?

"Thank you. Some other time," he replied; the saleswoman hid the tickets without saying a word and just as silently handed him a crumpled ten ruble note. Obviously, she wasn't too happy about Maxim not wanting to play on.

But Maxim couldn't care less. Having hidden the bill in his pocket, he took out the pad and marked the ten of clubs. That's it, he really had won!

The remaining part of the chain didn't matter now. Still, Maxim did see it through – those were the rules. Whether the chain came together or not, you still couldn't leave it to the mercy of fate. That was explained by the fact that an unfinished chain, left unguarded, still continued its realization. And no one knew what it could lead to. Finally, the idea of doing things perfectly required one to see the chain through: if a magician took on something, he had to finish it. With such an approach, the magician's word became the law.

Maxim couldn't wait to get home. Having reached the gate – or rather, the metallic door decorated with forged embellishments – he pressed the bell-button. The door immediately opened; Maxim remembered that the area in front of the house was controlled by surveillance cameras. Safety was a very serious matter around there.

The guards had already changed; Maxim was greeted by Ivan, a big kindhearted fellow about two meters tall. He already knew Maxim, and that's why he immediately, and with a smile, stretched out his big palm. Somewhat embarrassed, Maxim shook Ivan's hand and after exchanging a couple of words with the big guy, went into the house. He was still not used to his new status and felt a bit uneasy.

They had guests. Maxim realized that as he heard loud voices and a soft female laughter coming from the kitchen. It wasn't Oxana; Maxim would have recognized her voice right away.

Not knowing what to do next – to go up to his room or to say hello to the guests - Maxim halted in the hall. He decided to go up to his room after all. That seemed to be the right thing to do. He didn't want to feel out of place.

But, he didn't get far. The door to the kitchen opened and Oxana appeared on the threshold.

"Come on Maxim," she said, clearly having a hard time keeping herself from laughing. "Boris is calling you."

It was as if a load was lifted off his mind. Maxim drew a sigh of relief and entered the kitchen.

"Here's our stalker," Boris greeted him. "Maxim, let me introduce you. This is Rada." A young woman was sitting on Boris's left. At first, Maxim thought her to be about twenty-five years old then he decided that she was probably a little older than that.

From the very first sight Maxim felt a strange calm in Rada's appearance. Her gaze was particularly amazing – a pure, radiant gaze – and, nevertheless, it contained strange inner power. There was a little piece of indulgence in it, too. Rada was looking at Maxim the way a wise teacher looks at a toddler first-grader.

In her outward appearance, Rada also reminded Maxim of a teacher. She was quite slim, dressed in a strict business suit, and her chestnut hair was braided and carefully put up on the back of her head. She had a high forehead, clear face, soft smile and wonderful eyes...

"Good day," Maxim greeted her.

"Hi, Maxim," Rada replied; there was softness and calm in her voice. "Let's just drop the formalities, ok? From now on we'll be seeing a lot of each other. Take a seat."

"Rada is a dreamer," Roman explained; he had made himself comfortable on a small sofa by the wall. "She is the one who's going to teach you lucid dreaming."

"And you've already met her," Boris added. "That you probably don't remember it is a completely different story."

"I don't remember it," Maxim admitted and sat down next to Roman. "I am good at remembering faces. When did we meet?"

"Rather, where?" Boris said. Everyone started laughing. The laugh was frank and kind, Maxim also smiled, though, involuntarily.

"We've met in the Castle of Roses, in a dream," Rada softly answered. She spoke rather quietly, yet her words were perceived amazingly clearly and distinctly. "But this knowledge is on the left side of your consciousness and it is unavailable to you for the time being."

From Castaneda's books Maxim already knew that magicians separate consciousness into right side (everyday consciousness) and left side consciousness, responsible for magical perception of the world. One of the features of left side consciousness is that you couldn't access memories of being on the left side consciousness when in a regular state of mind. In other words, you just couldn't remember what you did when you were on the left side. Maxim thought that the notions – memory of the left and right side of the brain – only applied to the real world. So Rada saying that there is left side memory in dreams was a bit puzzling to him. He needed an explanation. Maxim was about to ask a question, but Boris stopped him by barely noticeably shaking his head.

"How was your walk?" he asked, looking at Maxim with a smile. "Did you win a million?" Everyone started laughing, but this laughter was kind, they meant no offence. Maxim smiled involuntarily.

"I won ten rubles," he said. "And the chain really did come together."

"What else could it have done?" Roman said; everyone smiled

again. Maxim sensed some kind of a trick.

"Maxim, everything is great," Boris calmed him down. "For the first time you saw the world answer your wishes. You saw events isolated externally and things in no way related to each other coming together into one chain. That's magic for you – the ability to interact with the world on a level that's unavailable to the logic of the average man. And the PM, in this case, is only the master key to the doors of the Spirit. One day there'll come a time when the world will answer even your thoughts."

"And that," Rada added, "also implies being responsible for your thoughts. If an evil thought belongs to an ordinary person, it won't do much harm. But a magician's thought carries power. In the heat of the moment, you sent someone to hell and then forgot about it, but that person will have problems. That's why the leading role in magic is the idea of perfection."

"I've read about it. To be perfect means to do your best in everything you're involved in," Maxim said.

"Yes," Rada agreed. "And at the same time, perfection is something much greater than that."

"Here they are, teachers," Roman grinned. "Just give them full rein, and they'll keep preaching days on end."

"I don't really mind," Maxim shrugged his shoulders. Smiles slipped across the faces of those present.

"We'll take you at your word!" Boris raised a finger. "So, Rada. Will you take upon yourself the task of his education?"

"Sure," the young woman agreed, looking at Maxim with a light smile. "We'll do a course – a month of intense therapy. Our mission – to teach you how to have lucid dreams on your own. It's just that a dream searcher that doesn't know how to have lucid dreams is nonsense."

"You may start right away," Boris recommended. "While Roman and I have something to discuss – to have a chat about our bustling days."

"All right." Rada got up from her chair and glanced at Maxim.

"Let's go."

Rada's room was located on the South side of the house; sun beams were breaking through the heavy green drapes.

"Take a seat," Rada suggested. Maxim sat down in an armchair standing next to a coffee table. He examined the room with interest. The walls were covered with greenish tapestry; flowerpots were hanging on the walls. Spiderwort, Elephant's Ear, Coleus, the magnificent golden Devil's Ivy – Maxim identified these plants without any difficulty.

Rada seated herself in an armchair opposite to Maxim's, and looked at him with a soft smile. Despite the obvious relaxed manner, Rada's appearance radiated power. It seemed that she was overflowing with hidden energy, and only her eyes gave vent to this inner power of hers. Her gaze was of substantial weight; Maxim involuntarily lowered his eyes. Rada smiled again.

"We have a lot of work ahead of us," she said. "I know many things, but in the end it's up to you whether you succeed or not. Firstly, I need to get your consent to study under me. This is not just a simple formality; your consent will allow me to enter you into the flow of my power. Without such consent our classes won't be of proper strength."

"I consent," Maxim said, feeling a bit nervous. The combination of the semi-darkness of the room and Rada's soft voice seemed just overwhelming to him. There was incredible harmony in all of this.

"All right, then we'll cut to the chase. First, I want to ask you a question: what is a lucid dream? I want to know what you understand by it."

"It's the ability of being aware of yourself in a dream," Maxim answered. "I've already been in a lucid dream once, together with Boris."

"You've been in a lucid dream about five times already," Rada corrected him. "You just don't remember the other times right now."

"Actually, I just wanted to ask you about that: how come I don't remember? If I got this right, there are two worlds: the real world and the dream world. The real world is the Tonal, the right side. The dream world is the Nagual, the left side. When we wake up we can bring our memories from the Nagual to the Tonal. Or I got it all wrong?"

"Yes, you did," Rada agreed. "First of all, one cannot equal the dream world to the Nagual. It's a mistake. There is the Tonal, consisting of the real world and the dream world. There are other planes of the Tonal, but we'll leave them for now. When you fall asleep, you simply exchange one Tonal plane for another, and nothing more. That is, the Tonal is everything that we have a description for. It's the domain of the mind. We may talk about dreams; we can study them, describe them; consequently, the dream world belongs to the Tonal. The Nagual, however, is beyond comprehension. You cannot speak of it in reasonable terms; we can only witness its manifestations. As for memory, it is directly linked to the location of the assemblage point."

Maxim had already read about the assemblage point in Castaneda's books. This point was located in the human energy body, two feet back from a person's shoulder-blade. Magicians saw it as a point of intense light, surrounded by a paler halo. It was considered that the assemblage point was responsible for our perception. If it shifted to one side or the other, the person's perception changed too. As far as Maxim had understood, the point of assemblage could be likened to the arrow on the tuning scale of a radio receiver: You're turning the knob, the arrow is moving, allowing you to tune into other radio stations; by moving the point of assemblage, not only could you change your perception of this world, but you could also 'assemble' completely new worlds. In fact, man disappeared from this world and travelled to the world he was tuned into at that moment. Magicians attached great importance to the mobility of the assemblage point, trying to shake its usual position with all available methods.

"In Castaneda's books, you've read that man has two types of consciousness – the right side consciousness and the left side consciousness," Rada continued. "The right side consciousness has to do with the usual position of the assemblage point. During the shift of the assemblage point you can enter the left side consciousness. What's special about this is that memory in this position of the assemblage point is not connected to your regular memory. In the real world you can be on the right side as well as on the left side. The exact same maneuver can be done in a dream. And in the real world you won't remember what happened to you on the left side, and similarly your left side memories will become unavailable to your memory. Imagine that you have two hard drives on your computer: you are using one but for some reason you don't have access to the other one – your operative system doesn't see it at all. You don't even have a clue about its existence – that's how left side memory works. It could hold huge amounts of information, but it is all unavailable to us. But one day comes a moment when two parts of the whole start integrating. You suddenly start remembering things that sort of never happened to you. Fragments of your left side memory start seeping through onto the right part, you start remembering more and more, until your memory comes together into a whole. You do not yet have any experience of being on the left side in the real world, but you have experienced the left side, or Nagual, dreams. Someday you'll definitely remember it all."

For some time Maxim was quiet, thinking about what he'd just heard. Then he looked up at Rada.

"Okay, but dreams have also something to do with the shifting of the assemblage point. And hence we shouldn't remember what we dreamt of, but we often remember dreams – how do you explain that?"

"That is explained by the position of the assemblage point," Rada said. "Imagine a piece of paper and a circle drawn on it. Put a dot in the center of the circle. The dot is the usual position of the assemblage point. It may move within the circle, during which our consciousness is slightly altered. You may perceive such fluctuations of the point as mood changes. The whole area inside the circle corresponds to a state of wakefulness in a person. Beyond this circle is the dream world. That is, when the assemblage point moves outside of the circle, you fall asleep. The nature of dreams is determined by where the point of assemblage has gone. But notice this: no matter where the assemblage point is, it doesn't leave the surface of the paper in our model. That is, all of this is right side consciousness. But, if you give the assemblage point the ability of moving not only along the plane, but also up and down, we'll get another scale of reference. Such movement, deviation from moving along the two-dimensional plane, will be the passage to left side consciousness."

"Yes, it's getting a bit clearer." Maxim thought about it for a little while. "There is another thing I wanted to ask you: on the net, I saw searchers mentioning something about lucid dreaming and controlled dreaming. What's the difference between these two?"

"The difference is in the level of your awareness. In lucid dreaming it could go from a minimal level of awareness, when you barely understand that you are asleep, to a rather high level of awareness, when you are quite capable of adequately assessing the surroundings and you are able to do some kind of research. Nevertheless, you still remain a guest in the dream. You get controlled dreaming when you become the master. This is the stage of absolute control. You enter the dream whenever you want, and you stay there as long as you need to. The dream world is no longer exotic to you – something that's available to you at rare signs of consciousness; instead it's a full-blown living environment. The line between that world and this one is erased.

"You are talking about living in a dream?"

"Not quite. I am just saying that the two worlds become of

equal value to you. You are now residing in this world as a master and you enter the dream world as a guest. I am equally good at controlling both worlds – it doesn't matter to me where I am. Say, for you this room and the room next to it are basically of equal value. You can be in one of them, you can go to another. They are different in some respects, but to you they are equal by their status; it doesn't matter to you where you are – in one room or the other. To searchers, this world and the dream world are just as equal. When it comes to living in a dream, it's a slightly different matter. Let's take our example with the rooms – they could be equal, yet at the same time they remain separated one from the other. You can be in one room, you could be in the other room, but you would still have to go from one room into another room. But if you'd want to, you could break the wall separating these rooms, thus joining them. In our case we are joining the real world and the dream world, and in that process, each of them obtains the features of the other. Is that clear?" Rada smiled.

"Not really," Maxim admitted. "I get it in theory, but what does it give you in practice?"

"Quite a few things; look here." Rada pointed at the flowerpot with the Devil's Ivy. "This flower is a predator. It's not advisable to keep it in your bedroom. It is in this room only because I study the energy of plants. Now it's just a plant, a rather beautiful one too. But let's join the ordinary world with the dream world." Rada glanced at the plant with a smile.

Nothing happened. Maxim was just about to ask a question, when he suddenly noticed the plant move. He looked closer – it really was moving! Beautiful spotted leaves were slowly turning, as if sniffing the space around it; little thin predator tendrils appeared on the flexible stem. They were fumbling about the tapestry, digging into it. In front of Maxim's very eyes, the plant started rapidly stretching up, throwing out more and more new leaves. Everything was happening almost in complete silence, in a few minutes the predatory creature managed to cover almost one third of the wall.

His heart was pounding with a hollow sound, Maxim clutched at the armrests of the chair. It seemed to him he was witnessing a miracle...

"Stretch out your hand to him," Rada commanded. "Don't worry, nothing horrible will happen. By the way, his name is Hector."

Maxim slowly rose from his chair; fear was struggling with curiosity in his heart. He walked up to the wall and carefully stretched out his hand.

The plant obviously sensed him approaching. It suddenly stopped; its leaves turned around to face Maxim. It was a very unpleasant feeling; Maxim suddenly realized that the plant was looking at him. It was unclear how and what it was doing this with, but the feeling of the plant looking at Maxim, with a cold stare, did not pass. Maxim was looking at the plant and the plant, at Maxim.

"Touch him," Rada suggested. "Go on."

Maxim really didn't want to do that, but he couldn't refuse Rada's directions. He stretched out his hand to touch one of the leaves; the leaf recoiled a little. In these moments, the plant reminded him of some unusual animal rather than a plant. Maxim persistently reached for the little leaf and carefully touched it. And at the same moment he shrieked and leaped back; the predatory green little tendril, having swiftly unfolded, slashed Maxim's finger as if with a blade.

"Damn it," Maxim mumbled, cautiously examining his finger. There was already a row of tiny red spots emerging.

"I think that's enough," Rada said. Maxim looked at the plant again and almost twitched. The profuse green that had taken over one quarter of the wall was now gone. Growing in the pot was now the same Devil's Ivy, habitual to the eye. The only thing serving as a reminder of what had happened was the dull pain in his finger.

"I'm sorry, he didn't like you," Rada said with a smile. "Hector doesn't care for strangers. Don't worry, it will soon pass. Take a seat."

Maxim sat down; he glanced at the row of bloody little stains stretched across his finger. Then he looked at the plant and, only after that, he turned his gaze back to Rada. The young woman smiled.

"You see, the plant hasn't changed at all. But your finger is hurting. That is living in a dream – the merging of two worlds, two cosmographies."

"And so what, all plants behave this way?" Maxim asked.

"Not really, no," Rada shrugged. "In this particular case, the plant was simply reflecting my intention. If I wanted, it could have bitten off your hand. And why?" Rada looked closely at Maxim. "Because in the space of this room you are a guest, and I – a mistress. And I am the one in here laying down the rules of the game. Do you understand?"

"Yes," Maxim said. "I do."

Rada smiled again, her smile was very soft.

"Now you see how the surrounding reality can change. You shall learn how to change it yourself. Not now, thought – it will take you years and years. But, you've got to see the whole picture; you must know the point of what you are doing." Rada went quiet for a couple of seconds, collecting her thoughts. "You already know that magicians are split into dreamers and stalkers. Dreamers start working with the dream world, stalkers – with the real world. But the end result for both is practically the same. It's like a double-edged sword: it has two edges, but it also has a middle. Stalkers move towards the middle from one end, dreamers – from the other. The end result – complete control over reality, communication – or rather – becoming one with the Spirit. You've got a talent for dreaming. That's why I'm the one talking to you, and not, for instance, Iris. I can say that you've been very fortunate." Rada smiled.

"Because of you?" Maxim smiled involuntarily.

"No," Rada shook her head, her eyes glistened. "You are fortunate that you didn't end up with Iris. If she had gotten her hands on you, you would definitely not have gotten away with a few scratches on your hand." Rada softly laughed, Maxim thought her laughter very pleasant.

"But let's continue," she said. "As I've already told you, your task is to learn how to enter a dream. And to do that you'll need to create a dream portal; or, as Boris would have said, an entry point into the system. He just likes computer terminology," Rada explained. "There are different ways of creating an entry point. For example, you can learn how to visualize a stain of a particular color – that's the method I use. My color is green. To enter a dream, I just need to close my eyes; I see a green light then it dissipates much like fog, and the dream stage shows through. But this method is difficult; it requires a lot of practice. That's why I'll suggest you another method. This is how it goes: when you go to bed, lie there for a while – wind down. When you feel that you can go to sleep, imagine a long hall lined with doors on its sides. This could be a hall that you're familiar with or a creation of your imagination. The second alternative is better because then there won't be a focus on familiar elements. Your task is to imagine this hall the best way you can; notice the floor, the walls, the ceiling, the illuminating lamps. There could be torches instead of lamps. Once you feel yourself in the hall, walk along it. At the end of the corridor you'll see a door. Behind it is the dream world; the door is the entry point. Women must choose one of the doors to their side – either the left one, or the right one. Although," Rada smiled, "that doesn't concern you; the door for men is located right in the middle. Having seen the door, try to examine it as closely as you can. In addition, you may paint it in your color right away. As I've said, I have the color green; you may have some other color – for instance, yellow, orange or any other shade of these colors. The important thing is that you like the color, that the color is yours. Then, open the door, enter and calmly fall asleep, not thinking about anything. Right now you cannot enter the dream at once; your first dreams will appear around morning time. With time you'll learn to become aware of the moment when you fall asleep and enter the dream at once. The corridor and the door will transform down to just a door, and then there'll only be the green color. You closed your eyes, you saw the stain – and you are in a dream. But you must start with the corridor and the door; start visualizing these every night. I think everything is clear so far?"

"Yes," Maxim nodded, thinking that he should make sure to write all of this down.

"Wonderful," Rada smiled. "Let's move on." She grew silent for a second, then continued.

"The ability of being aware of yourself in a dream is directly linked to the level of our life force and to how well-trained your attention is. As you remember, Don Juan recommended Castaneda to not waste his energy on nonsense – to become a real miser in this sense. That's absolutely true. You too must follow this advice and not waste your power on empty tricks. But what do we do with the power that we've already spent?" Rada raised her eyebrows, inviting Maxim to answer this question.

"I don't know," Maxim admitted. "If we've spent it, then we've spent it; we must draw conclusions from that and not allow for similar mistakes in the future."

"That is true," Rada admitted, "but searchers went a bit further. Remember Castaneda recommended reviewing one's life by recreating former events in their memory? By reliving them, magicians take back their energy and give away energy that's not theirs. This is a working method, but a method that's both difficult and time consuming. If you remember, Dona Soledad spent five years in a recapitulating crate. Searchers are not as patient." A grin flashed in Rada's eyes. "We are freeloaders in that sense, and instead of ramming against the impenetrable wall, we dig a tunnel under it, or even fit a master key to the door. That's what we did with life force restoration. There are two main ways of doing it: the stalker way, using the Patience of Medici, and the dreamer way, where you look for lost energy in dreams. You will use both methods. You should ask Boris about how to restore energy with the help of the patience; he'll explain it better than me. I'll tell you about the second method; it's called regaining luminosity. It entails the following..." Rada again grew quiet for a short while.

"When studying dreams," she continued, "searchers noted something interesting: visiting certain dream places causes a dramatic inflow of energy. As the ability to be aware of yourself improves, your vitality increases. You can even tell by the way you look – your skin gets elastic, wrinkles disappear. Deriving from this and other observations, searchers concluded that there is a regeneration of our own energy that was once lost – or rather – taken from us. There are five main places where we can regain our luminosity; each such place finds its reflection on the dream map. They may be different for different people, but they have one thing in common – they are being guarded and we are not allowed there. Usually guards, enemies of some kind or various monsters, are in your way. Your task is to get there, despite the crafty designs of the enemy, and to find a certain item. Often it is something beautiful – a charm of sorts; a jewel, or an ancient tome. You'll recognize the right item right away. If you manage to get to the item and take it, you get a bonus in the form of an energy boost. We can get our luminosity from four places. The fifth place is different in that sense – no matter how many times we take the luminosity; it still slips away from us. Usually, dreamers associate this fifth place with a jail, barracks, places where we studied, large administrative buildings and other similar constructions. Obtaining luminosity from these places is easy, keeping it doesn't work. However, regaining luminosity from the other four places allows us to significantly boost our life force."

"But in order to regain luminosity, you have to be able to have lucid dreams?" Maxim asked. "And to boost one's life force and reach lucid dreams, you need to regain your luminosity. So, it's a vicious circle?"

"In some sense, yes," Rada smiled. "You just have to practice all of these methods by the means of integration. But the energy that's usually at our disposal is enough to reach dreams. So, for now create your entry point, map out your dreams and regain your energy with the help of the Patience of Medici. In the evening we'll talk about attention. But that's all for now." Rada smiled and rose from her chair.

Maxim only managed to have a chat with Boris about an hour later. To the question, how to use the PM to get back one's energy, Boris only smiled.

"All of that is on the CD I gave you," he answered. "You just need to look for it. But since you asked, I guess, I can explain. Let's go to my room."

Once in the room, Boris immediately started explaining.

"I think you have already noticed that in the Patience of Medici we use a not so ordinary link of elements. When carrying out the chain by the rules of the PM, we attribute certain qualities to the elements of this world. One can say that we're tagging them. The question is: what do we need that for? We need it because that's the conditions of our game. When you are working on the Patience of Medici, creating a programming language that's inherent only to you, you are creating a virtual space – a subprogram of sorts – which starts influencing the events that happen around you. You could say that you are specifying the conditions on which the real world should be operating. That is the first important feature. Let's proceed," Boris continued after a short pause. "You ask how to regain your energy with the help of the PM. But to understand that you'd first need to get your head around something else – how exactly are we spending this energy, what determines these expenses? Let's take a situation as an example – let's say you decided to set up a firm. You've got a partner and you are eager to realize your project. You start working, you get into a dispute. Let's look at the two ways of how these events might develop: first one – you have disputes, you argue, but all these arguments are purely business. Finally, you arrive at certain decisions, set up the firm and work, pleased with each other. And the second alternative: you cannot reach a compromise and so you go your separate ways, with a whole set of negative emotions and the weight of disappointment on your shoulders because of the hope that went unfulfilled. On the whole, these are quite normal situations, but let's examine them from the energy point of view. In the first case, the chain did come together; you got what you planned for. And that means that all of the energy that was put into this chain comes back to you – keep this in mind; this is very important. The project has been realized, and you don't have the weight of unfinished business on your shoulders. And the second alternative, where you went your separate ways – nothing came of your project, the chain of events did not come together and you didn't get back the energy that you put into the project. And now think about the 'tail' of unfinished business each and every one of us has. How many undertakings, big and small ones that we, for some reason, didn't see through, had there been in our lives? We think that we've forgotten all about it – not by any means, all of these chains are still hanging on us like a dead weight, pressing us down to the ground. We need to free ourselves from these, but how? You can do the recapitulation, as recommended by Castaneda, but it's a slow and dull process – we want something quicker. Searchers learned how to put together uncompleted chains with the help of the PM, restoring lost energy. The idea is very simple: we look for an uncompleted chain in our life. Then in a goal-oriented fashion we're working with the largest chains hanging over us like a dead weight. For example, let's say it's an unanswered love." Boris grinned and made himself comfortable in the armchair. "Since the chain didn't come together, there was some kind of an obstacle – let's call it the ace of spades. We can mark everything that preceded the ace of spades with another card. Love – that's hearts, so our prehistory could be designated with the '8H'. Eight – because you were interacting with someone," Boris explained. "Of course, you may designate any other card to mark the events preceding the 'AS' in a way you feel is right that would correspond to your assessment of the situation. Then we create the chain of the PM with the starting cards '8H'and 'AS', and we carry it out in a short time – let's say within a couple of hours. With this simple action we are bringing together the hanging chain, all of the energy that we've lost comes back to us. Having purposefully worked with the most important events, we may move onto the next stage; namely, to start hitting all targets. Here we are no longer fixating specific events; we are simply carrying out the chains of the PM, several a day, each time introducing small changes to their beginning. Let's say that the chain started with the '6S' and the 'AS', then the '7S' and the 'AS', then the '8S' and the 'AS', the '9S' and the 'AS' and so on. Having done the spades, we move on to the clubs – the '6C', the 'AS'; the '7C', the 'AS'; the '8C', the 'AS'... Then we take diamonds and hearts, going through the whole pack of cards this way. Each initial card, in this case, corresponds to a chain that you've initiated but have not completed; the 'AS' stands for the obstacle that stopped you from completing the chain. By carrying out these chains, we, each time, put together an uncompleted chain of the past. After that, you can change the conditions of the task; for example, you can take the 'AH', instead of the 'AS'. Here, the 'AH' will symbolize any emotional expenses – from laughter and joy, to hatred and tears. And after that, it's all the same: we put the 'AH' on the second place and go through the whole pack. Here you need to grasp the actual principle of the unit that has changed. Having realized how it works, you can create and 'chase away' a chain in order to solve a hanging problem whenever you want. Working with the chains of the past lets us restore lots of spent energy and free ourselves of all the garbage from the past. Your energy level increases, which has immediate effects on your present life. After that, the most important thing is to avoid accumulating new weight from uncompleted chains. And that's why you need to adopt the rule of seeing all your undertakings to the end. Stalkers assume that any task must be done with maximum speed and efficiency; it shouldn't be spread out over several years. Again, you need to act so that you won't create excessive chains of events; take note of this – this is a very important point. Let's say when a ship is moving it is leaving waves behind. In exactly the same way man, when sailing through life, leaves a track in the shape of the many chains that he has created. A stalker, in this sense, is not sailing; he's sliding on the sea of life, leaving on its surface a barely noticeable trace."

"And if I had many chains in my life with the same beginning?" Maxim inquired. "Then one chain with the appropriate beginning won't be enough to close the whole 'tail' of similar chains?"

"That's right, it won't," Boris agreed. "Yet no one stops you from repeating this process a couple of times. The most important thing here is to get involved in the process, to induce the appropriate flow. And then the flow will take you in the right direction. Try it, and you'll see yourself."

"I will," Maxim agreed. "For sure."

The day turned out to be very intense; Maxim could barely handle the stream of information that swept over him. Right after lunch he retired to his room and spent a couple of hours getting his ideas into shape, writing down the most important points in Rada's and Boris's explanations in his notebook. At six o'clock he had another session at the sports hall, after which Maxim came out covered in sweat. After a shower, they had supper, then an hour of spare time, and a new meeting with Rada.

This time they talked about attention. Rather, Rada did all the talking, Maxim had only to listen and ask questions when something was unclear.

"The main role in this world, just like in the world of dreams, is played by our attention," she began. "Attention creates this world. As you recall, Castaneda divided attention into primary – ordinary attention, and secondary – magical attention. Searchers agreed with Castaneda on this point. Still, they introduced a couple of new terms. One of them is cosmography charts. Practically, it's an inventory bill of everything that surrounds us, that exists for our consciousness. It's a model that determines our behavior and our assessment – the way we treat the world around us. The cosmography charts are formed early in our childhood, gradually becoming more and more solid and unshakable. That is the prism through which we are looking at the world – our rose-colored glasses. And if we examine the process of perception, it will look something like this: you perceive something; the received information is instantly checked against the data in your cosmography charts. Practically speaking, it is a way of testing the validity of what you perceive, and the validity is determined by what is in these charts. If the incoming information does not contradict the existing data, our mind grants it passage into our consciousness. If the information doesn't match the data, there is a conflict. This conflict could be resolved in different ways. First one – providing the conflicting information with an acceptable configuration. For example, a man sees a UFO in the night sky. If he doesn't believe in all these 'saucers', then the cosmography charts will throw in a non-conflicting solution – the man will think that he saw an airplane, a rocket or just a very rare natural phenomenon. The second option – the man concedes that he saw something unusual, and this phenomenon requires further investigation. This is a mild alternative, where the cosmography charts start changing and new entries are gradually made. And when this person sees another UFO, he'll already be ready to adequately perceive this phenomenon, his cosmography charts have changed, and the conflict situation does not arise. Finally, there is the third option, where what he sees is so removed from the contents of his cosmography charts that these simply block his perception channel. If there's no information, there's no problem. Recall the situation with Castaneda, when Don Juan and Genaro introduced him to the old seers. These beings entered their house, but Castaneda couldn't perceive them. All he felt was a gust of cold wind that burst in through the open door. His cosmography charts remained stable, there was no place in them for ancient magicians – and that means that Castaneda didn't see them. The barrier of cosmography charts is in every one of us. It is what separates us from unusual perception. I can assure you that the left side memory of each person holds plenty of episodes of unusual perception, but these memories cannot break through onto the right side – the hard barrier of cosmography charts is in the way."

"Yes, but when you showed me this flower," Maxim nodded in the direction of the Devil's Ivy, "I had no problem seeing it. That is, I saw it move, I saw that it was alive. What were my cosmography charts doing then?"

"Good question," Rada smiled. "You see, any explanation carries but a part of the truth, and it should not be perceived as a rigid scheme. The cosmography charts of each person have their peculiarities. Someone is ready to accept miracles, someone is not. Some phenomena could be ignored; others are so vividly manifested in our Tonal layer that they cannot be ignored even if we'd want to. And that means that each person will have his own level of perception, which depends on his personal characteristics and the situation. Finally, don't forget that I am the one controlling the space of this room. You are in the flow of my power, and I determine what you may perceive here and what you may not. For example, a very strange creature is now crawling on the ceiling." With a smile, Rada pointed at a corner of the room. "Do you see it?"

Maxim examined the ceiling and didn't notice anything.

"No," he said and shook his head. "There is nothing there."

"Perception is about your mindset," Rada continued. "You could say that we are usually firmly fixed on perceiving one wavelength. It's like with a radio, where the tuning knob is fixed on one radio station. There are many different radio stations, but your radio picks only one – the one it's tuned into. You may perceive the creature crawling on the ceiling in two cases: either it moves into your area of perception – into your frequency range – or you change your setting. And then there's the third option." Rada smiled again. "I change your setting."

Maxim wanted to ask another question but he couldn't. There was a slight ringing in his ears, his vision blurred. He started blinking rapidly and his vision cleared. He looked at Rada, then moved his gaze over onto the ceiling and started.

Indeed, something was crawling on the ceiling. It reminded him of a crocodile without a tail or a huge hideous toad. It seemed that the force of gravity did not apply to this creature. Having made a step, the creature froze for a few moments then it threw forward another paw and froze again.

"Is it real?" Maxim asked; his voice was quiet and somewhat frightened.

"Quite real. I just slightly altered your band of perception. And now I stop holding you."

His vision blurred again, Maxim started blinking. When he looked at the ceiling again, there was nothing there.

"It's still here," Rada explained. "But you are separated by your barrier of perception.

I can tell you what will happen next. First of all, the unusual experience you just had will induce a change in your cosmography charts. Before, you thought that there are only the things that you can see. Now you begin to understand that there is another range of frequencies – other bands of perception. And you can reach these bands of perception. However, you must

remember that the cosmography charts do not change immediately, they are very stable. And if you, for example, would now
break up with us and return to the world of ordinary people, then
there's a strong possibility that your consciousness, having
played with miracles, will find some reasonable explanation for
everything that has happened. You will think that I hypnotized
you, fed you a magic mushroom broth or whatever. It doesn't
matter if the explanation will sound silly; the important thing is
that it corresponds to what's in the charts. On the other hand, if
you won't leave and will proceed deeper and deeper into the
world of magic, your cosmography charts will start changing
involuntarily, in accordance with the new settings. And one day,
when new entries have completely settled in the charts, you'll get
new abilities. The nature of these depends on your intention – on
the direction that you are working in. Remember how Don Juan
was trying to convince Castaneda? He told him that magic is very
easy, that it is at the tips of our fingers; the difficult part is in
convincing yourself that it is all possible. And to convince
yourself means to make an entry in the cosmography charts that
allows for miracles of one kind or another."

"And portals? Are they also about a change in the cosmography charts?"

"It's rather about entering a new record. The ordinary state
does not allow for the possibility of portals, as it doesn't allow for
the existence of many other unusual things. And often, even the
fear of death is unable to convince it otherwise. Recall Castaneda
jumping into an abyss – his attention was supposed to assemble
another world. Castaneda was successful in doing this; he crossed
over to another world, not having reached the bottom of the
abyss. His cosmography charts allowed that, they were prepared
by long and laborious work. But there were others, those who
followed Castaneda's example and stepped into the abyss, hoping
for a miracle. They died – and why? Because they had another
record in their cosmography charts: 'he, who falls from a high

height, always dies'. And courage in this case won't, by any means, save you from foolishness. A person like that jumps into the abyss and yells at the top of his lungs 'I believe!' While his inner voice replies "But I don't..." Miracles are only possible when you are ready for them."

"So, I must convince myself that portals are possible?"

"You won't be able to simply convince yourself," Rada smiled. "And that's the whole difficulty of it; as constant dripping wears away the stone, so are the cosmography charts changed by long laborious work. In the case with the portals, you need to start with becoming aware of the structure of the world – you need to understand how it works. You need to know about the laws controlling it. This will provide you with hints to understand how you may move through a portal. You will get some leads, which will allow you to find ways of practically accessing these abilities. As a result, you really will open a portal, yet it won't be a lucky coincidence, but a result of long and hard work."

"Okay, but where does attention come into play?"

Rada softly laughed, then shook her head, pretending to disapprove. "There's an old joke," she said. "At the dawn of automobile industry there was a lecture on how the automobile works. Everyone was listening, admiring, nodding. Finally the lecture was over and the lecturer asks: 'Any questions?' Then one lady raises her hand and says: 'It was all very interesting and educational. But there is only one thing I don't understand: where do you harness the horse?'"

Maxim smiled. Rada was looking at him, her eyes were shining.

"You just asked me a similar question," she said. "We've been talking about attention all this time – or rather about the filters of our primary attention, the Tonal filters."

"I'm just having a hard time taking it all in at once," Maxim answered.

"Don't make excuses!" Rada shook her slim finger at him.

"Forget about this silly habit. So, one more time: our attention creates the world. And attention is based on cosmography charts, which determine the existence of things in this world. We see the edited world, not the actual world. Our attention has been trained to perceive only the things for which there are records in the cosmography charts. In this sense attention is really creating the world – or rather, the projection of the world that reaches our mind. The charts have the label 'default setting'. Magicians don't like that, and so they change these settings the way they want. As a result we start perceiving things that we didn't notice before. And the function of noticing and not noticing is the main function of attention. Thus, when working with cosmography charts, we are working with attention. Now, only dare say that you didn't get it, and Hector and I..." Rada glanced at the plant, "...will have a massacre.

"Then we'll assume that I got it," Maxim answered and laughed together with Rada then he added, "I'll work it out. I just need time for it all to sink into a comprehensive picture."

"We'll hope so," Rada said. "All right, let's talk about the type of attention that you are more used to. To be aware of what is going on in a dream, we need to train our attention – our ability to focus. To do that, all kinds of methods will do; for example, meditation, as described in Castaneda's books. On this shelf," Rada pointed at one of the wall-mounted book shelves, "there's plenty of relevant garbage for meditating. Choose a couple of things that you like, I'll give you a mat." Rada got up from her armchair, opened the cupboard and took out a couple of neatly folded thin mats or rather little cloths. "Choose," she offered. "It's better if the color matches the color of your dream portal."

There were ten cloths in total, all of different colors.

"This one," Maxim asked, choosing the brownish-orange color.

"Are you sure?" Rada asked. "Mark you; magicians do not change their decisions. You must really be drawn to this color."

"I like it," Maxim replied. "It's warm, but not too bright."

"Good," Rada agreed and put away the other mats. "You'll meditate the following way: get yourself seated by the wall on a small mattress – it's in your closet. Put a pillow under your back. If you need, you can put little pillows under your knees. Comfort is of importance here. Unfold the mat a meter away from where you're sitting and place the item you've chosen for mediation on it. Your eyelids should be slightly lowered, gaze calmly – relaxed. All your attention is focused on the object of mediation. Try just looking at it, without analyzing what it is you are seeing – that is very important. You must spend at least two hours a day doing this exercise. If you want to do more – great, but you shouldn't do less. You can start right away, once I am finished," a smile slipped across Rada's lips. "Besides, you'll have one more task: learn to focus on what you are doing in the present moment. In other words, your thoughts should not rush about like a horde of frightened monkeys; your attention must be focused on one thing. All of this strengthens your attention." Rada became quiet then she smiled. "I think it's enough for today," she said. "Choose three things to meditate on and don't forget your mat."

Maxim got up from the armchair and approached the shelf.

"And what's a good choice?" Maxim inquired. There were all kinds of things on the shelf – little figurines, jewelry, small busts of poets and musicians, children's cubes, dry chestnuts, a lot of stones of various colors and many, many other things…

"Anything," Rada answered. "Better if it's something natural. Items created by people often carry their imprint."

Having thought about it a little, Maxim chose a dry chestnut and two beautiful stones.

"That will do," Rada said, having assessed his choice. "You must meditate on one item at a time, preferably not changing them too often. That is, you may meditate on one item several months. That's it – we'll talk about the rest tomorrow."

"I got it, Rada. Thank you." Maxim took his mat and went out of the room.

Once he got back to his room, Maxim stated with regret that he was really pushed for time. The patience, mapping, the training sessions at the sports hall, meditating... Now he had to go and meditate, but instead he got himself seated by the table and started making notes in his notebook – he just had a feeling that he needed to somehow organize the obtained knowledge. And he'd do some meditating right before going to bed...

Chapter Six

The Legion Attacks

The search for the boy didn't bring any results. Ten days had passed from the moment of his disappearance; Kramer was frowning, realizing that he had nothing to tell Dags. The Sovereign didn't like losers, and another meeting with him could have a very bad ending. It was somewhat comforting that he had had some progress in other areas of his job; namely, he had been able to launch the activity of one of the major religious sects. They didn't spare strength or money for that. Thousands of sect activists were calling people into their organization right on the streets, handing out colorful promotional pamphlets. All of this was a part of the systematic activity against the Russian Orthodox Church; the Hierarchs of the Legion attached great importance to the struggle against the Church. If there's no Orthodox Church – there's no Russia.

Nevertheless, the successful activity of the members of the sect was a cold comfort – Dags would probably not appreciate it. The searchers had been and remain his headache.

Yana was the one to save the situation – according to her; she had managed to find a few followers of the dream searchers. A while ago, Kramer had made her his personal assistant, paying tribute to her intellect and talents. Sometimes he thought she was worth as much as all of his assistants combined. And so this time she was the one to bring the good news.

"It's all very simple," Yana explained to Kramer. "Our techs tried to get into the computers of some of the participants from the searcher forums. They had created a new 'Trojan' for that purpose. There was no problem with most of the machines, but they were unable to hack into three of them. Moreover, all hacking attempts had the same outcome; I won't go into details, but our guys think that all three machines have the same security system installed, and it's a nonstandard one. Now tell me, why are these three computers different? What is the reason for that?"

"That's interesting," Kramer agreed. "But it's not the searchers?"

"That's highly unlikely," Yana shook her head. "These guys ask questions on the forums, and there are a lot of things they don't know. But they are very smart, and have rather interesting ideas. I have a suspicion that they are talking to searchers using secret channels. And to avoid a leak, the searchers helped them protect their machines."

Kramer thought about it.

"We must start investigating these guys right away," he said. "Who are they? What are their nicks?"

"And what do you think I am doing?" Yana inquired with a touch of sarcasm in her voice. "As for their nicks, it's Serpent, Evelina and Felix."

The situation looked reassuring; Kramer perked up. Now he knew he wasn't going to Dags empty handed.

"Just don't scare them off," he asked Yana. "Act carefully. Don't stick your neck out."

"Don't worry, sweetie," Yana reached out for Kramer and gave him a tender kiss. "Everything will be ok – you know me."

"That's why I am warning you," Kramer muttered, feeling Yana's skilled hands undo his belt. "Not now, I have a meeting with the mayor in ten minutes," He reluctantly stopped the young woman – Yana smiled.

"If you say so," she said. "Oh, I completely forgot to tell you: I am flying to Samara this evening."

"To tease me?" Kramer guessed.

"Not at all," Yana smiled. "I need to meet up with a guy."

"From that trio?" Kramer asked warily.

"Maybe," Yana smiled mysteriously. "Don't worry, it'll be ok.

That fool thinks I am going on a business trip, and he wouldn't mind meeting up – since the opportunity arose..." Yana laughed; however, her gaze remained cold. "After this meeting he'll be mine, in both body and spirit."

"Now that's something I don't doubt," Kramer ran a hungry gaze over her fine figure then looked at the watch. He hesitated for a couple of seconds, then put his arms around Yana and held her tight; his hands slipped under her shirt.

"And what about the mayor?" Yana inquired.

"He'll wait," said Kramer sourly.

Boris stayed at the searcher residence for a couple of days and then left again. When Maxim asked him where he was going, he only grinned and patted him on the shoulder.

"Business, Maxim. Very urgent business. I'll come back and tell you all about it."

"And when will you be back?" Maxim inquired.

"Everything is in the power of the Spirit," Boris demonstratively lifted up his eyes. "But I think I'll manage in one or two weeks."

Maxim smiled; the last time Boris was going away he also spoke of a week or two. But that was an answer that really didn't tell much.

"And until then, do as Rada tells you," Boris added. "She knows what she's doing." Indeed, Maxim had great respect for Rada. It seemed inconceivable that this fragile pretty young woman possessed such fantastic power over reality. The most surprising was that in order to demonstrate miracles – namely, her predatory favorite Hector and the cuttlefish crawling on the ceiling – she didn't use any external actions. She didn't utter spells, perform magic rituals or use miracle potions or amulets. For her, Intention was enough...

Maxim carried out Rada's assignments with great enthusiasm – he simply understood that they were worth it. The first two weeks had been just crazy. But soon to his surprise Maxim discovered that he now even had some spare time. Getting into the life rhythm of this house wasn't too easy – now that he had accomplished that, everything was taking a turn for the better.

Practicing magic was interesting, yet Maxim also tried to enjoy the other sides of life of the habitants of this house. When Boris was gone, Roman was the one in charge and he was the one to gradually familiarize Maxim with the power arrangement of the city. He explained to Maxim what was what. Right now the city was getting ready for new elections: Legionaries expected to leave the present mayor, one of their guys, for another run. Searchers actively tried to stop that from happening. The forces were unequal, but Roman was not put off by that.

"It's easy to explain failures by attributing them to the circumstances," he told Maxim. "And it's a completely different story when you succeed come hell or high water."

Maxim really liked Roman because of his calm and fine sense of humor. Boris told him that in the beginning of the nineties, Roman was working as a manager at a small security firm in Volgograd. At some point, he sensed there was a new power in town. At first he thought it to be an ordinary criminal gang, but then it became clear that it was much more serious than that. That's how Roman first came across the Legion. Back then, he didn't know anything about it, that's why he thought that a large financial-industrial group was trying to move in on the city. These people were rather skillful, and they always got their way. At some point, Roman's interests and the interests of the Legion crossed. It was really a trifle matter, but to the Legion it became the excuse to lay hands on a prospective security business. They gave Roman an ultimatum, as he was the manager of the firm – either he'd work under them, or he wouldn't work at all. Having weighted all pros and cons, he agreed. It's just that he understood realities well, and besides, working together with a large structure had its unquestionable advantages. However, it soon became clear that the activity of his new masters was of rather specific nature – everything they touched either fell apart or dragged out a miserable existence. At some point, Roman realized that he could not work with these people; their orders required coming to terms with his conscience – something he couldn't do. His attempt to have it out with his new boss ended with a fight. Only a year later did Roman find out that he gave a thrashing to no one less than the Legion Deputy of the Volgograd area. He managed to get out that time, with a group of people devoted to him, including Denis. Roman went underground. Realizing that he wouldn't achieve anything by legal methods, he and his companions chose the option of force resistance. It was a war without rules – Roman and his people were hunting Legionaries, and those, in turn, were hunting them. Both sides bore losses. That's when Roman met Boris…

That meeting changed everything. Roman found out about the Legion from Boris, and Boris was the one to help Roman realize the futility of a violent struggle – the forces were way too unequal. As a result, Roman and his fighters moved to Siberia – that was the only way to get the surviving co-workers out of Volgograd alive. Gradually, Roman and his people got so close to the searchers that they became an integral part of their group. Roman and his fighters provided safety and were responsible for all searchers' operations that involved force. With time, Roman joined the ranks of searchers – turned out he was a natural born searcher. He left all direct supervision of the group to Denis, who brilliantly managed his new responsibilities.

Now, having found out about the upcoming mayor election, Maxim volunteered to help the searchers in their work – of course, to the best of his ability; that was taken for granted. And so it came about that Maxim, from time to time, ran various small errands.

Now he had to pay a visit to the south garage – that was the name of one of the places where searchers kept their 'work' cars. Not one of these cars had ever been close to the searcher residence

– the strict safety rules demanded that. The car park itself was regularly updated; sometimes cars were replaced after only one operation.

Maxim arrived at the south garage by eight thirty in the morning. He got there on the tram, having followed all Roman's instructions – he had to make sure that he was not being followed. On the whole, they had not noticed anything suspicious these last few weeks, but you can never be too sure, and so Maxim did his best in everything.

"There are no trifles in our job," Roman told him two days ago. "Learn to always work with a guarantee, never leaving anything to chance. If there is even a shadow of a doubt, don't wave it away – check everything thoroughly, so there won't be any surprises later. Don't be in a rush; don't try to do everything in one go. Remember, straight paths often lead to the cemetery. Watch, notice; trust your intuition. Always pay attention, but stay relaxed; be on your guard but remain calm. There are no contradictions here, with time you'll understand what I'm talking about."

Actually, this time around everything was calm. Maxim got off the tram and walked along a shady poplar alley then he turned to a side street and was soon approaching the unremarkable housing estate. In the front yard of this old house were three big garages; there was the heavy Kamaz truck with tainted windows and, in the two remaining garages, a couple of passenger cars. These were the 'work' cars – cars that were used for important trips. Each had several sets of license plates and documents to go with them.

The house itself was inhabited by Stepanych, a bearded man about sixty years old. He had taken part in many armed conflicts and was a former commanding officer of an elite subversive unit. His career came to an end thirty years ago, in one of the hot African countries; coming back from an assignment in a car, Stepanych and his people got under fire. That's when his service ended. The doctors were unable to salvage his smashed-up arm, but they saved his life.

Fate brought Stepanych and the searchers together in the year of ninety eight – it so happened that three opportunistic youngsters thought that the lonely old man, living in a three room flat, was a sitting duck. Apartments were of good value back then, and so the guys considered the issue solved. However, the events took quite a different turn. The one-armed old man turned out to be extremely stubborn, and when the three fine young men tried to explain to him in plain language – with the help of a knife and a gun – who is who in this world, the old fighter was forced to remember his youth. Although, later he actually admitted that he got too worked up. Be that as it may, everything ended rather quickly – the old man called 911 and then went to the kitchen for a cup of tea.

The ambulance arrived in twenty minutes; having assessed the situation, the medical worker immediately called the police. Two young people no longer required any medical attention; the third one was taken to the emergency unit. The old man, having finished his tea, handed the knife and the Tokarev gun he took from the raiders to the arrived police. There were exactly two cartridges missing from the charger...

The old man could very well end up in jail – supposedly for exceeding the limits of self-defense. Besides, the crippled teenager turned out to be the son of a very well-known man in the city. He was so well known that the two lawyers refused to take part in the process after a little chat with the representatives of the enraged dad. Parity had to be maintained, and so Roman's team got involved in the incident. Phone calls didn't bring the desired effect, the enraged dad promised to grind to dust all the bad guys. So they had to take some 'third degree action' – not even a week went by, until the paternal wrath appeased and the dad's voice sounded rather human on the phone. In the end, Stepanych got away with a suspended sentence, but he still had to move out of his flat, mainly because of Roman, who had reasons to believe that it wouldn't be safe for the old man to stay there after all.

However, Stepanych had no complaints. He liked his new place, and besides, he now had a job. And so it came about that Stepanych has been looking after the cars for many years now, getting more than a considerable sum of money to his pension. He didn't know anything about searcher business, but he was firmly convinced that he was working for some government special agency, which made his officer heart very pleased.

Stepanych already knew Maxim, so he answered the bell without hesitating. The old fighter's handshake turned out to be exceptionally firm. Maxim thought that he wouldn't want to meet this old man in a dark alley.

"Which one will you be taking?" Stepanych looked at Maxim questioningly.

"The Lada 2110."

"You got it." The old man rummaged in the little closet, attached to a wall in the hall and handed Maxim the car keys.

"Here you go."

Maxim took the keys, Stepanych closed the closet then they both went outside. The old man removed two massive locks from the outer garage. Maxim helped him open the heavy doors.

At the very edge of the garage was a luxurious grey BMW, behind it was a white Lada 2110.

"Wait here, while I'll get the 'German' out of the way, otherwise you won't be able to get out." The old man opened the door of the BMW and got into the car with impressive agility for his age. It is probably not the easiest thing in the world, driving a car with one hand, but Stepanych obviously didn't care about that. The engine started gently spinning; the wonder of foreign technology smoothly drove out into the front yard.

When starting up the engine of the Lada, Maxim was smiling – that's how vivid a sight it was, watching the bearded Stepanych behind the wheel of the foreign car. Maxim had barely driven out of the garage, as Stepanych, with the skill of a daredevil, got the car back inside the garage.

Maxim helped the old man close the garage doors, then waited while he put the locks back on. Finally, Stepanych hid the keys in his pocket and looked at Maxim.

"When will you bring it back?" the old man said in a lordly tone.

"Tomorrow morning. Probably," Maxim added, and the old man smiled knowingly.

"I'll be waiting," he said, and went to open the gates. Maxim didn't know who needed that car or why. His assignment was very simple: to pick the car up from the garage at such and such time and to leave it by one of the city shops. They'd drive it back without his help or tell him where and when he could pick it up. Maxim wasn't offended by the fact that he was not yet let in on all the details of what Roman and his people were doing. It all had a very simple explanation – why know the details of things you have no active part in? If he'd get into the hands of the Legionaries, the excess knowledge could lead to the ruin of them all.

He talked about that with Roman yesterday. Maxim let it slip that, on the whole, he was surprised at how good he had been treated. Or rather, by the extreme, in his opinion, trust they had been showing him.

"Because any way you slice it," he said, "you don't know me at all. And still you brought me here, to your residence. Even if this is all purely theoretical, but what if I, all of a sudden, cross over to the Legionaries' side for some reason? In my opinion, you are being too reckless."

"It's not quite the way you think," Roman smiled. "Any person that comes into contact with us is most thoroughly checked. It's another thing entirely that he doesn't know anything about it. Can you guess how this is possible?"

"No," Maxim admitted honestly.

"The testing of potential candidates to join our ranks is led by experienced dreamers. Boris and Rada were the ones who took care of you. You passed several very strict tests, but they all took place in your dreams. What's more, it all happened on the left side of your consciousness – I believe, you already know what it is?"

"Yes," Maxim nodded. "I do."

"Then you must know that the left side memory is buried so deep inside that it's inaccessible to our ordinary consciousness. You've passed four tests out of five. That's a very good sign."

Maxim didn't reply. For a few seconds he thought about what he had just heard then he looked up at Roman.

"But a dream is only a dream. Can you really evaluate a person by his dream?"

"You can," Roman nodded. "In a dream, a person throws all his masks away and acts in line with his true self. This is what happens during the actual test: searchers create a training ground – that is, they create a specific dream situation, then they drag you over into that dream and leave you alone with the problem. And then they observe what you'll do. For example, you are put into a situation where you have to choose between your life and betrayal, or between your life and the life of your friend. They check your greediness; your sexual preferences. For example, can you be seduced by some young female Legionary?" Roman grinned. "Off the record, that's the test you didn't pass."

Maxim twitched then blushed. Roman laughed.

"Don't get embarrassed," he said. "In the end, all guys are the same. Ninety percent of male participants who take this test fail. Women do better, but even they flunk it in about sixty percent of cases."

"And each candidate for the position of a searcher goes through the dream tests?" Maxim asked in disbelief.

"Each and every one. If you've been surfing the net, you've probably seen a lot of smart guys and girls interested in searcher techniques. However, only a few of them will become searchers.

Why? Because most of them fail the first couple of tests. These people will continue hanging out on dream forums, and taking part in searcher workshops; they will even create their own groups. We may sincerely wish them good luck, but they won't have anything to do with us anymore. And that's because they showed weakness in one of the important tests."

"And is it possible to find something out from a person? For example, his secrets?"

"You can," Roman nodded. "Searchers came up with a technique of dream interrogation. It's reminiscent of neuro-linguistic programming (NLP). The function of critical reasoning is very low in a dream, so a person could blurt out his innermost secrets. I can tell you that the special agencies of many countries in this world are after this technique. Searchers use it to inter-rogate Legionaries and their accomplices in dreams, and to unmask the 'moles' on searcher forums."

"Moles? You mean spies?"

"Yes. Legionaries are always trying to send us their people, and we keep unmasking them. Having done that, we either smoothly stop any further contact or use them in our games, providing them with disinformation. The last option is often used online: we organize some kind of workshop, and Legionaries always sign up. First, the workshop takes place in an open mode then it moves into closed mode. Not everyone gets to the closed part of the workshop, yet we intentionally take in one of the Legionaries. Once we've moved the participants to the closed stage, we discuss a few topics that are of little importance – for example, the Patience of Medici or simple dreaming techniques. Usually, these forums are lead by one of the new guys; to them, it's a way of polishing their stalker techniques. Legionaries take this bait; they keep the forum under close watch and try to find us through this forum. We know this, and that's why nothing ever comes of their attempts. While the Legionaries are busying themselves with dummy forums, we are calmly leading a few truly prospective groups in closed workshops. Finally, there's our own private forum on the net – we call it the inner forum. Only those people who we are absolutely sure about get invited there."

"And isn't it unfair to the average forum participants?" Maxim inquired. "Turns out you are leading them down the garden path."

"No," Roman shook his head. "Don't forget that each of the participants has a real chance of showing his worth and getting into one of the groups that actually is operating. So, it's all in their hands; no one will drag anyone against their will, but if a person shows promise and passes the tests, he'll get invited. Wouldn't you agree that to have a chance to touch upon real knowledge is already something?"

"Perhaps," Maxim agreed then he glanced at his watch. "Roman, I must go. Rada is waiting."

Yana got back four days later. Kramer already knew that she was back in town, and was now impatiently waiting for her to show up. The hands of the clock standing on the mantelpiece were crawling up to noon, when the soft tap of little heels was finally heard outside the office door.

"And here I am," Yana said, closing the door behind her. She glanced at Kramer, and by her radiant smile he understood that everything went well.

"Did it work?" he asked, raising himself a little in the armchair.

"You forgot to say 'hello'," Yana replied, coming closer. She leaned on the edge of the table and pecked Kramer on the lips then she tiredly lowered herself into the armchair opposite his.

"Did you succeed?" Kramer repeated.

"Could you really have doubts about that?" the young woman inquired, making herself more comfortable in the armchair. "Two nights were not spent in vain. I hope you are not jealous."

"Don't be ridiculous," Kramer brushed that idea away. "I'm

waiting for details."

"About these two nights?" Yana asked and burst out with ringing laughter. Sometimes she was insufferable.

"What did you manage to find out?"

"Not a great deal so far," Yana replied. "The boy is smart, well-read, good looking; works as a manager in a prestigious firm. We talked a lot about searchers and their techniques, but he didn't blab out anything that could be of use to us. But he knows something, I can feel it. He could hardly keep himself from telling me his secrets."

"And that's it?" Kramer frowned. "I expected more."

"That's almost it," Yana smiled. "While that silly was in the shower, I managed to upload a 'Trojan' to his computer from a CD. There's already information coming in. Our guys are working on it right now. By the way, our Felix turned out to be Sergey Kondratenko – twenty-six years old."

"That's already better." Kramer relaxed a little. "Is there anything specific in that information?"

"The guys are working on it," Yana repeated, stressing her words. "I doubt there's need for haste. As soon as there is a report, I'll forward it to you in a heartbeat."

"Good," Kramer muttered. "I'll be waiting."

The report came in late in the day. Having received the folder from a messenger, Kramer with trembling hands took out the papers with printed text and immersed himself in the information. And the more he was reading, the happier he got.

Yana was right – Felix was one of the closest followers of the dream searchers. The information transmitted by the 'Trojan' turned out to be very important – here was the link to the closed forum of the searchers and a few of their emails. A certain somebody with the nickname, Moran, was of particular interest; he was obviously one of the DH. A couple of his emails had already passed to the cryptography unit; there it would be compared with the messages of the other searchers. Based on his style of expression, the frequency of use of certain words, experts will be able to accurately determine whether Moran is one of the new searchers, or if one of the old guys has simply changed his nickname.

That was already something to go on; Kramer was rubbing his hands with impatience. There was now a real possibility of not only locating separate searchers, but even their base, at least their regional one. And a base equals an archive; it contains truly invaluable data on the dream searchers' methods. One would give everything for that...

For the last week Maxim had already made it his rule to each day do at least one chain of the Patience of Medici. If the first chain worked and he won a laughable sum of money, but he won nonetheless, then the few next chains were less successful. Maxim didn't restrict himself to chains where he'd win the lottery. Instead, he compiled chains for all kinds of goals: for example, he ordered a scenario where someone would ask him the time. Strange, but it didn't work. And if the first couple of chains worked somehow, then soon everything completely got out of order. Magic waved to him and disappeared – that was seriously annoying. After several unsuccessful attempts Maxim decided to consult Rada.

"The first chain went excellent," he explained, "then they started to go worse and worse. Now I don't feel them at all, it's all random. Could you tell me what I am doing wrong?"

"You're doing everything right," Rada smiled. "You have just bumped into one of the defense mechanisms of the real world. Remember the chemistry classes in school – or rather, Le Chatelier's Principle. I don't remember the exact phrasing, but the general idea is that a system is always trying to restore the equilibrium. When doing the chains of the Patience of Medici, you disturb the system, and, in complete compliance with Le

Chatelier's Principle, the system launches a resistance mechanism. In computer terminology – they cut off your traffic. There is only one way out: to not back down. If you won't give up and continue your research, then the following will happen: the point of equilibrium in the system will gradually start shifting in the, for you, desired direction. In other words, your interference with the business of the real world will cause less and less resistance, and one day it will disappear all together. You will get a new upgraded status; magic to you will become an ordinary phenomenon. There will be a new entry in your cosmography charts. I can say that the same mechanism of resistance also exists in dreams. If the dreamer doesn't know about it, he may encounter serious problems, the simplest of which – lucid dreams go away. On a more serious level you can get real physical ailments – for example, diseases of the liver."

"It's getting somewhat clearer," Maxim said, evaluating what Rada just told him. "But isn't there some kind of trick you can do to avoid this resistance?"

"You are reasoning like a searcher," the young woman smiled. "Unfortunately, there are no methods for getting rid of the resistance of the real world that work a hundred percent. The thing is that it is the natural defense mechanism of the universe, the Tonal's immunity of sorts. You are breaking into the subtle mechanisms of the universe; the system immediately notices the intruder and tries to put him back in his place. That's why, at the moment, the only useful recommendation for you would be to not expose yourself. What that means for your dreaming we'll talk about later. And in the real world, try not to have any obsessions. The more you want something, the fewer chances you have of getting it. Recall the words of Don Juan: even if success does come, it must come without fixed ideas and shocks. Note this is a very delicate point: you just go and get what you want. Here's a direct link to intention, and intention is not the same as desire. Intention is rather unconditional knowledge. Say, you're playing the lottery; the more you want to win, the fewer chances you'll have of doing that. With your desire to win you are launching the mechanism of resistance; the configuration of the real world will change as to not let you win. And you won't win. Why not? Only because you exposed yourself; you told the whole world about your desire to win. And the world punished you for that. Conclusion: don't let the world know about your desires, instead – just go and take what you need. The same with the chains of the PM – treat them more calmly. Many try to influence this world by force, not realizing that that is the easiest way of getting a scolding. At first, it seems as if something is working, the world gives in to you. But then it strikes back, and in one go you lose everything you've got, or even more. Thus, learn to just know what you need. Let's say, it's cloudy outside, but there's no rain. If I want – there could be no rain at all. Then again, in five minutes I'll start a real heavy shower – it's time to give this town a little washing. It's very easy for me to do, because I know how to intend the right way, my connection with intention is very pure. Correct intention – it's not a hit with a sledgehammer, but a breath of air. It's not about force, but about sliding in the flows of the forces around you. Look, it has already started raining – only because I thought about it a couple of minutes ago."

Maxim looked out the window – the first drops had already slipped across the glass. Rada smiled.

"You see?" she said. "No force, no 'wrecking' will; I just marked the route and paved the way with my intention, and the chain of events was realized the way I wanted it to. In reality, it's all very easy."

Rada was looking out the window, the rain was getting heavier. Another minute went by, and it turned into a heavy shower.

"You see?" Rada asked again and looked at Maxim with a smile. "This world does as I tell it."

"And can you stop the rain?" Maxim inquired. "Right now?"

"I can," Rada answered. "But I won't. It just wouldn't be right. You cannot change the direction of the flow twice in a short period of time. A magician must always be consistent in his actions. And if I summoned the rain, then let it pour."

"Got it," Maxim nodded, watching the rain drops crawling on the glass. "So, I just need to practice the PM, and everything will be all right?"

"Yes, Maxim. But it would be better if you'd take a week's break. Let the universe get some rest from you," a smile slipped across the young woman's lips, "and let yourself get some rest from the universe."

"Okay," Maxim agreed. "I'll do that."

"All the better. And now let's talk a little about dreaming. I saw you this night; you were very close to lucidity. But your assemblage point is too rigid for you to reach lucidity yourself." Rada got up from her armchair and walked over to the closed closet. "Here," she said, having picked out a light-colored crystal the size of a finger from the closet. "Take this, it will help you."

"What is it?" Maxim asked, carefully taking the crystal. The crystal was drilled through on one end – apparently, it could be worn as an amulet. On the surface of the crystal, Maxim made out strange symbols carved out with some unknown tool.

"It's mica," Rada replied, taking a seat back in the chair. "I found this crystal some time ago by the sea. Rather, by a water reservoir. I rounded it off and polished it then carved the appropriate runes on its surface. Now this crystal helps one become aware of oneself in a dream. More precisely, it helps the assemblage point shift to a place, where awareness can be most easily achieved. Wear it around your neck; adjust the string so that the crystal is in the depression – in the place where your chest borders with your belly." Rada smiled once again. "Fall asleep on your back; the crystal must lie in this little depression. When falling asleep, focus on the contact point between the crystal and your body."

"Thank you," Maxim said, carefully examining the crystal. "I'll try it."

And so he did. If the first two nights didn't bring anything, then on the third night something unusual happened. Maxim already knew that to enter a dream right at the moment of falling asleep was almost impossible for a beginner, so he didn't think about it too much. He simply focused on the contact point between the crystal and his body, and at the same time his thoughts kept crawling away someplace different. At some point Maxim suddenly saw a school class; it just appeared out of nowhere. And immediately his consciousness prevailed; Maxim was in rapture over the fact that he managed to enter a dream! And not just anyhow, but at the moment of falling asleep. He looked around, trying to remember how one should act in a dream, and at the same instant he sensed that he was losing control. The world around him grew dark; Maxim opened his eyes and lay there for a few seconds, reliving over and over again what had just happened. Then he felt the crystal – turns out that thing really did help him...

He didn't have any more dreams that night. Nor the night after that, yet something had started to change. The actual quality of the dreams was changing – they became more 'transparent'. Maxim sensed that he was on the threshold of lucidity, there was just a tiny bit to go. And Rada confirmed that.

"You are now very close to the dream world. And the most important thing for you now is not to overdo it. Remember what we talked about a couple of days ago. Don't push yourself. Don't strive towards success – just go and take it. Treat it as if it is already in your pocket. When you are in a dream, control your emotions. It's a difficult thing to do, but you will have to learn how to control yourself. Otherwise, the dream program with notice your emotions and will try to slightly press down against you so that you won't disturb the equilibrium with your bursts of emotions."

"I got it," Maxim nodded. "Tell me, what can you do in a dream? Say, I got there then what's next?"

"Start studying it. Don't forget that searchers are, first of all, researchers. Look around – examine your body. If there is a mirror nearby, look at your reflection. Try to go through a wall. Fly around. Try talking to someone. Does the conversation make any sense? Finally, assess your own level of consciousness. Namely, do you remember where you are sleeping right now? What month, what year it is? The important thing for you now is to familiarize yourself with the dream world – learn how to enter it at will and to remain there at least for a couple of minutes. Then you'll be able to move on to more serious research and exercises. Again, you must remember that the energy of this house helps you dream, and the percentage of your own effort in your achievements is still very low."

"Yes, I understand that," Maxim agreed. Rada barely noticeably smiled.

"And in general, you should just lighten up," she said. "You are way too serious. I still haven't heard you laugh, not even once. Learn to enjoy this world, become friends with it. Don't load yourself with problems. Then everything will start happening by itself. We are the ones increasing the significance of the problems that appear before us – learn not to attach too much importance to problems, and they will run away from you. You'll see."

Maxim smiled.

"He, who slides on the sea of life?" he said.

"Exactly," Rada confirmed. "You can't even imagine how much meaning there is hidden in this simple phrase. It could be considered the motto of dream searchers – their way of life. Most people are too preoccupied with themselves and their own problems; they have forgotten how to enjoy life. Someone's making money, someone's raising children, someone's busy with his career or with buying a house. Millions of people – millions of problems. We don't notice how we transform our life into a small, personal hell. And then one day comes a moment, when a person finds himself on his death bed and realizes that he has ruined his life – that it flew by in vain. It was consumed like gunpowder, and the wind carried away the smoke. But he did have dreams, dreams about great accomplishments. And where did it all go, huh?" Rada stared at Maxim.

"I don't know," he shrugged his shoulders. "Everyone lives as they can."

"You just don't get it yet," Rada said with a sad smile. "You don't get what Castaneda called the Abstract Cores. But it will come to you; you will learn to see the world differently. And there, where the regular person only sees an external chain of events, you'll see its true meaning."

"Let's hope so," Maxim said; Rada smiled once again. Her gaze was very soft and a little sad.

"Do you have any other questions? On anything?"

"I always have plenty of questions," Maxim answered. "Could you tell me about the DNA of the Tonal?"

"I can," Rada said. "But it's a topic for another time, so let's leave it for now. Ask me something else."

"Okay," Maxim agreed. "Then another question: what comes after the Patience of Medici? Because you don't use it, right? And I didn't see any cards in Boris's room."

"You see, the Patience of Medici helps you come into contact with the universe. With its help you can pull a few divine strings. But for practical problem solving it is very cumbersome and inconvenient. There are not just one, but four active chains of events in the Patience of Medici, each of which is responsible for a particular area in life. Spades is the area of will; clubs is everyday life, work, and so on. But we're usually interested in a specific goal, and four areas to achieve this goal are simply super-fluous. Four suits, in this sense, represent four flows. Sorting the patience according to suit is moving in the flow; sorting the patience according to the value of the cards is moving from one flow to another. Now in your hands you have got all the necessary information to come up with a new, more convenient tool for interacting with the real world. I'd like it if you'd take some time to think about all of this and tell me about your conclusions. But today, I think, we'll stop there."

"All right." Maxim got up from the armchair. "I'll have a think about all of this."

Unfortunately, the subsequent events of the evening messed up all of Maxim's plans. Everything started with Boris' homecoming; he returned together with Roman. They both looked pretty gloom. Maxim knew something had happened.

"What happened?" Oxana voiced his unexpressed question.

"The Legionaries have overrun the Voronezh group," Boris said. "An hour ago. They took Mariana and Kostya. Danila got a bullet in his shoulder; our guys are now taking him to Belgorod. The others managed to escape."

It became very quiet, in this silence you could clearly hear the stairs creak – Rada was coming down to them. Apparently, she heard everything.

"Who is with Danila?" Rada asked, approaching.

"Kirill and Stas," Boris answered.

"The archive?"

"They did manage to destroy it in time. I don't know the details yet."

"Let's go to the main room," Roman suggested. "We need to decide what to do. I called Denis, he'll be here shortly."

In the main room, Maxim sat down on a small sofa next to Oxana. Rada took a seat in an armchair by the window. Roman and Boris made themselves comfortable in the armchairs by the coffee table.

"First, let's assess our risks," Boris began. "Kostya and Mariana have never been here, so there won't be a leak there. They know the Moscow and St.Petersburg guys, but they will take care of themselves. The archive is destroyed and they can't find us through the email addresses. So, it's safe here. Any elaborations?"

"Mariana knows Goncharov," Rada said. "And he has been here. We have to warn him at once."

"Damn it!" It burst from Boris. "That didn't occur to me." He took out his cell and dialed. Everyone was waiting with tension. "Ilya? It's Boris. They might find you. You need to leave right away... I don't know, the sooner, the better... Just sit snug at somebody's place... No, the others are not in any danger yet. All the details later. That's all. Bye." Boris ended the call. "They won't be able to get to anyone else." Boris heaved a sigh. "Now we only have to decide what to do about Kostya and Mariana."

"We have to get them out of there," Rada said quietly. "Give me one hour, and I'll tell you where they are. Meanwhile, get in touch with Iris; we won't be able to pull this off just the two of us."

"Okay." Boris jerked up his head, having heard someone knocking on the front door.

It was Denis. Rada went up to her room, and Denis was told all the details about what happened. He left right after that to give directions to the guards, to warn his people about a raised security level.

"You've never done that before," Oxana said and glanced at Boris. "Will it work?"

"It was going to happen someday," Boris replied. "Besides, we've got the surprise factor working for us. I'll warn Iris." Boris got up and went out to the hall, retrieving his phone on his way out.

Maxim didn't break into the conversation; however, he had already realized that the searchers had to do something unusual. He didn't know the people they were talking about now, but he understood that they were in the hands of the Legionaries. Boris and Rada decided to pull them out of there – but how? Through a portal? Was that possible?

"I didn't know there were searchers in Voronezh," Maxim

said, feeling that he could no longer just keep watching what was happening. "Do they have any way of leaving on their own? Using that very same portal?"

"The Voronezh group is barely three years old, they had just started working properly. And such an ending..." Roman shook his head regretfully. "I don't even know where they could have made a mistake. They do not know how to open portals yet. It's not that easy."

"Danila led the group 'searcheros'," Oxana reminded.

Maxim already knew that the term 'searcheros' was used to refer to the groups of dream searchers' followers. Classes with such groups were usually conducted by searchers on closed forums.

"One of the new guys?" Roman suggested.

"Perhaps," Oxana shrugged. "It's too early to accuse anyone, but that's the most likely option so far. If Legionaries had reached their forum, they could have gradually figured out the addresses of all the members of that group."

"There was a base in Voronezh, just like this one?" Maxim asked.

"No," Roman shook his head. "They lived in the most ordinary houses and apartments. I told you that they've just started working. Danila moved to Voronezh just to help them consolidate their position. It's an important region; we didn't want to leave them on their own."

Boris returned.

"Iris is already up to speed," he said. "And this time the Legionaries have pissed her off."

"Because of Danila?" A vague smile slipped across Oxana's lips.

"Yes. They shouldn't have touched him," Boris smiled too. "Now she'll definitely vent her anger on them."

Maxim felt slight relief. If they are all smiling, hope remained...

Rada returned about forty minutes later; all that time they were discussing all kinds of unimportant things. Maxim got the impression that the tenants of this house deviated from the main topic on purpose.

"They are in the basement of a large estate," Rada said. "Kostya is tied to a chair – he's being beaten. And his foot is shot. Mariana is, so far, alone in a separate cell. She's unharmed by the looks of it, only her lip is broken. She's also strapped to a chair."

"Did you warn her?" Oxana asked.

"No," Rada shook her head. "There are surveillance cameras. And it seems they both have been drugged. How's Iris?"

"She said she's going to wait for us at the Glade. We better hurry up. Roman, fill the bathtubs with water. We're going," Boris took Rada by the hand and they quickly went upstairs.

"Oxana, fill the bathtubs," Roman ordered. "I'll call Gerasimov. We're going to need a doctor." He didn't wait for a reply and quickly left the room.

Maxim and Oxana were left alone.

"Maxim, fill the bathtub with cold water," Oxana said. "And I'll fill up the top one."

"With cold water?" Maxim asked.

"Yes. And we're also going to need clothes and blankets." Deep in thought, Oxana left the main room and went upstairs.

Maxim hurried to the bathroom. He plugged the bathtub and opened the tap. Then he sat down on the edge of the bathtub and started waiting for it to fill up…

Only a week ago Kramer couldn't even dream about such luck. While reading the forwarded reports, he kept getting amazed at Yana's talents. What would he do without her?

The implanted 'Trojan' in Felix's computer did its job, providing Kramer's people with the necessary threads. Having pulled at them, they uncoiled the whole ball of strings. It turned out that this particular group was based in Voronezh. The hardest part was to figure out the first member of the group. The searchers had a well-thought out security system. But they worked it out, the rest was very easy: having traced the contacts of this person, they revealed the entire group. Its core consisted of at least four people. Kramer didn't go on to reveal the group's other contacts – a bird in the hand is worth the proverbial two in the bush. If these people sense danger, everything would go to pieces.

They decided to attack on the evening of June seventh, yet problems arose right after the beginning of the operation. It started with the Keeper, Mariana Krutikova. She got delayed at work and, instead of getting out of her university at five thirty, she came out only at quarter past six. She was immediately grabbed, pulled into a minivan and taken away, yet the hitch had its effect – one of her colleagues sensed danger, having noticed an unfamiliar van and suspicious movements in his front yard. He immediately made a few calls on his cell phone, warning his friends that the hunt had begun; the traced calls worked as a signal for immediate attack. The door turned out to be more solid than they thought. They managed to break it open only a couple of minutes later. The searcher showed fierce resistance against the attack force; however he didn't manage to escape.

The two remaining members of the searcher group did. One of them, already warned of danger, made a phone call to the police and reported an armed assault on his apartment. Then he called the fire brigade, who came surprisingly quickly – sooner than the attack group was able to break in the steel double door. The fighters of the group were forced to quickly retreat, and the searcher, having thrown a few smoke bombs into the entrance of the house and taken advantage of the panic, managed to slip away. He disappeared among the people leaving their apartments in a rush.

They made another blunder with the fourth searcher. He lived in a private house, and, when the attack group broke inside, the only thing that appeared before the fighters' eyes was an open basement hatch. Once in the basement, they found a narrow manhole leading to the sewage system. Having noticed some kind of movement in the dark, the fighters immediately started firing at the suspicious place where they saw the movement, but they didn't manage to catch the searcher. However, the most unpleasant thing was that the searcher had time to destroy the hard drive of his computer. Kramer knew that it had to contain something very valuable, because the searcher didn't try to take it with him, but destroyed it instead. Hence, he thought it possible that he would not manage to escape. There were indications that the disc contained very valuable information, and that the searcher who got away was the leader of the group.

Despite the unfortunate mistakes, Kramer was satisfied with the operation. Two searchers had been captured, and that was already quite a big deal, they could tell many interesting things. Having told his people in Voronezh not to overdo it and await his arrival, Kramer went to Dags.

The conversation didn't go as well as Kramer thought; Dags immediately pointed out the mistakes. Yet, in the end of the conversation he still complimented Kramer for his efforts.

"Tomorrow we're flying to Voronezh," he said. "I'll tell them to get a plane ready. You are going with me."

"Good, Sovereign," Kramer answered, pleased that things were developing this way. Very few people got invited up to his airplane, and that Kramer got invited surely meant something. They flew out in the morning and already by eleven o'clock they were in Voronezh. While the black armored limo was driving through the streets of the town, Kramer now and then cast a glance at his boss. Dags was obviously in a good mood, and that made Kramer happy.

And there was the Legion residence; the massive metallic gates silently opened and the limo smoothly drove into the front yard and stopped. Guards run up to the car and immediately opened the doors.

Dags was the first one to step out of the car, Kramer followed. He sighed with satisfaction; his eyes met the eyes of Malygin, the local Legionary supervisor, and twitched. Malygin looked too pale; there was no joy in his eyes. And the guards seemed a bit dejected – did something happen?

"Good morning, Mr. Dags," Malygin murmured with a faltering voice. "You've already arrived?"

"No, I'm still in Moscow," Dags answered, his voice was getting heavier by the second. "Report the situation."

"They disappeared, Mr. Dags," Malygin answered; he was a sorry sight. "I…don't know how it could have happened… We took everything into account, we drugged them… We even tied them to the chairs; guards were watching them… But about two o'clock in the morning the surveillance cameras… stopped working. We got there immediately, but there was nobody there… Their clothes were still there, but they… they were gone… Forgive us, Mr. Dags." Malygin lowered his head; his lips were quivering.

"Why didn't you report this at once?" Kramer spoke, sensing that he had to save the situation somehow. More precisely, he had to relieve himself of the responsibility for what had happened. "Do you realize that you've made us come here all for nothing?"

"We tried to work it out," Malygin sobbed. "We searched through their houses again; we thought that maybe they were there. They had to appear somewhere after all."

"I'll think about your fate," Dags said with a sullen voice. Then he glanced at one of the guards. "Take us to the cells."

Escaping these cells was impossible. Still, the searchers managed to get away. Dags looked at the metallic chair embedded into the concrete floor with the fugitive's clothes hanging on it – Kostya Prilukov was kept in this cell – and became thoughtful.

Something wasn't right. It is one thing, if the apprehended searchers were experienced searchers like Sly, then their disappearance, even after an injection of a very strong antipsychotic drug, could have some kind of explanation. But, the searchers that got away were clearly not too experienced. The whole intercepted correspondence was evidence of that. Besides – Dags looked at the armored wire that had been torn out of the surveillance camera – this is something the tied up Kostya Prilukov definitely could not have done.

There was only one final logical explanation: more experienced searchers helped these people escape. And that means that they are even more powerful than he thought. It is one thing to disappear yourself; it's a different thing entirely to be able to enter a closed room and pull someone out of there. It's no longer magic; it's some kind of devilry…

"We'll have to draw certain conclusions from this situation," he said. Kramer, standing behind him, was hanging on his every word. "We're going home." Dags looked at Kramer with dislike and sighed. "We're done here."

More than two hours had passed before footsteps were heard on the stairs. It was Boris, he looked a bit pale.

"So far, it's not working," he said. "There are two men in Kostya's cell; they won't let us take him away. And we can't save only Mariana, then we will definitely not be able to get Kostya out of there. We have to wait."

"Hot tea?" Oxana jumped up from the armchair and asked. "Everything is ready; I'll bring you a cup."

"Do that," Boris nodded, then turned around and slowly walked upstairs.

Oxana ran away to the kitchen, and Maxim looked at Roman.

"And why do they need tea?" he asked. "Does that somehow help you dream?"

"They are not just dreaming – they are leaving their bodies," Roman explained. "Even if you wrap yourself up, it's still cold. Experiments like these are hard on the human body. So before making another attempt they need to come around. The best thing to do is to drink some hot sweet tea."

"And what's the difference between a dream and what they are doing right now?" Maxim inquired. "I don't catch the difference."

"The difference is in the level of the energies they are using. Boris, Rada and Iris are not simply dreaming, but they are watching our real world. That's what people usually call astral projection. Boris or Rada will explain the details." Roman smiled. "I'm not the expert on these things."

Again the wearisome hours dragged on. The conversations soon faded; all they could do now was wait. To occupy himself somehow, Maxim picked up one of the books by Castaneda and immersed himself in reading.

Things came to a head at about four am. A door creaked on the second floor – there were voices. Roman and Oxana jumped up from their armchairs and rushed upstairs. Maxim hurried after them.

It was pretty crowded in Boris's room. Excluding Boris and Rada, there was Iris, a very pale, blond young woman that Maxim didn't know, and, sitting on the bed, a guy about twenty-five years old. Yet, it wasn't the miraculous appearance of Iris and the strangers that surprised him, but the fact that all three of them were naked.

However, no one seemed to care about that. Rada and Iris grabbed the near-unconscious Mariana and dragged her to the bathroom; Oxana was helping them, opening the doors. Boris and Roman were carrying down the guy. Only now did Maxim notice that he had been severely beaten; he was bleeding from a wound on his left leg. They were taking him to the bathroom on the first floor; Maxim started helping.

Kostya was put into the bathtub with water up to his chin. His wounded leg was also left above the water. The searcher was very pale; his absent gaze was wandering the room. At some point Kostya tried to get out of the bathtub, and Boris tried to hold him back.

"It's ok, Kostya, we're home now," Boris said, holding him

back. "Hang in there, just a little more."

Maxim already knew that cold water helped you get yourself together after such journeys. He had already come across something similar in Castaneda's books.

Kostya remained in the water for about fifteen minutes, during that time Roman managed to hastily irrigate and bandage the wound on his leg. The doctor would do the treating later. Then Kostya was pulled out of the tub, wrapped into a blanket and carried to the bedroom. There they made him drink a few pills and some hot tea; as Kostya was drinking, his teeth loudly knocking against the edge of the cup. Nevertheless, there was life in his eyes now.

Boris too looked very tired, but a smile was already playing on his lips.

"So, how are you?" he asked Kostya. "Okay?"

"Yeah." Kostya gave a weak nod. "What a fine mess we've got ourselves in. How's Mariana?"

"She's fine; she's in the next room. That's it, get some rest now. If you need anything – call."

Kostya was left alone as Boris said, he'd be okay now. Tomorrow morning a doctor would examine the wound.

"Let's go to the kitchen," he suggested, having come downstairs. "I wouldn't say no to a cup of hot tea myself."

Soon they were joined by the girls. If Rada looked tired, then Iris was energy impersonated.

"They're a bit tight, but it's okay," she said, clearly talking about her clothes. Maxim recognized them; these were Oxana's jeans and sweater. "Make room for a lady. Half a kingdom for a cup of tea!"

They drank tea for more than two hours; everyone was cheerful and truly happy. Maxim could almost feel what a load had lifted from the shoulders of his friends. Iris didn't miss the opportunity to make game of him, having said that this was surely the first time in his life that he got to see two naked young women at the same time and so beautiful at that.

"That," she said, "was easy to tell by the way Maxim's jaw dropped."

Maxim had the only option to agree.

The doctor came at six o'clock. It was a short elderly man with a very pleasant smile. He examined Kostya's leg and said that there's nothing to worry about – the bone was intact. Nevertheless, he fiddled with Kostya's leg more than half an hour – Oxana was helping him. When the doctor left, everyone went to sleep, tired, but feeling pretty good about themselves...

Having woken up, Maxim glanced at the watch – it was two o'clock. Being half asleep, he couldn't figure out how that could be, as it was already bright outside. Then he remembered that they went to bed at seven in the morning...

Once downstairs, he was surprised to hear the clang of swords coming from the sports hall. He walked over and shook his head. It was just as he thought, they were already here.

As usual, Roman and Oxana were practicing sword fighting, and Boris was busy pulling weights. There was no one else in the sports hall. Having seen Maxim, Boris smiled.

"Join us," he said. "War is war, but we do sports according to the schedule."

Boris didn't have to tell him about the schedule; still, Maxim was quite enthusiastic as he approached the gym equipment installed on the right side of the hall. For some time now he'd been enjoying physical exercise.

He worked out for almost forty minutes then Iris popped by the hall and called everyone for lunch. After a quick shower, Maxim headed for the kitchen.

Right after lunch the girls went upstairs to Rada's room, while Maxim, Boris and Roman stayed and made themselves comfortable in the main room. Naturally, the conversation immediately turned to the events of this night.

"You, Rada and Iris pulled them out through a portal?" Maxim asked, he meant the miraculous rescue of Kostya and Mariana.

"Not quite," Boris shook his head. "In this case we used dream techniques. First, Rada found Mariana and Kostya, and found out how they were being guarded. Then the three of us – Iris, Rada and me – gathered at the Glade. That's our meeting place in the dream world. From there Rada lead us to the residence of the Legionaries. After that, I was taking care of Mariana, while Rada and Iris were helping Kostya.

"And why not the other way around?" Maxim inquired.

"Mariana knows how to dream; dragging her over is easier than Kostya. I could handle her on my own. But Kostya needed the combined efforts of Rada and Iris. Promptly, at four fifteen am, we appeared in their cells so that we wouldn't be noticed by the surveillance cameras."

"What do you mean – you appeared?" Maxim put in. "Literally?"

"Almost," Boris smiled. "It's what Castaneda calls 'the time of the double'. Your dream body becomes visible and tangible. When in it, you can interact with the ordinary physical world. After that, I cut the cord of the camera – for a double with his strength it's pure child's play. Then I got up to Mariana. Having shifted her level of consciousness, I dragged her dream body out and redirected it to the bedroom of this house. And then I helped her wake up. To her it was waking up in a remote dream position. This trick entails a 'transfusion' of a person from one point in space to another. First the dream body moves over, then the rest of his physical emanations are pulled over to the new position. The person really does disappear; the only thing that remains are his clothes. Then I had only to wake up in my body and go to Mariana."

"And your double?" Maxim inquired. "Where did he go?"

"A double exists only as long as he is needed," Boris explained. "Someday I'll show you. Right now I'm a bit too tired for experiments like that. As for Kostya, our witches pulled him out in the exact same way. After that Iris could have gone to her place, but she too preferred to wake up here, and that's why she had nothing on."

"Clothes are always lost in the process?"

"No. You can take clothes with you as well, but Iris had other things on her mind."

Maxim was silent for a little while, thinking about what Boris had just told him. Then he looked up at Boris.

"All right. And how is traveling through a portal different from traveling using a dream? Is the only difference that you are not asleep when moving through a portal?"

"No," Boris shook his head. "You see, there are many different schemes. And your classical type of portal is a monumental construction like the Stonehenge. Heard about it?"

"Of course," Maxim nodded. "A circle made out of blocks of stones."

"Exactly. The scientists still can't say what it is – a cult construction, some kind of an astronomical observatory or something else. Searchers believe that Stonehenge is a central element of an ancient portal system. Remember how it's built: several stone blocks are arranged in a circle, separated by a certain distance; on top, they are covered by the same kind of stone flags. What we get is a circle with a lot of π-like cells. And now imagine a wheel – say, from a cart – where the central hub is the Stonehenge. The spokes specify the direction of the travel. And the rim of the wheel is represented by reciprocal π-like elements – that is, two vertical stone flags and a third one overlapping them. Thus, we have a central junction – the actual Stonehenge – and a system of outlying portals. Traveling from one remote portal to another always happened through the center: the magician entered a faraway portal, exited through the cell in the central junction corresponding to that portal. Once inside the Stonehenge, he approached the cell leading to another outlying junction – the place where he wanted to go. He entered the cell, and exited in the right place. In that sense, Stonehenge played the role of a central interchange station."

"Awesome," Maxim smiled. "And all of that actually worked?"

"And why not? It's just that modern people don't believe in portals. To them, it's science fiction. And so they think Stonehenge to be anything else but what it really was. I can say that such portal systems existed even on Russian territory. The simplest version of a portal was massive stones arranged in a circle – obviously, with a certain distance between them. The space between two stones determined the direction of the travel. You can find the remains of such structures even today."

"But that means that these are all stationary portals," Maxim said. "You cannot take a portal like that with you. Yet there were no stones when you escaped from the internet cafe."

"True," Boris agreed. "It was a slightly different situation. Have you read about the searchers' view on the structure of the world?"

"It's more like I've heard about it," Maxim shrugged. "I've seen something about the world having either a holographic, or a network-like structure – either one of those things or both of them together. But what it really means, I haven't manage to figure out yet."

"Then that's what we'll talk about," Boris smiled, then looked at Roman. "If Roman doesn't mind."

"I'm all ears, actually," Roman replied, making himself more comfortable in the armchair. Then he smiled at Maxim and explained to him in confidence: "When Rada and he start explaining things this way, you can listen to them for hours."

"Then listen," Boris said. "I'll start by saying that the universe operates according to the holographic principle. What does it mean? First, let's recall what a hologram is. A hologram is a three-dimensional photograph created with the help of a laser. The photographed object is illuminated with one beam; the reflected light interacts with the second laser beam, creating an interferential image. This image is then fixed on a film. If we look at the photograph, we'll see a chaotic image of black and light colored stripes and stains that don't make much sense. But if this film was to be illuminated with a laser beam, then we'll immediately see a holographic representation of the photographed object in space. So, the most interesting thing for us is the fact that, if we were to cut the photographic plate in two, when illuminated with a laser beam, each of the two halves will produce a complete image of the object. A complete image and not an image cut in two. No matter how many times we cut the photographic plate, each little piece, even the tiniest one, will still produce the image of the photographed object. Hence – attention! – each part of the photographic plate contains information about the whole object. That's the principle the universe is based on. Namely, the world that we consider to be the world of separate objects and phenomena is not anything of the kind. Everything is tightly interlinked. Each atom of the universe is connected with all the other atoms and carries information about all objects in the universe. All in all, everything is interconnected. In addition, time does not exist on that level of communication, which I am talking about. This is an extrachronal level, where the past, present and future exist simultaneously. With the world operating this way, time travel becomes possible, and the world itself acquires the property of multivariation and branches out like a tree. And our reality, which we have the honor of beholding, is only one cut of the universe – only one side of it. Its dimension is smaller, so the apparent connection between objects disappears, and the flow of time appears. Note – this is a very important point: on the level of a holographic universe everything is as one. On our level, the universe starts organizing into structures – the way that water steam, condensing onto glass, creates ice patterns on the windows – an excellent example of the network-like organization of the world. The primordial chaos of high dimensions, when falling out into our reality starts self-organizing into hierarchical network structures. We can witness some of it with our own eyes – for example, rivers with their central stream beds, smaller feeders and a lot of little inflowing rivers; mountains, with their central ridges and smaller arms; trees, with a thick trunk, thinner branches and really thin small twigs. That and many other things are on the surface. On the other hand, some other network-like structures are less apparent – we do not notice them. But that doesn't mean that they do not exist. And if we look closely at the world around us, we will be able to see the manifestation of a network-like organization of the world. Even in this room." Boris contoured the room with his hand.

"For example?" Maxim immediately asked.

"The chairs in which we are sitting; the paintings on the walls; the books on the shelves; ourselves; everything that your gaze stumbles upon is an element of the Net."

Maxim spent a couple of minutes thoughtfully examining the room then turned his gaze back at Boris. "I don't get it," he admitted honestly. "I get the thing with the ice patterns on the glass or with the rivers; it really does look like a Net. But how are our armchairs interconnected?"

"You just see one level of the Net," Boris smiled. "That, which lies on the surface. But let's take a different look at the things around you. Let's take, for example, a bunch of grapes: each grape is on its own, they do not grow together. In this sense each grape is a separate berry. But that doesn't mean that it is not connected to the other grapes through the leafstalk. And the same ant that started crawling on one grape could very well end up on another grape – right?"

"Right," Maxim confirmed, already seeing what Boris was getting at.

"And now imagine our armchairs instead of the grapes. Of course, you won't see any leafstalks, but that doesn't mean they are not there." Boris was looking attentively at Maxim. "And in that sense all homogenous objects are interconnected, just as the berries in a bunch of grapes. Moreover, even heterogeneous objects are interconnected, but these are already elements of different bunches; do you catch the difference? The connection is still there, it's just that it is more remote between an armchair and a painting, than between two armchairs or two paintings. And so it turns out that everywhere you go there is the Net. The network of poles and street lamps, the sewage network, the network of female shoes, the network of handbags and plastic bags, the network of garbage cans and piles of dog shit on the lawns."

"Yes, but where is hierarchy in all of this? Large piles or small piles of shit?"

Boris laughed. Roman was trying to control himself, but he too was chuckling. He was clearly enjoying this conversation.

"The hierarchy is not between piles," Boris shook his head. "When talking about homogeneous objects, we are making a certain cut – examining elements of one level. Let's say the nails on your hand are an example of such a connection. They do not have a hierarchy, they are equal. The hierarchy in this case would be the movement from the nail along the finger. That is, the phalanges – what do we have next? – the metacarpus, the wrist, the radial bones, the humerus and so on. When examining the Net, you need to consider two aspects: the succession of the elements – that is, the movement in the stream bed of the flow – and the interconnection of the elements of one level of the hierarchy. If you were to make a link between this and the Patience of Medici, then the movement from the nail to the shoulder will be sorting the patience according to suit – the movement in the stream bed. While jumping from one nail to another will be sorting according to the nominal value, moving to another flow – that is, to another finger. As you see, it all ties up." Boris smiled.

Basically, Maxim was starting to get the idea. He had not yet completely caught the subtleties of this scheme, but the actual principle of a networked organization of the world started to acquire certain contours.

"Well, all right, that's clear," he said. "But what does this network-like organization of the world really give us? Rather, what do we get from knowing about this organization?"

"Knowing about it gets you everything," Boris answered. "Let's say that you are now sitting in an armchair. But, there are a huge amount of armchairs in the world, and among these there are probably armchairs that are familiar to you. And if you'd think about it, what stops you from moving along the Net from one armchair to another? You see what I am talking about? They are interconnected, and that means that a transfer – a transit – could form between them."

"You can even move from a toilet bowl," Roman added. "Onto a toilet bowl in a house you're familiar with."

"That's right," Boris confirmed. "The important thing is that the second toilet bowl doesn't turn out to be occupied." He laughed; Roman too started laughing.

Maxim smiled. Indeed, seemingly there was some logic to it all. And still he couldn't believe he could move from one armchair to another. Or from a toilet bowl to another...

"Ok, fine," he said. "Let's assume that everything is the way you've just told me, and that I now know about the networked organization of the world. But how do I go about the actual moving, say, from this armchair to the armchair in my room? What do I need to do? I see this armchair; I feel it with my behind." Maxim demonstratively jumped up and down in the armchair. "I know the chair upstairs as well. But this knowledge doesn't help me move between them."

"There are difficulties in any business," Boris agreed; he and Roman looked at each other and laughed again. They were indeed in a good mood. Having finished laughing, Boris continued more seriously this time. "You see, Maxim, the knowledge by itself doesn't give you anything; you need to be able to use it. I'll tell you one radical thing: the Net is a conscious structure – a global network mind, if you will. And it rests wholly with the magician, whether he'll be able to get along with the Net or not. Remember Don Juan's words about the Earth being alive – he knew what he was talking about. The Net mind could be called the mind of the Earth, although that wouldn't be entirely correct either. Rather, we're talking about an earthly level of hierarchy. But what's important to us, is the fact that the Net is a global world mind. It is self-conscious and can interact with us: It can, but it won't do that with anyone. It's like working online – to get online, you need to have permission, access. But if you can buy or even steal some online time, you cannot do that with the universe. Here you need long and niggling work; the Net must understand that you are a researcher, and not a thief – that you can be inter-acted with. The difficulty is that the Net cannot go over to our level; we must take the step towards it. How do we do that? By becoming aware of the presence of the Net – by detecting its manifestations in the world around us. You must introduce the Net into the context of your life; you must understand that every-thing that surrounds you is also part of the Net. But even that is only the beginning. Then you will have to study the properties of the Net – the laws by which it operates. With time you will see the manifestations of the Net in everything. The things happening to you and around you, you will no longer perceive as whims of fate, but as a consequence of getting dragged into a particular flow. And one day a miracle will occur: you'll become so aligned with the Net that you will start resonating with it. And then all the miracles we've been talking about here will stop being tales of power."

"And does it take a lot of time? How long does it take, roughly?"

"There are no exact time frames," Boris shrugged. "It all depends on you and on you only. It's like with foreign languages – you can learn it in a year, or you can study it your whole life."

"I got it," Maxim nodded and smiled. "I'll be learning…"

Kostya and Mariana stayed with them for about a week. They could have stayed longer, but they simply didn't want to – as Kostya put it, it was time for someone to pay their bills. He was obviously talking about the Legionaries.

"Just don't get too carried away!" Roman warned them before their departure. "That is, we'll do everything like we've discussed: first – you'll gather information and we'll discuss it. And only then we will all make a decision, together."

"Of course," Kostya smiled. "That's how we're going to do it."

"I know you," Roman muttered. "This time you were lucky, but that doesn't mean that somebody will always fix your mistakes. So be more careful."

"Roman, I understand completely," Kostya answered. "Everything is going to be okay." Maxim liked Kostya. They were of the same age, yet there was power in Kostya's appearance, in his behavior and way of talking – something that Maxim couldn't yet boast of. They quickly found an understanding and were left rather pleased with each other. As for Mariana, she seemed to Maxim like a shy grey mouse – quiet and calm, with a soft sad gaze. The young woman rarely was the one to speak first. Still, a couple of times Maxim had caught a fire flash by in her eyes and he realized then, that even she is not that simple. And how could it be any different?

"Mariana is a good stalker," Boris had told him once. "Usually, she tries to stay in the shadows; yet, at the same time she's in complete control of the situation. Remember yesterday evening – we were all chatting away, while Mariana was reading a book. But I assure you, she didn't miss a single word of what was being said. And the image that she creates is only a mask, and a very efficient one at that. People usually don't take Mariana seriously. And that's too bad." Boris grinned. "As everyone knows – still waters are the ones that run deep."

Mariana and Kostya left for Belgorod. According to Roman, they would stay there for some time, until they found out exactly why they failed. After that they'll move to another city, and another group will take their place in Voronezh.

"If a group has been exposed, then they are better off leaving their former home base. It could be dangerous to stay," Roman explained. "It's easier to start all over in a new city."

Iris returned to Rostov already the following night after the rescue of Kostya and Mariana. As she explained to Maxim, she still had business there.

"Come back to Rostov," she suggested to Maxim with a smile during supper. "You are such a nice boy."

Maxim only smiled. He had already learned not to react to Iris's provoking comments, simply ignoring them. And so even this time he only noticed the essence of the sentence, and not the 'nice boy' bit.

"Maybe I will," he shrugged. "Sometime in autumn."

"Then I'll be getting ready for that event," Iris answered; everyone laughed.

In the morning Iris didn't leave her room. Maxim wanted to know whether she had really relocated or was still sleeping. He carefully knocked on her door – no answer. He knocked harder then pushed the door open.

"Iris?"

There was no one in the room; the clothes Iris had borrowed from Oxana were lying on a chair. The carefully-made bed indicated that Iris didn't sleep there. Looks like this time she simply used a portal...

Having caught himself on that thought, Maxim grinned. "Simply used!" ...If only it was that simple for him...

Again, rather calm days dragged on. Maxim picked up the chains of the Patience of Medici; they passed pretty well. He made maps of his dreams, and tried to create a point of entry into the dream world. He was learning meditation – trying to make sense of the network-like structure of the world. Finally, he continued studying martial arts. Maxim really liked the combat sessions in the sports hall; he diligently listened to Denis's explanations and fine-tuned technical elements together with him. And even though there were things he still couldn't master, he kept going to the sports hall with increasingly greater pleasure.

The training sessions had their effect; Maxim noticed with surprise and joy that his body was gradually transforming. No, not on the outside – it remained the same as before, except it was a bit more muscular now. It was something else; there was now a previously unknown sense of lightness and fluidity – a cat-like gracefulness. His movements were now filled with meaning, their initial roughness disappeared. To his surprise, Maxim noticed that this had also become evident on the ordinary every day level. Less than a month's training, and there were already such changes…

"Not bad," Denis evaluated his results after another sparring. "At least, you'll be able to fight off the riffraff."

But a rather unpleasant incident that happened one evening in a small café helped Maxim appreciate the results of these training sessions in full. Maxim liked the evening town; he often walked the quiet streets, breathing the fresh air and thinking about his new life. In the café he had a pastry and a glass of apple juice, and sat down by a cozy little table in the very end of the small lounge. He had only started eating, when three young spruced-up cool guys entered the café. Cheerful and roaring with laughter, without paying any attention to those around them, they got some beer and looked around, choosing a table for themselves. Then they came up to Maxim.

"Hey, dude, clear the table." These guys looked like they owned the place, so Maxim was a bit taken aback by such impudence and couldn't find the right thing to say. Having quietly glanced up at the guys, he just took a bite out of his pastry and a sip of his juice. However, his silence was interpreted differently.

"Hey, you, bro; are you deaf, or what?" The guy standing

closest to him grabbed him by the collar and dragged him out from the table. In the process, Maxim accidentally knocked over the glass, some juice spilled right on the guy's stylish tracksuit.

"You mother..." the guy drawled, having jumped back, and started brushing drops of juice off his pants. "You freak!" He cast an angry glance at Maxim and rushed towards him. Then, almost without raising his hand, he whacked him shortly and neatly in the jaw.

Maxim didn't understand what happened and how it happened. His hand let go of the pastry and in a reflex-like manner knocked away the fist rushing his way, while his stretched out fingers automatically shoved the enemy in the throat.

Perhaps he was not the only one who didn't get what just happened. Everything happened very quickly; Maxim's movement was more like an awkwardly delivered block, that's how the other two guys saw it. But then why was their leader now wheezing, with his hands grasping at the desired table?

Maxim decided not to wait for the conflict to escalate. He dashed towards the exit and in the process managed to, with his knuckles, whack the biceps of an arm trying to stop him, and quickly slipped out the door.

Only now had anger finally started to stir in his heart, having noticed, by the very entrance, the BMW shamelessly sprawled across the sidewalk; Maxim kicked the car door with all his might, leaving an impressive dent on the polished metal, and hared off under the anguished wailing of the activated alarm. Already turning a corner, he had time to notice the guys that had just rushed outside, or hear their infuriated screams.

Maxim never thought of himself as a hero, and so he ran all he could. One lane, another, and here's the tram, right on the button... Maxim jumped into the closing door and looked around – no one was pursuing him anymore...

Be that as it may, this incident made him respect Denis's teaching methods even more, and Maxim's desire to learn all the subtleties of this art grew only bigger. But he was in for a disappointment; after yet another session, Denis said that this was the end of his short course.

"Why?" Maxim asked, somewhat saddened by such a turn of events, he had already learned to love these sessions.

"You are not bad. It's enough for a start." Denis softly smiled. "Then begins the magic of combat, and that is beyond my competency."

Chapter Seven

Searchers Strike Back

Information about what had caused the incident in Voronezh arrived from Belgorod by the end of June. It turned out that Felix, a participant of the closed internet forum, was the one to blame. He had leaked information as the Legionaries managed to upload a "Trojan" to his computer. Through the forum, the Legionaries found Danila, who was the leader of this forum and the coach of the Voronezh group. And, having tracked down his contacts, the Legionaries located the other members of the group. However, upon investigating the incident, the searchers discovered such interesting details that no one dared to accuse Felix of not being careful enough. He had absolutely no chance of resisting Yana...

"Let this be a lesson to us," Boris said, when everyone, including Denis, had gathered in the kitchen for an evening get-together. "Even a computer's defense system on its own could cause suspicion. If a computer of a seemingly average user is that well protected, then his owner has something to hide. The Legionaries could not access Felix's computer through the internet, so Yana just met up with him. With her talents, making a fool of the guy was easy."

"Maybe, we should do something?" Maxim asked carefully. "Fight back somehow? And if the Legionaries are after us, then we too must be after them."

"It's all not that simple," Boris sighed. "Fighting ordinary Legionaries is pointless. It won't solve anything. They are pawns – if you get rid of one, he will be immediately replaced by another. And we cannot get to Dags or his closest assistants – the project curators – just yet."

"Why not?" Maxim inquired. "Seems to me, that with your

skills nothing is impossible."

Boris smiled.

"Everything is really much more complicated than that," he said. "If you try to get to Dags or that very same Kramer in a dream, you won't succeed. Why? Because they too are magicians, and we should not underestimate their skill level. A good magician can almost always avoid an unwanted conflict. Thus, finding Dags in a dream is extremely difficult. But that's not all; even if you manage to find him, you probably won't be able to do him any harm. Firstly, that's hard to do in itself. Secondly, all influential Legionaries have dream guardians. This is something like the 'allies' in Castaneda's books. They are very aggressive and protect their master with devotion. Dags is guarded by three guardians; Kramer has a couple. The regional managers have one each. Legionaries of lower rank can get a guardian only as a reward for some kind of service. A guardian is a very serious enemy, I advise you not to cross his path just yet. It's not too pleasant." Boris grinned once again.

"It's not a joke?" Maxim asked distrustfully. "About the guardians?"

"Maxim, if there is something that you do not see, it doesn't mean that it doesn't exist. Reality is much more multifaceted than we can imagine. Consider that only recently you didn't know anything about searchers or Legionaries. Now you've found out about dream guardians, and that is not the last thing you will familiarize yourself with."

"It's just really hard to believe," Maxim answered. "But I'll try... And these guardians... can't you just... you know... nail them?" Maxim raised his eyebrows inquiringly.

Instead of Boris, Rada was the one to answer: "Of course you can," she said. "Though, it is very difficult. The problem is that a guardian still manages to push his master out of a dream. After that, he goes to work on you, and that is really unpleasant."

"Have you seen the movie *Alien*?" Oxana put in. "Imagine an ugly mug like that attacking you, and you'll understand what we're talking about."

"You've seen them?" Maxim asked.

"Only once," Oxana admitted.

"And what did you think?"

"Impressive," the girl answered; everyone laughed.

"And so," Boris continued. "You cannot get to Dags through a dream. It's too much trouble and Dags is not one to expose himself. And getting to him in the real world is even harder."

"Because he is too well guarded?" Maxim guessed.

"It's not about the guards – although he's probably guarded much like the president – the problem is that we have absolutely no information on Dags. The Legionaries sacredly keep the secret about his identity. We do not know who he is; we don't even know what he looks like or where he lives. We tried to get to him through a chain of Legionaries, starting with managers of lower rank, but we have nothing so far. Average Legionaries know as much as we do about Dags. The Curators and the Deputies could have told us who he is, but we have more or less the same problem with them." Boris fell quiet for a couple of seconds. "You cannot get to them in a dream. They too are protected," he continued. "Rada has tried about five times, and I about the same – all for nothing. You are attacked before you have a chance to get close. Then we tried to capture a Deputy in the real world. Roman and Denis organized an operation. Everything went like clockwork; we kidnapped the Deputy of the Krasnoyarsk Territory right out of the sauna. We brought him to our place; he was sound as a bell – clean, rosy cheeks. We started questioning him, and a couple of minutes later he died."

"Why?" Maxim didn't understand.

"He was killed by his own guardian. That's when we realized that guardians are not just bodyguards, but also overseers. The Supreme Hierarchs provide their servants with guardians, and they are also the ones to provide the guardians with the right qualities. While a Legionary is true to the Legion, the guardian takes care of him and protects him. But if a possibility of treason arises, the guardian, obeying the will of the Supreme Hierarchs, immediately destroys his master."

"A guardian can kill an ordinary person?" Maxim inquired.

"No," Boris shook his head. "The life force of a guardian is tightly interlinked with the life force of his master. That's why the guardian can manipulate him. The guardian's power does not apply to other people; although, Legionaries have been experimenting with that too."

"So you see, Maxim," Roman summarized, "finding Dags is almost impossible."

"Nevertheless," Roman smiled, "we're looking for ways of doing it."

"And what about Yana?" Maxim remembered. "She too has a guardian?"

"No," Roman shook his head. "First off, she simply doesn't need one; her experience is enough to let her slip away at first signs of danger. Secondly, no doubt she suspects what a guardian really is, and doesn't want to have an overseer by her side."

"Maxim is right that we need to get to work," Rada said. "True, we cannot get to Dags just yet. Let's leave that problem for later. But Kramer is not Dags. He is the one who is in charge of our persecution, and right now he is our main enemy. And if we try hard, we have a chance of getting to him. Having dealt with Kramer, we'll get a break to organize our forces against Dags. In the meantime we'll have to coordinate the work of all regional groups. There are enough of them now to cause Legionaries serious trouble. On top of all of this we need to accelerate our work on training Keepers. We need to make that a mass event. We have to cover all regions with our groups, otherwise there's no point."

"I agree," Denis said, who had been quiet all this time. "Isolated pricks won't change anything, but a massive and well-prepared attack may give pretty good results. My guys long for some serious work." He looked at Boris and smiled.

Everyone was quiet, waiting for what Boris was going to say. Maxim realized long ago that his opinion was respected around there.

"I agree with everything you just said," Boris started quietly. "But all our actions must be sensible; we can't let our emotions guide us. We've already seen what mistakes can lead to. So, I suggest that everyone think about possible ways of going about things and present their suggestions by Saturday. And that's when we'll decide what do to and how to do it – at least when it comes to the strategy bit. In any case," Boris made a long pause, "we'll make them pay for Dana."

The talk with Dags went pretty smoothly for Kramer. Dags didn't accuse Kramer or rub his nose into the mistakes; apparently, he realized himself that the situation developed in a rather unusual way. Never before had searchers rescued anyone this way. It made him wonder.

"They are progressing very rapidly," Dags said, thoughtfully looking through the window at the clouds passing under him; the airplane was going back to Moscow, staying in Voronezh was pointless now. "Before, only some of them, such as Sly, could use portals, and then only sometimes and for their personal use. Now they managed to find and drag away two people. They managed to disable the surveillance cameras, which means that they have already mastered the technique of influencing the real world from the astral plane. They are getting more and more skilled, and if we don't take some decisive action very soon, the balance could sway in their favor."

"That's hardly possible," Kramer, sitting in the opposite armchair, didn't agree with his boss. "How many searchers actually know enough to be a real threat to us? Not more than a few. The skills of the others are, at best, only enough to hide from us. We are the hunters now, not them."

"You are being too optimistic, my dear Kramer." Dags gloomily looked at his companion. "Don't forget that searchers always come up with something new. And where's the guarantee that one of their ideas won't become the last one for you and me?"

"That's true," Kramer tactfully agreed. "I'll look over our actions, keeping in mind the recent events."

"You won't just look them over, Kramer." Dags pursed his lips in an unfriendly manner. "You will change them completely. Two days ago I spoke to the Supreme Hierarch. He was very displeased with our work. And not only because of the searchers, he's displeased with everything. We've messed up things in Chechnya; we could not change the power in Belarus. We've completely failed the job with the workers of research institutions – the FSB is getting stricter at cutting off any of our attempts to obtain the information we need. These are no longer coincidences, Kramer. It's a trend."

"But I wasn't in charge of any of these projects," Kramer noticed logically.

"And that's why you are still alive," Dags retorted with a deeper grimness and turned away to the window.

The motors were softly humming; there was a tense silence in the air. Not able to stand it anymore, Kramer made an attempt to resume the conversation.

"Mr. Dags, I can handle the searchers. I promise that soon no one will even remember them."

"As I recall, you promised me the same thing a year ago," Dags grinned gloomily. "And so what? The popularity of the searchers is growing; they are calmly walking the whole Net, organizing forums. Moreover, they even plan on publishing a couple of books on their subject area. And books – that's already serious. Millions of people could find out about searchers, and then you can't get rid of them just like that."

"I won't allow it," Kramer answered, feeling rather uneasy.

"We are tracking the work of possible authors; we have good positions in the publishing business. Not a single searcher book will ever see the light."

"I hope so," Dags sighed tiredly. He looked pretty bad. Kramer noted that the Sovereign looked much older than just a couple of years ago.

"I have one interesting idea," Kramer said, hoping to turn the conversation to a more pleasant subject. "There is no point in dissuading people from searcher ideas – flies will always be drawn to sweets. But what if we create an alternative to the searcher movement? Organize our own popular youth movement, using searcher approaches? We'll come up with a new terminology, about ten myths of great achievements, get together a team of leaders. We'll serve searchers' ideas in our own sauce, and we'll gradually compromise the searchers themselves and squeeze them out from the Net."

This was Yana's idea, yet Kramer didn't feel it necessary to mention such petty details. Kramer liked the plan himself, now he was closely watching Dags, waiting for his verdict.

"Actually, it's not a bad idea."- Dags thoughtfully moved his lips. "It would be nice to execute it. What do you need to make it happen?"

"Only your decision," Kramer responded. "I'll assign Yana to this project, she'll get together a suitable team and come up with a plan."

"Good," Dags agreed. "Act. And don't forget that the Supreme Hierarch doesn't care for losers."

For Maxim, the following night was marked by a joyous occasion – he had, once again, managed to enter a dream. All his last attempts to enter a dream in the moment of falling asleep had failed, so now, following Rada's advice, Maxim decided to 'let himself go' a little. If it works – great. If not – that's ok too. As he was falling asleep, he was simply thinking his own thoughts, only some part of his consciousness reminded him from time to time about the necessity to enter a dream. He had almost fallen asleep, when some indistinct images started flashing before his eyes. One image turned out to be very stable. Something made Maxim focus on that image. An instant, and he, completely conscious, found himself inside of the scene he was watching. Again, his heart was overflowing with joy; Maxim later remembered that you shouldn't show strong emotions. You should not expose yourself; the dream program will notice the violator and kick him out of the dream. Although, he noted that, just for appearances' sake, he was completely engrossed by the sight opening in front of him.

He was standing on the sidewalk, to his left towered grey buildings of some kind of factory. They looked empty; Maxim felt an urge to enter.

The control post was not guarded; no one stopped Maxim. He entered the territory of the factory without any difficulties, and soon he found himself inside a huge workshop. They made ceramic tiles there – Maxim noticed the stacks of already finished goods and a conveyor for putting a pattern on the tiles. He went through the workshop, trying not to touch anything, and came out on the other side. The following view unfolded before his eyes: there was a wide river with a few docks and submarines. The combination of submarines and a workshop making tiles was so absurd that Maxim even started laughing. He wanted to fly – he pushed off and flew over the river, going higher and higher, his consciousness was again overflowing with delight. Flying while being fully conscious – what could compare to that?

Changing his direction a little to the left, Maxim started crossing the river at an angle, already thinking that when he'd wake up, he would make sure to note all of this on his dream map.

On the other side of the river were city quarters. The quay ended with a vertical wall partly submerged under water. Tire casings were hanging on this wall – apparently, this was the place where motor ships were moored. Having descended, Maxim got down onto the levee and surveyed the place. The road to town was rather steep, Maxim really liked the place. It occurred to him that living here would probably be pretty nice. It's quiet, cozy and beautiful...

There was a chocolate bar on the road curb. Maxim picked it up and started unwrapping it and at the same time, to his surprise, he realized that he was now in a different dream. For some reason, there was now only the wrapper left from the chocolate bar. There were people walking around him; Maxim crumpled the wrapper and put it into his pocket, then he looked around.

He was in a big store. The shelves were crammed with products; everything looked very beautiful and appealing. He approached one of the display cases and saw coins scattered behind the glass. One coin caught his attention; it was a large coin – the size of a pal and encrusted with precious stones. It was very beautiful.

"Can I see this coin?" he asked a young female shop assistant.

"Of course," she answered, retrieving the coin from the display case, which contained gold, diamonds and rubies, the age of Ludwig XV.

Maxim took the coin from the hands of the young woman – it turned out to be exceptionally heavy. He ran his finger over its surface, and touched the precious stones; a beautiful thing – a real masterpiece. If it's only a dream, then who made this coin?

He wanted to wake up. Holding the coin tight in his hand, Maxim started waking up; the world around him quickly dissolved. He opened his eyes and realized that he was lying in his bed. The coin was no longer in his hand. He sat up and felt the bed – empty...

In the morning he told Rada about his dream and inquired whether it is possible to bring something back from a dream.

"It's possible," Rada replied. "But very difficult. That process is akin to alchemy when certain substances turn into others. Take a look at these earrings." Rada pointed at her elegant emerald earrings. "I brought them from a dream, but in so doing I lost several kilos. If I was a fatty," Rada softly smiled, "I'd have definitely liked that. Otherwise, I prefer not to accomplish any more feats of this nature."

"All right, but who created the coin I saw? My mind?"

"That's a very good question," Rada agreed. "But let's change it a bit: what creates all of that we are able to see in a dream? The answer is the dream program, plus our cosmography charts. Usually, we take things at face value." Rada smiled. "However, the greater part of what we see is, in essence, an illusion. Remember, Castaneda was learning how to see energy in a dream – pointing at items with his little finger. This method works, but why was he doing that? To be able to separate illusion from real energy formations. 'Real' means containing energy, and not dream phantoms. Let's take computer games as an example; we happily chase around various monsters, fighters, footballers on the screen, they will perform certain actions – run, fight, kill each other and score goals – but how real are the things happening on the screen? Wouldn't you agree that it's only an illusion, created by the computer software and the phosphor luminescence on the surface of the screen? What we see on the screen doesn't actually exist, and if it does, then it's in a completely different form. In a dream, we encounter the exact same situation – we are handed an illusion, and we take it at face value. Finding out whether that is the case is very easy: next time, try to find some kind of object in your dream. Anything. It's up to you what it will be. Take it in your hands and focus your attention on that object. The important thing is to not interrupt the flow of attention even for a second. I can tell you what will happen next, but it'll be more interesting to you to find that out on your own. And then we'll continue this conversation – agreed? Besides, we are already due for breakfast."

Maxim could only agree.

To his indescribable joy, the following night was also marked by a dream of very high quality. It began in the wee hours; having become aware of himself, Maxim instantly recalled Rada's assignment.

In this dream, he was back at his house in Rostov. Realizing that he was at home made his heart ache a little. Maxim went through to the kitchen – a tablespoon caught his eye. Maxim grabbed it by the tip, focused his gaze on the spoon and started waiting.

At first nothing happened, then the spoon twitched and turned into a fork right before the eyes of a dumbfounded Maxim. A knife with a beautiful decorative handle and a ravenous blade replaced the fork, and then the knife immediately turned into a big nail. The nail started rusting right before Maxim's eyes; it gave off a little smoke and then curved. The metamorphoses stopped; in Maxim's hands was a rusty bent twig of unknown nature. And Maxim immediately felt himself being thrown out of the dream, all attempts to linger on proved fruitless...

He managed to have a talk with Rada only in the evening; they continued the conversation in her room. Each time he visited her room, Maxim got astonished by the calm reigning there. This silence simply was there, it seemed almost tangible. Even voices in Rada's room sounded a bit damped, not like in the other rooms of this house. Upon his first visit to Rada's room, Maxim ascribed that quality to the heavy green curtains, but he soon decided that the curtains had nothing to do with it.

"You've carried out my assignment to the letter," Rada said, having finished listening to Maxim's report. "Now let's examine what you saw and why. As you've seen, your spoon turned out to be something completely different. It was both a knife, and a fork, and God knows what. This happens for the following reason..." Rada thought to herself for a couple of seconds, collecting her thoughts. "Remember, when you are working on the computer, looking for some lost files, and messages sometimes appear on your screen: 'Requested file not found.' 'The following file is the closest to your search input.' 'Match the found file with the requested one.'? In this case, the computer program selects a file that's the best match to the file you've requested. The same happens in a dream; when designing the sphere of perception for us, the dream program selects its elements according to our cosmography charts. You saw a kitchen table – if it was a kitchen table." Again, a smile slipped across Rada's lips. "And what can be on a table? Your cosmography charts hold the answers to these questions. That is why you see a spoon there as the item most suitable for the situation, and not a gun or a sewing machine. But then you took the spoon in your hand and started examining it – is it really a spoon? The dream program feels your hesitation and immediately tries to hand you something suitable – a knife, a fork, a nail. That is, something that would have satisfied your request. However, you must keep in mind that the dream program was obviously created by amateurs – it's full of bugs. Everything was thrown together in a hurry. For an ordinary person that will do quite well, but when you start studying the elements of dreams, the program keeps malfunctioning now and then. Specifically, the number of objects to be matched – as in the case with your spoon – is very limited. Three, five, seven metamorphoses at the very most – and that's it; after that the program cannot slip you anything else. Instead, it simply chucks you out of the dream – the same way a teacher, not knowing the answer to a student's question beats the pointer on the table and orders not to ask stupid questions. So you should keep in mind that everything we see in a dream is usually quite embellished. When you learn how to enter the dreams of other people, you'll see it yourself. This is what usually happens: a person is walking around in his dream like in a museum; his attention is engrossed with various pretty things. But a searcher inside this dream is walking around and smirking, seeing the squalor around them."

"And how do you enter the dream of another person?" Maxim couldn't resist asking that question.

"There are different ways of doing that. But let's consider this question in the vein of our former discussion: who is the person that we see in our dream? How real is he?" Rada raised her brows, urging Maxim to answer her questions.

"I don't know," Maxim admitted. "That's what I'd like to find out."

"Everyone we meet in a dream are usually called sprites, or apparitions, but that's too general of a term – it doesn't always reflect the real meaning. As you know from Castaneda's books, in our dreams we sometimes come across quite real entities, be it spies, inorganic beings or some other creatures. Many of them can take on human appearance and interact with us in that form. Sometimes that could prove quite dangerous. Besides, in the dream world there is a myriad of different powers which we, thanks to the models of our cosmography charts, will also perceive as people. Let's say, if it is a friendly force, we'll perceive it as a friend. If the force is negative, it will appear before us in the shape of an enemy. Each time, our consciousness is trying to add known qualities to something unknown – turn it into something familiar. Usually it succeeds, but there are situations when, despite the will to do so, our consciousness cannot pull it off. This happens when there is no matching record in the cosmography charts. That's what happens with the scouts: when we see a scout in a dream, our consciousness comes to a full stop – how do you describe something that has no description? The way out of this is the same – the scout is matched to any suitable object. In the end we get a surprising result: things that we're used to seeing start surrounding themselves with absurdities. We may see a flying elephant in a dream, a parrot bathing in a bathtub, moving stones and so on, and so forth. The appearance is familiar, but its essence is different – hence all the nonsense. That's why absurdities in dreams are an unmistakable sign that there is a scout nearby. We'll talk about scouts later." Rada smiled again, "And now let's get back to your question. So, in a dream you see your good friend. First, evaluate your sensations: if you feel even a shadow of worry, then it's not your friend, but something that has taken on his appearance. Our body is usually very good at sensing that something's wrong, so it is never wrong. Having sensed danger, just turn around and walk away – interacting with alien forms of life is very dangerous. If there is no danger, then you are probably dealing with an ordinary sprite – that is, a dream phantom, an apparition. The connection between the sprite and your real friend is pretty much the same as between a phone number and the user that you can reach on this number. A sprite is a phantom; a projection; a vague shadow of your real friend. But thanks to that shadow you have the opportunity to actually meet your friend in a dream. This is how it happens: having found the sprite of your friend, start interacting with it. The principle of interactions completely agrees with the well-known scheme from neuro-linguistic programming – 'matching, pacing, leading'. First you start talking with the sprite of your friend – you ask him what he's doing and where he's going, what's on his mind and what worries him – that will be the matching bit. Then comes the pacing; if he's going somewhere, you go with him; if he's doing something, you help him. By interacting with the sprite, you are performing a maneuver – changing the settings of a dream – as a result, the scenario of the dream usually changes, and you find yourself next to the dream body of your friend. Basically, you enter his dream, his sphere of perception, while the initial sprite becomes a transit of sorts. Once you're next to your friend, you initiate the leading phase; that is, you gradually take over the reins of government. You start asking your friend questions about the things around you. For example, you put your hand through a wall, make him notice this peculiarity and ask him how this could be? Could it be happening because it is a dream? Usually, it leads to your friend becoming aware of himself. There is glitter in his eyes – he gets brighter; having seen this once, you'll know what I'm talking about. After that, it all depends on the power of your friend. An ordinary person disappears at once – that is, he wakes up. Someone, who is at least somewhat familiar with lucid dreams, can for some time remain in the dream together with you – you can talk to him in quite a normal fashion. What I've just described could seem complicated, but it's actually a very simple maneuver; entering somebody's dream this way is easy. To make a person become aware of himself is harder; as I've already mentioned, if prompted, a person usually wakes up and disappears. And he could also drag you out with him." Rada smiled. "It's a very interesting trick, but it requires strong nerves. Imagine – your friend wakes up, and you wake up in his bed next to him. At that point you'll be in your dream body. However, you will only be able to remain there for a few seconds – your mind will immediately raise an alarm and throw you back."

"And will my friend be able to see me?" Maxim inquired.

"It's not impossible. However, being half-asleep he'll probably think that he's just seeing things."

"Amusing," Maxim smirked. "And all of this is actually real?"

"Maxim, I never tell fairy tales," Rada replied. "Everything I am describing is a real technique."

"Sorry, it just slipped out." Maxim smiled with a guilty look on his face.

"No worries, I forgot how to take offence a long time ago. It's just when you are standing on the threshold of eternity," Rada's eyes glistened, "any grudges lose their sense."

"I see," Maxim nodded.

"If you have more questions, go ahead and ask them."

"Okay. Tell me, does the dream map actually help you become conscious? It's just that the couple of times that I've found myself in a dream, I simply realized that I was dreaming without any dream landscapes."

"The thing is that it very much depends on your own talents,"

Rada explained. "After all, people are very different; everyone has their own likings and talents. And the same mapping… it's just a method – one out of many. Someone likes it, someone doesn't. If you feel that mapping doesn't help you become lucid, then just become lucid the way you feel is best. You can try some other method, there are plenty of them. For instance, introduce into your practice moments of consciousness, control points of sorts while you are actually awake. The idea is simple: from time to time you need to remember that you wanted to become conscious and test reality – is it real or is it a dream? Try it right now – your thoughts freeze, you look around. At the same time try perceiving the environment not only with your eyes, but also with your body, it's very important. Go ahead, try it."

Maxim looked around hesitantly.

"Do you feel a pause in your consciousness? You don't need to look around for too long, the important thing here is the moment of remembering. The ordinary routine of life, and then suddenly – bang! – you remember that you wanted to become conscious and you immediately test reality. Only a couple of seconds, and you continue doing whatever you were doing. At the same time your goal must be to become conscious as often as possible. At first, you'll remember to do it maybe once a day, then more and more often, until you learn to be in the present at all times. It is very important, Maxim, especially for stalkers – it is one of their main methodologies. Usually, there is an endless stream of thoughts spinning in a person's head; most of these thoughts are silly. Even when doing something, we manage to wander off in our mind. Introducing conscious moments in the real world leads to you immersing in the state of being – you are here, in a specific moment. All your attention is concentrated into a beam – it's not wandering all over the place. This is how you introduce magic into your real life. It is one of the best shortcuts to magic. As a result of such practice, the inner dialogue stops, and even Don Juan said that the inner dialogue is what presses us down to the ground. Well, and for dreamers this technique is useful, as it begins to manifest in their dreams. Say, you are in an ordinary dream and because of your acquired habit you start looking around, testing the things around you. You realize that it is a dream and thereby find yourself in a lucid dream. It's all very simple." Rada sighed and smiled.

"So, I don't have to do mapping?" Maxim asked.

"I didn't say that. Mapping still gives you a lot of useful things, so I don't recommend dropping it all together. At the very least, it develops our dream memory – helps us regain our luminosity. And that is only the beginning." Rada glanced at the watch and smiled again. "Well, let's call it a day?"

"Yes," Maxim agreed, getting up from the chair. "Thank you, Rada. I'll go and try to get my head around it."

Throughout the week Maxim honestly practiced the methodology of becoming conscious IRL, as suggested by Rada. And if, at first, he remembered the assignment only sometimes, then towards the end of the week he caught conscious moments more and more often. Maxim expected this practice to have a positive effect on his dreaming, but it was the other way around – throughout the whole week he didn't have one single lucid dream. Moreover, Maxim even stopped remembering his ordinary dreams. That alarmed him – perhaps he was doing something wrong.

"You are doing everything right," Rada calmed him. "Every magician has periods of ups and downs. In your case, the down has quite objective causes – namely, your increased consciousness IRL. That happens to all who practice this technique: first, you feel as if there is a decline, however later there'll be a sudden and big quality jump. Your attention is progressing, and soon you'll actually be able to sense it. And one more thing: it wouldn't be a bad idea for you to work on the techniques of stopping the inner dialogue. There's no time like the present. If you'll learn to stop the ID, you'll learn to enter dreams."

"I've tried to stop the ID using the methods described by Castaneda," Maxim responded. "I've walked around town with my eyes defocused and my attention concentrated on my fingers squeezed together. But so far I haven't sensed anything."

"That method takes time," Rada smiled. "Try stopping the ID with the help of the Patience of Medici."

Maxim wrinkled his nose.

"I haven't made sense of that yet," he said. "I've looked through it, but it sounds very sophisticated: Hexagrams, Yin-Yang…"

"Ask Boris," Rada suggested. "And don't be shy, there's no room for shyness around here. He's going away tomorrow, so I suggest you talk to him today."

"Okay," Maxim agreed. "I'll do that."

Only around midnight did he get a chance to talk to Boris – all that evening Boris was busy, discussing something with Denis and Roman. When he saw Maxim, Boris smiled.

"Rada already told me," he said, without waiting for Maxim to ask the question. "Let's go to my room."

In his room, Boris opened a small bar built into a closet and retrieved two beer cans. With a grin, he threw one to Maxim, sat down in an armchair and sighed with satisfaction.

"So, now we can rest from our daily chores." Boris opened the can and, with great pleasure, took a sip. "So, what are we going to talk about?"

"About stopping the inner dialogue with the help of the PM," Maxim replied, opening his beer can. "Could you explain how it works?"

Boris thought about it for a couple of seconds. Then, having sipped some more beer, he looked up at Maxim. "It's a really complicated topic," he agreed. "And we'd have to start not with stopping of the ID, but with I-Ching, the Chinese Book of Changes – I think, you've heard of it. According to this book, everything that happens around us does not develop randomly, but in accordance with certain templates. Say, if you'd go and punch a police officer in the head, you probably won't be awarded a medal – they could put you in jail. If you try to stop a train and get onto the tracks in front of it, the train will, probably, spread you all over the tracks. In this case we're talking about prioritized alternatives of further developments. That doesn't mean that things will happen one way and not any other way, but the probability of them happening according to a specified scenario is extremely high. There are very different situations, and each of them has its own logic of development. Still, even with the diversity of various situations, they could all be described using a rather limited amount of templates. And that's what the Chinese did; they got sixty-four alternatives in total. Each alternative is represented by a hexagram – a system consisting of six lines arranged one above the other. Each line has its own meaning; they are numbered from the bottom up. The first line reflects our desires and incentives. The second line – our resources and the opportunities for making our desires real. The third line – action, leading towards achieving a result. The three first lines are the inner sphere of a person. Searchers prefer to interpret these as 'I want, I can, I do'. The next three lines form the external sphere: the fourth is interpreted as external agents, the fifth – the law, the sixth – the Spirit; the Power." Boris went quiet for a little while. "Let's move on," he continued. "Each of the lines reflects its stage in the development of the situation. It could have two states: Yang – an active position, marked with a solid line. And Yin – a passive position, marked with a line broken in the middle. What does that actually mean? For example, you decided to go someplace. You have a wish – so the first line is Yang. You have the means to implement your plan – namely, you've got time and money – the second line is Yang. Finally, you buy the ticket and go – the third line is Yang. And now let's look at a different situation – you are being drafted into the army and taken someplace. You didn't have the desire to travel, but no one asked you, you were drawn into the situation. That means that you could go ahead and put down zeroes in the inner sphere – that is Ying. The three lines of the external sphere will reflect the details of the actual trip – namely, how the trip will go. By analyzing a situation this way, we can determine which hexagram is capable of describing it. If you know your I-Ching well, you can, on the intuitive level and without any calculations, feel the course of the situation – its potential development. This helps us orient ourselves in the combination of events around us – to glide on the sea of life." Boris softly smiled and took another sip from the can.

"But aren't the laws of the Eagle what determines the course of events?" Maxim asked. "Then what on earth do hexagrams have to do with this?"

"That's right," Boris agreed. "Hexagrams reflect the laws of the Eagle."

Maxim frowned. It just didn't add up.

"But there are only sixty-four hexagrams, right? And there are thousands and thousands of laws of the Eagle."

"And that is true," Boris grinned. "You're just forgetting the fact that we are living in a holographic universe, the principles of which are inheritance and infinite divisibility. Let's take, for instance, a Russian doll – it is one, but inside it is a whole stack of other dolls. The same with the hexagrams: each corresponds to a particular situation, but any situation could be described with a whole train of hexagrams of a lower rank. Here's a book." Boris picked up from the side table a little volume with the views of Lao-Tzu. "It's only one. But if I open it, I'll see a whole lot of pages. And on each page, a whole lot of letters. That is the principle of inheritance. Or let's take the folders on a computer – you click on it with your mouse, and the folder opens, inside could be a pile of other folders; In our case – sixty-four. And each of them contains another sixty-four, and so on without end. Get it?"

"Roughly," Maxim answered. "Then all laws that exist in this world could be divided into sixty-four types?"

"Perhaps," Boris shrugged. "You see, the problem is that our mind is potentially unable to grasp the entire greatness of the universe. And in order to make sense of all of this, somehow, we have to create certain descriptive models. Recall the parable about the four blind men feeling an elephant. One was feeling its ear, another – its leg, yet another – its tail, and the fourth one – its belly. Each of them felt the elephant, but they each got a different idea of an elephant. The same thing with us – when creating descriptive models, each time we look at the universe from one particular point of view. Each of the models is defective, but together they allow us to form at least some kind of a representation about the immenseness surrounding us. So, don't try to be a nit-picker when going through these descriptions, instead acquire common links – common principles. At the same time, what's most important here is that your description might be different from the descriptions of other people. At the end of the day, it's not that important how you describe the universe; the attempt to structure it is what matters. Basically, you are creating your magic world, where you are the master. The world is the way we want to see it. If there are portals in your model, then one day you will find them. If you accept the fact that there could be time corridors, they'll open for you and you will get the possibility of traveling in time. Nothing is impossible in magic; its limits are defined only by your imagination. And creating your world of magic is like making a painting: first we see a clean canvas, then an underpainting appears – the rough elaboration of contours. Finally, the finishing touches, the glazing and the painting is done. As soon as you've painted the magic painting of the world, it will start working." Boris sipped some beer then put the can down on the side table.

"I'll give it some thought," Maxim agreed. "So what's the deal with the hexagrams and stopping the inner dialogue?"

"It's all good with the hexagrams and the SID," Boris answered, crossing his legs. "As you've already realized, we are able to describe any event with the help of the hexagrams, and in so doing the hexagram will reflect the process of further development of the situation. In the chain of the PM, we have four strings of events, consistent with the four suits. And that means, we can describe a chain of the PM with four hexagrams. The cards of the PM are substituted, for hexagram lines, according to a specific system – you'll sort this out later on your own, it's hard for me to explain it in a simple way. Hence, in order to get the right hexagrams in a spread, you'd have to put together the actual chain in a very strictly defined fashion. In fact, a chain created this way has a certain energy pattern. The rest depends on what hexagrams we get in the chain. In the sixty-two hexagrams, we have the alternation of strong and weak lines, and only in two hexagrams – number one and number two – we've got either Yang-lines, or Ying-lines. Consequently, we can make the assumption that these hexagrams have a special status. You know, when you fall asleep, there are always thoughts spinning in your consciousness. The thought process could be called the infinite wandering from one hexagram to another, and the alteration of strong and weak lines gives rise to an inner dialogue. But in the moment of falling asleep, for a brief instant there is a pause in your consciousness. This is the point of transfer between the real world and the dream world. Imagine the following picture: like a mirror image of each other, two pyramids are connected through their tops in one place. The real world, going through the focal point, moves into the dream world. And the point itself is created by the hexagrams one and two. These hexagrams create a little bridge; when falling asleep, first you get into one hexagram, let's say it's hexagram number one. All lines are Yang – the inner dialogue has stopped. You hover in emptiness without a single thought; that's the state Castaneda called restful vigil. Then you start leaving hexagram number one, moving into the narrowest region; in that moment your perception for an instant disappears, it grows foggy. This is the moment of complete emptiness, immediately after this moment lies hexagram number two. This hexagram already belongs to the dream world – it is the top of another pyramid. In hexagram number two, the inner dialogue cannot take place either. When you leave the hexagram and enter your dream, the inner dialogue resumes. All night we are moving from one dream sphere of perception to another, and each of them has a corresponding hexagram – their own scenario. And so on until we wake up. In the moment of transfer, we again pass through hexagrams one and two, getting a short moment where the ID stops. This is a general and very rough description; a beta-version, so to say." Boris smiled. "As you know, searchers don't take the trouble of creating detailed and thoroughly crafted theories – there's just no point. It's quite enough that the model is functioning and that it gives practical results. The rest is the work of the devil. That is, of the mind." Boris grinned again and stretched out with his hands in the air. His bones made a cracking sound. "And now look: if stopping the inner dialogue is caused by us being in hexagrams one or two, then what prevents us from obtaining these hexagrams with the help of the PM and stop the inner dialogue? We've tried this option, and it proved to be quite operational. Now we and our followers know how to put together the right chains that would allow us to stop the inner dialogue. And the best thing is…" Boris looked closely at Maxim, "…it's enough to stop the inner dialogue a couple of times this way, in order to get the same result without any PM. Any questions?"

"Yes," Maxim nodded. "I've come across something about the balancing of lines – what is that?"

"It's one of the subtleties you'd need to consider when putting the chains together. How can I explain this?" Boris became thoughtful. "As you know, any system strives towards the state of calm – equilibrium. In the chain of the PM we have four hexagrams. Each of the hexagram lines can have the states Yang or

Ying. Let's assume that we're looking at the first lines of the first hexagrams. They could all turn out to be Yang or Ying. There could be equality – two Ying and two Yang. Finally, there could be a situation where we'd have three lines of one type and one of the other. So, in a situation when there's no equality, the system balances itself; namely, the excess line of any type turns into its opposite. As a result, on each line there are always two Yang and two Ying. Here we're, first of all, interested in the energy produced during the balancing process. That energy is what shifts the assemblage point to the desired position. And here's one other very important detail: it's not enough to just get hexagram number one or two in a chain. We need to get it while balancing the lines. Picture the following: we take a Rubik's cube and slightly modify it; namely, we install a system of springs that, each time, brings it back into its original position. That is, you start turning it, twisting the sides of the cube every which way, but should you only let go of it, the sides start moving on their own – everything is twisting and buzzing, and the cube returns to the original, assembled state. We've got the same thing going on here; we put together the chain so that there is an imbalance present from the beginning – the greater the imbalance, the better. Then the chain undergoes self-balancing, and the energy produced during that process drags our assemblage point into the position of the SID. That's the reason why putting together the right chain is pretty hard – you'd need to know all the subtleties of the balancing. You may use the already-made chains; they are on the disc I gave you. Although it is better to put them together yourself – own chains work always better. The same principle is at work here: first you plough the field, then the field works for you."

"That's complicated," Maxim said thoughtfully. "I'll try to figure it out."

"There's nothing complicated about this at all," Boris didn't agree. "The really difficult stuff is still ahead. And now, it would be nice to get a little nap. What do you think?" Boris looked at his watch and yawned demonstratively.

"All right," Maxim agreed, getting up from the chair. "Thanks, Boris. Oh, and one more thing – Rada and you have mentioned the Glade a couple of times. Could you show me this place sometime?"

"Of course," Boris agreed, his eyes were glowing. "We'll take you there someday. But not today, this night Rada and I have a bit of a job to do."

"I'll wait, there's no rush. Good night, Boris." Maxim exited the room and carefully closed the door behind him.

Making sense of the subtleties of stopping the inner dialogue turned out to be exceptionally difficult. Still, Maxim kept moving towards his aim – he drew hexagram schemes and arranged cards on the lines. He messed about with the PM calculator – the computer program for assembling the patience, trying to put together the right chain on his own. He had already understood what it should look like, but he couldn't yet put it together – each time, when everything was pretty much ready, he found several errors. Finally, not wanting to waste time, Maxim decided to start with the already available chains. He'd try, and then he might just make his own. Having looked through the chains on the disc, Maxim picked the following one:

< JS 9H 10S> <QS 7C QH > <8S 8C 6S > <10H KS > < 10C> <JD KC> <6C QD AS QC> <KD 9C> <9S 6H 9D> <AD AC KH 8D AC> <7H 8H> <6D 10D JC 7D> <JH>

It would seem odd that an ordinary card sequence could bring about some kind of changes in one's consciousness. Nevertheless, that remained to be tested.

Maxim starting doing the chain the following morning, right after breakfast. He went to the grove he'd come to love at the far side of town. Good thing he could get there by foot.

The walk turned out well; however, the chain did not come

together – Maxim had a very real feeling that he'd made a mistake somewhere. At first the chain worked pretty good, then it disappeared somewhere, he had to look for the events. No wonder that the chain didn't produce any results.

He had to do it all over the next morning. This time the chain passed pretty smoothly, yet Maxim didn't feel the inner dialogue stop. He was going back to the searcher residence with a feeling of disappointment, thinking that he should assemble his own chain, or ask Boris for advice – maybe he could give him a hint.

Boris was not at home, he and Roman had gone on business in the early morning. Just to be sure, Maxim checked the chain he'd been using – what if there were mistakes or typos? He pored over the chain for almost forty minutes, yet he didn't find any errors. The chain was put together correctly, and it went okay this time, but for some reason it didn't bring any results.

Two hours passed this way. Maxim was drawing objects on the dream map, when he suddenly felt something changing in his consciousness. Something was not the way it used to be, but what it was exactly, Maxim couldn't make out just yet. He carefully looked around, trying to get a feel of what was going on inside of him. Maxim noticed a soft ringing in his ears and a strange sluggish feeling. Was he just imagining? Maxim returned to the map. He worked for about twenty minutes, then put it aside and looked around with interest.

Something did actually change, Maxim was now certain of that. There was still the soft ringing in his ears, his head was strangely heavy. Whatever was happening to him could only have been the consequence of the chain he had carried out earlier. Having realized that, Maxim started studying the peculiarities of the new state he was in.

About an hour later it reached its peak. The inner dialogue did not stop; Maxim was still able to think. But to not think turned out to be much more enjoyable – his thoughts froze automatically. There was a strange sensation of being – being here and now – in the present moment. He even perceived his body differently – it seemed to Maxim that he was looking out from inside of himself. The dream map and the dream journal were put aside long ago, the desire to write and sketch was gone. On the whole, his perception was very reminiscent of dream perception, with the only exception that nothing stopped him from examining the surroundings. His gaze picked out one or another detail and focused on it. Maxim noted with delight that he could look at the chosen object without a single thought in his head. His attention was now focused into a beam; it was no longer jumping around all over the place like a horde of monkeys. But the nicest thing Maxim thought to be the sensation of power, the strange stoutness, fullness – it was hard to find the right word. This was the power that distinguished all of the searchers, and now for the first time Maxim had experienced it himself.

To Maxim's surprise, the new state had no intention of going away. When about five o'clock in the evening he heard voiced coming from the first floor, Maxim exited his room and went downstairs. He wanted to talk to someone about his new state – at the same time, something was holding him back. He even thought it was a little funny – a part of Maxim was telling him that he had to immediately make sense of it all, write it down – systematize. And the other part – the part that made him feel the power – was telling him that it couldn't give a damn about all of this fuss. And that part prevailed.

In the hall, Maxim met Boris and Oxana, they were discussing something. What it is they were discussing, Maxim didn't care.

"Hi, Boris," he greeted his friend.

"Hi," Boris answered. His gaze quickly and thoroughly examined Maxim; a smile appeared on his lips. "Oh, I see you are making progress," Boris said, his eyes glistened. "Take a look at him, Oxana."

"Yeah, so what?" Oxana didn't get it.

"His assemblage point has shifted," Boris explained.

"Apparently, it's the PM chain working?"

"Yes," Maxim confirmed. "I carried it out this morning. I thought it didn't work."

"It is working, and very well, I might add. The powers are favoring you. Try to maintain this state as long as possible."

"I'll try. Actually, it's quite amusing; I'm wandering around like a sleepwalker. Or like I've had too much to drink."

"Shifting the assemblage point always brings about changes in perception," Boris explained. "Note all the peculiarities of this state, the whole spectrum of sensations, it'll come in handy."

"That's what I am doing," Maxim nodded.

"And I still can't manage," Oxana complained. "Even though I've tried several times."

"Each of us has things that he or she is better or worse at," Boris answered. "Maxim has a very good connection with the Spirit. It's a rare thing these days. The Spirit opens up to him easily. By the way, try meditating now." Boris again glanced at Maxim. "You have a chance of not just stopping the ID, but the world."

"I thought it was the same thing," Maxim remarked.

"Not quite." Boris shook his head. "Stopping the world is a qualitatively new level; the world around you acquires new traits. What has changed for you now is the quality of your perception of the world, but not the world itself. There's still time until supper, do some meditating. It's kind of an advice." Boris smiled.

"Okay," Maxim agreed. "I'll give it a go."

"Good luck!" Boris instructed him. "And don't get scared if you see something out of the ordinary."

The whole remaining hour Maxim honestly meditated on the dry chestnut; however, he didn't manage to stop the world. At some point he realized that the inner dialogue was gradually resuming. When the arm of the clock on the wall reached seven in the evening, he went back downstairs...

Boris, Roman, Denis, Rada and Oxana were already sitting at

the table; Galina was there as well, bustling about. Apparently, Boris and Oxana had already told everyone about Maxim's achievements, so they met him with laughter and applause.

"You're almost back to normal," Boris said. "Take a seat."

"Yeah, it's almost gone now," Maxim agreed. "It was interesting, but I expected something more spectacular." He smiled with an apologetic look on his face.

Rada answered instead of Boris. "You've only made the first step," she started quietly as usual. "Right now your assemblage point is still very rigid, so it quickly gets back into place. Give yourself some rest then try again. I assure you, the effect will be much more lasting."

"I'll try," Maxim agreed. "I liked it."

At about eleven o'clock he came into Rada's room; earlier that evening he'd asked her to tell him about the DNA of the Tonal.

"Sit down," Rada offered, Maxim took a seat. "So, let's talk about the DNA of the Tonal. You probably know that DNA, or deoxyribonucleic acid, holds genetic information about the structure of living organisms. For a protein to synthesize in a cell, information about the protein is first rewritten from DNA to RNA, and then from RNA, ribosomes make protein during the translation process. Consequently, the initial information about the making of proteins is within the DNA. In DNA, there is a chain of so-called triplets, or codons, that correspond to each protein. And each triplet codes for one amino acid. The coding mechanism is what's important to us. Each triplet is made out of three nucleotides, and there are only four nucleotides in DNA: adenine, guanine, cytosine and thymine. Four nucleotides in different combinations can potentially make out sixty-four different triplets. Do you get the idea?"

"Yes," Maxim nodded. "I've read up on DNA on purpose. If we were to take three nucleotides out of four and change their places, we could get sixty-four different combinations. Hence, each triplet that we'd get as a result of this could code for something."

"Precisely," Rada agreed. "Searchers got primarily interested in the number sixty-four. There are direct analogies both with I-Ching with its sixty-four hexagrams, and with the chess board and its squares. There was the idea that this number – sixty-four – is not a random number, that it reflects profound mechanisms of the universe. And if in regular DNA we have four nucleotides, then in the table of I-Ching hexagrams there are the same nucleotides – the pair combinations of lines Ying and Yang. There are also four alternatives in the I-Ching: both lines Yang, both lines Ying, upper line Yang, bottom line Ying, and the other way around, upper one Ying, bottom one Yang. The combination of three out of these four 'nucleotides' yields one or the other hexagram. The analogy with the actual DNA is just striking. And if DNA codes for the structure of living organisms, then the Tonal too could be coded for by a similar principle. Do you get the picture?"

"Well, actually not quite," Maxim admitted. "It's pretty clear with the regular DNA; triplets code amino acids and those, in turn, make protein. But what is being coded in the Tonal?"

"The spheres of perception," Rada replied. "The order of alteration of situations. Situations are arranged in chains, like proteins, where each amino acid is a sphere of perception. Recall the algorithm: "I slipped, fell down, a closed fracture. I was knocked out; I came to – a plaster cast". That's humor, but it describes precisely the main principle behind the building of chains. Events of one type pull others along and, in so doing, the chains are not just intertwined randomly, but they correspond to the DNA chains of the Tonal. That is, there are certain templates, algorithms, which determine the course of events. Searchers found out how this mechanism works. So now they've got the ability to, in some sense, control the course of events. A searcher simply knows how a particular situation could develop, so he can control it, making it follow the course that he wants it to follow. He knows how the spheres of perception are connected, and he acts like a pointsman, moving the arrow. Thus, a seemingly insignificant effort directs the situations along the needed course – that's how moving the arrow directs the train along a different track. And the important thing is that each sphere of perception is connected to several others next to it. Usually there are four of them. One of these spheres is the previous situation – the sphere that we've come out of to enter the one we are in at the moment. The other three spheres are the three different ways in which the situation might develop. And that is the number of ways in which a situation usually can develop. For example, a person could be healthy, sick or dead; hungry, full or stuffed; and so on."

"I disagree," Maxim objected. "There are plenty of situations that you could call binary – dual. For example, you've caught the train or you've missed the train; it's either one thing or the other, there is no third alternative."

"Really?" Rada smiled. "There's always a third option. For example, to refrain from going all together."

Maxim also smiled then he started laughing. Not even once has he been able to defeat Rada in an argument.

"I accept your argument," he agreed. "I'm listening, what's next?"

"Next, it all depends on which option we choose," Rada answered. "And one of these three options is a priority option, another – less likely, and the last, third one – the most complicated one. A simple example: you fell off a high cliff; three options: first one – you fall to pieces; second – you'll survive, but you'll get injured; and the third one – you'll survive the fall unharmed."

"But how can you choose an option when you are flying off a cliff?" Maxim snorted.

"And here's where the magic starts," Rada smiled. "Of course, in a situation like that it is very difficult to do anything at all. And to choose the third option is only possible with the power of your intention – there's simply no time left for anything else. You have the intention to survive; it probably wouldn't help an ordinary person. But a magician could get the situation onto the needed course by simply using his intention. And it will turn out that there's a haycock or a lake, or a tree that will cushion your fall. That is, all things will conspire for you to stay alive."

"But a tree can't just grow up, while the magician is falling down?" Maxim objected.

"It can't," Rada agreed. "But you forget about the fact that, in this case, we're dealing with intention. And intention – attention! – is of timeless nature. Hence, your present intention could lead to a seed sprouting beneath that cliff some hundred years ago. And at the moment of your fall, there was already a large tree growing and you landed on the branches of that tree. Do you see? The event that's a hundred years old was determined by your present intention."

"But is it actually possible?" Maxim couldn't believe it.

"Quite so." Rada mysteriously smiled, then added in confidence: "Being with Iris has a bad influence on me. I am slowly adopting her ways. Tell me, where's your switchblade?"

"In my pocket." Maxim went into his pocket and realized that the knife wasn't there. "I've probably taken it out."

"You didn't take it out, you lost it," Rada corrected Maxim. "There's a hole in your pocket." "Damn it!" Maxim felt his pocket and indeed found a hole in the lining. "Maybe I did lose it."

"You did," Rada agreed with a smile. "And why? Because I, in the best traditions of our faithful Iris, have just demonstrated to you the power of intention. I remembered that you bring that knife with you everywhere, and then it all happened on its own." Rada lifted her hands in dismay. "So, you'll have to forgive me."

"But how can that be?" Maxim desperately tried to make sense of what just happened.

"My intention simply made you lose your knife. That's all there is to it. This is an illustrative example of intention acting outside of time. Some day you'll figure all of this out."

"Fine," Maxim sighed. "Let's get back to the DNA of the Tonal."

"Let's," Rada agreed. "Let's now examine another important point – how the spheres of perception are connected between each other. Regular DNA is in the shape of a helix, this helix is also twisted in a rather sophisticated way. The nucleotides are connected in pairs: adenine with thymine, guanine with cytosine. This way, and no other. The elements of each pair fit each other like a key fits a lock. It turned out that the spheres of perception are also connected in a similar fashion; so the Tonal DNA has a rather complex configuration. When going from one situation to another, we are traveling along the DNA of the Tonal – that is, we are moving from one sphere of perception to another. Usually, it's a linear movement, along the chain, from one sphere to another. And we, say, have to go from the first sphere to the tenth, we have to visit all intermediate spheres in line. It's like school: first grade, second grade and so on. Yet some gifted students manage to skip a class, or even two. Searchers do the same thing: having figured out the system of Tonal DNA, they can take a shortcut to the right sphere of perception. In other words, they can change the situation any way they want, and achieve their goals. Usually, people put a lot of effort into achieving something – they are practically feeling their way to their goal. Searchers achieve things much easier – only because they know how the universe works."

"That's interesting," Maxim agreed. "But how do you actually go from one sphere to another in practice?"

"Think about it," Rada suggested. "You've got all the keys in your hands; you'll find the DNA template of the Tonal in our archive. Just think about what we've discussed, and try to apply the model of the Tonal DNA to the world around you. Don't view events as separate; instead, try to see them as connected to other events – like chains. Think carefully about all of this, and you'll see how quickly you'll start acquiring an understanding of this topic. You'll notice how closely it's linked to the other topics, such as, for example, the PM or dream mapping. After all, dreams are spheres of perception, and they obey the same patterns of relationship, i.e. they come together in chains. In dreams you can find the transits, leading from one sphere of perception into another. With time, you will be able to find transits like this IRL as well. It's a very interesting topic."

"I believe you," Maxim agreed. "Thank you, Rada. If I have any questions, I'll come back – okay?"

"Okay," Rada agreed. "You're welcome."

That night Maxim expected to have a lucid dream, but it didn't happen – he couldn't even remember his regular dreams. But the following night he was in for a surprise.

It all started with an ordinary dream. Maxim was walking around on a steep bank, trying to find a way down. At some point he suddenly realized that he could fly. He was just about to push away from the edge of the steep and glide down, when he suddenly felt somebody take him by the arm. He turned around and saw Boris. A moment later, his consciousness prevailed.

"It's me," Boris said, his eyes were gleaming. "I remember I promised to show you the Glade. Let's go." Boris winked at Maxim and pulled him along.

The river bank got immediately hazy and disappeared. It was replaced with a flower-covered forest glade about thirty meters in diameter and surrounded by a thick wall of shrubbery and woods. A tall branchy cedar tree was growing on the very edge of the glade; a little closer to the center, Maxim saw four scroll benches. The benches made out a straight square, their edges did not touch, creating passages about one meter wide. Rada and Oxana were sitting on one bench; opposite them was Iris, and a young man about twenty-five years old that Maxim didn't know; they were talking. Having noticed Maxim and Boris, Oxana waved her hand bidding them welcome.

"That's our Glade," Boris said. "Our little island in the Nagual. You'll need to learn how to get here on your own. Go up to the benches and take a seat."

Maxim got up closer, looking at the girls and the guy with interest.

"Hi," he said. He got up to the guy and stretched out his hand. "I'm Maxim."

"I've heard a lot about you," the guy answered with a smile and shook Maxim's hand; Maxim thought he had a very pleasant smile. "I'm Danila. Take a seat."

Maxim sat down on the available bench; Boris seated himself next to him.

"Well, how do you like it here?" Rada looked at him and asked.

"Not bad," Maxim nodded. "It's a very cozy place. By the way, what are these benches made of?" he inquired, running his hand along the smooth surface of the bench. "Plastic?"

"Ivory," Rada explained. "To be more specific, it looks like they are made out of ivory, but in reality…" she smiled.

"Got it," Maxim said. "Another illusion?"

"Not quite." Rada shook her head. "This glade is by far more real than it may appear to be at first. Besides, it has a real prototype – an actual forest glade. We memorized its appearance and reproduced it here."

"Can you really reproduce each flower?" Maxim bowed down and ran his hand on the grass. "Can I pick?" He touched a rich chamomile bush, growing by the bench leg. "One flower?"

"Go ahead," Rada agreed; in her gaze Maxim sensed a little bit of mockery and leniency. "As for the way the glade looks, each of us contributes, in his own way, to the place. You are now also part of this process; your knowledge of biology helps detail the glade even more."

"The cosmography charts?" Maxim guessed.

"The very same. Your consciousness completes the glade, providing it with realistic traits, until the right level of truth has been reached."

"I got it," Maxim nodded. "Do you meet up here at some specific time?"

"Both yes and no," Rada smiled. "Usually, we meet here at midnight. But if you go to sleep at ten o'clock in the evening or even at two am, you still won't miss us. Just have the intention to get to the Glade at midnight and meet us there, that'll be more than enough."

Maxim frowned – it didn't make sense.

"How can that be?" he asked. "If I go to sleep at two am, the meeting would have already passed?"

"Maxim, the thing is that there is no time in this place." Danila entered the conversation. "Rather, it has nothing to do with our real world time. It's difficult to grasp, but there are usually no problems when it comes down to it. You can even go to sleep in the morning and you would still meet us at midnight."

"But what about the cause-effect links?" Maxim looked closely at Danila. "What if I find out something that happened in the morning, then I go to the Glade and tell you about it? Then you could wake up and somehow use the information about what has yet not happened."

"It won't work." Danila shook his head with a smile. "This glade is in the Nagual time. And the Nagual keeps everything weighted. If you try to tell us something this way, you simply won't find us, or something will stop you from getting to the Glade."

"Fine, but what if I let the cat out of the bag by accident, no foul play?"

"You won't be able to let the cat out," Danila replied. "The problem is that you are trying to operate with a linear flow of time, when it cannot be applied here, and on some level of the hierarchy it's already known that you won't be able to blab out anything like that. Do you think Boris and Rada wouldn't have warned us about the flop, if there was an opportunity to do so?

But you cannot do that: the laws of cause-effect links remain inviolable. On the other hand, the ban on linear flow of time is lifted here, and we can use that, meeting up at the Glade at the appointed time."

"It's that situation, when something is difficult to understand, but you can use it nonetheless," Boris put in. "In magic, that happens pretty often."

"Okay, but you always meet at different times? That is, the moment of meeting still moves from one day to another? Let's say there are six of us here today, tomorrow there might be four or eight. Someone comes, someone goes. So, it's still not the same moment?"

"So it isn't," Danila said; everyone laughed.

"You'd make an excellent theorist," Iris, who had been silent all of this time, said with a grin. Her piercing gaze made Maxim shudder. "You're worried about petty things, which a normal magician doesn't give a damn about."

"Yes, but man always strives towards understanding. Is that a bad thing?"

"Understanding can be different." Iris didn't agree. "Take, for instance, Castaneda; there are several rather complicated things in his descriptions, but this complexity never exceeds the threshold of reasonable sufficiency. Theory, in his books, walks hand in hand with practice, helping it out. We stick to the same approach. On the other hand, so many false naguals have bred lately. These little people don't really know how to do anything, yet they take on the responsibility to teach others. They churn out books; some of them even conduct paid seminars – forgetting that knowledge cannot be transferred for money. It just makes me sick looking at these people."

"I saw one of them the other day," Boris added. "In a dream – bald, fat guy, with the consciousness of an amoeba. But if you'd read his books, he's such a cool magician."

"The problem is not even that they are writing books," Iris

continued, "but that many of them create their own egregors. Such a person could be a worthless magician, yet if he creates his own egregor it will provide him with a real chance of maintaining his consciousness after death. All similar egregors are built according to one principle: a false nagual is in charge of everything, he's the king and god of that place. A couple of his closest assistants are helping him and all average members of the egregor have the role of milk cows. As a result, we get deception in an attractive package. It's a shame that a lot of people don't realize that."

"Don't searchers have their own egregor?" Maxim inquired. "After all, a great many people have become interested in your ideas."

"The question is not whether an egregor exists or not," Iris answered, "but rather what it is like. The DS egregor represents a network structure, we don't have and we cannot have a sole leader. Someone is more experienced, someone is less, someone has got more power, and someone has less; but that's not ground for glorifying some of us and depreciating others; in this sense we are all absolutely equal. And if in egregors with false naguals, everyone follows the example of their guru, all new ideas and instructions originate only from him, the network egregor favors the individual development of all its members. We consider personal research not only a right, but an obligation. You study the experience that has been gained before you, and you move on, so that someone else could study your research experience later."

"I think we started with theory," Oxana reminded. "Actually, I don't see anything bad about theory either. In my opinion, the more thorough the explanation the better – isn't that true?"

"Let Rada answer that," Iris waved away. "And, you know, I must be going, I still have an errand to run – I've promised to pinch a few feathers off a wise guy. Be seeing you!" Iris gave a charming smile, got up from the bench and disappeared.

"I don't envy the wise guy," Rada said, again chuckles were

heard. Rada was silent for a while, then continued. "As for theory, it's not all that simple. On the one hand, we need theory to have some kind of reference points. On the other hand, by logically trying to explain the world of magic, we are only extending our inventory list. If we take into account that magicians are doing everything in their power to go beyond the description of the real world, then extending the inventory list seems very harmful. Instead of collapsing this world, we continue to impose structure on it. Thus, we must observe a delicate balance. On the one hand, we need theory; we cannot do without some kind of a description of the world. On the other hand, a magician is always aware of the fact that all his knowledge is, in reality, not worth a thing. To believe without believing, to accept without accepting – a magician pays as much attention to theory as it is needed, and not more than that."

"The inventory list and the cosmography charts – is it the same thing?" Maxim inquired.

"In some sense," Rada agreed. "I'd say that the inventory list makes out a part of cosmography charts. It's all that rubbish that we accumulate in our consciousness. As for cosmography charts, they touch on a deeper level." Rada became thoughtful for a second. "Let's take, for example, the computer; there is data in it, and there's the operating system. In this case, data is the inventory list. And the operating system – the cosmography charts, responsible for the actual functioning of the system – for its parameters. And when I talk about entering new records into the cosmography charts, I mean acquiring real skills of some kind; in other words, changing the settings of the operating system. So, it's one thing to enter in the inventory list the knowledge that man can move through portals, and it's a completely different thing to enter a record into the cosmography charts, which allows us to do so in practice."

"It's like with a TV and a child," Boris put in. "The TV is kind of there, but Mom and Dad don't allow the child to turn it on –

only sometimes, and only to watch cartoons. He'll get a little older and he'll be allowed to turn on the TV on his own, yet watching whatever he wants – like erotica – is still not allowed. Finally, our toddler will grow up and become an adult; that's when he'll be able to watch whatever he likes. The same with the cosmography charts: first, either no miracles, or they happen only sometimes, then more and more often until the man becomes a magician."

"Just don't forget that excess rationality is very harmful, and any theory is but a way of getting our attention," Rada continued. "The truth, in this case, is like a foundation stone: even if we can reach it, everything left for us after that is a pile of ruins that no one cares about. So, being essentially pragmatic creatures, magicians give theory just enough attention as to benefit from it, and not more than that."

"Basically, fear the Greeks bearing gifts," Boris put in again. "I'm talking about those who try to litter your brain with empty philosophizing. Send these 'authorities' directly to the garden, and everything will be ok. If, all of a sudden, you'll get fed up with our teachings, you may even send us someplace hot."

"I think, he's had enough," Danila said, closely looking at Maxim. "Otherwise, he'll get completely phased out of his mind."

"End of supper – back to your cells," Boris agreed with a smirk. "The picnic is over, everyone is free to go."

In the morning Maxim didn't remember that he'd been at the Glade. He once again stated with disappointment that he didn't remember any of his dreams, and that really annoyed him. He got out of bed, got dressed and went to the bathroom.

He was washing his face, when the first unclear image flashed in his consciousness. Maxim froze with the toothbrush in his mouth, trying not to miss or scare away the vision. He grabbed on to the thin memory string, and that proved enough to gradually, out of nowhere, pull out the whole picture...

Once Maxim realized that he had been at the Glade and not alone at that, he turned absolutely euphoric. He didn't yet recall all of the details of their night talk, but fragments of the conversation started surfacing in his consciousness in blocks – theory, egregors, cosmography charts... While wiping himself with a towel, Maxim thought that he definitely had to write all of this down...

His story about the meeting at the Glade was received with satisfaction.

"You are doing well," Boris said at breakfast. "Carry on in the same way and don't think too much about your progress. Take everything for granted, without getting too worked up about it. Otherwise, your progress will fade like smoke."

After breakfast, Maxim went to the grove to carry out the PM chain. This time it was his own chain – he had finally managed to put it together, he was even a bit proud of this achievement. Unfortunately, this time around there was no result; he had to repeat it all over the following day; and again – down the drain. The chain just didn't want to come together. The third attempt didn't bring any luck either. Still, Maxim's stubbornness was rewarded. Having completed the fourth chain on Saturday morning, he returned home and soon, with satisfaction, sensed the first signs of altered consciousness.

Everything was just like the last time, with the only difference that the altered state of consciousness showed no indication of fading. All that day the searchers were making fun of Maxim. Oxana immediately named him sleepwalker. Maxim only smiled in response. During supper, all his attention was wholly absorbed by food. Not only did that make those present at the table laugh, but Maxim was very amused himself. It was extremely interesting observing the way attention worked when the inner dialogue was stopped. It was all here, in one spot. They were eating rice milk porridge for supper. Maxim took a spoonful of the porridge, raised it to his mouth and swallowed. His attention obediently tracked all these actions, without getting distracted by anything else.

After supper, they watched a movie – a comedy starring Jim Carrey. Maxim was sitting on the sofa, feeling the strange unreality of what was going on. All of this reminded him of a dream, and to such extent that at one point Maxim even tried to put his hand through the sofa cushion, trying to find out how real the things around him really were. His hand didn't go through the cushion – that convinced Maxim that he was not sleeping after all.

The movie ended, Maxim went up to his room. He had to do some mapping, but he didn't really want to. He only wanted one thing – silence. Any thoughts at this point caused unpleasant emotions – they worried him, disturbing the calm Maxim was shrouded in. Finally, he sat down by the wall and put a pillow under his back. He threw the dry chestnut on the floor in front of him. It rolled slightly to the side, but Maxim couldn't be bothered getting it back into place.

Maxim spent more than an hour meditating on the chestnut. On several occasions his vision blurred and there was a nauseating feeling, he had to cling to an item with his gaze and intensify his breathing in order to get back to normal. Finally, Maxim got fed up with it all, and went to bed shortly before midnight...

When he woke up the next morning, first of all he assessed his condition. Maxim's thoughts moved pretty slowly, yet the frightening silence that crept over him yesterday was no longer there. Having washed his face with cold water, Maxim felt almost normal.

He sensed that something had happened already during the morning warm-up in the sports hall, but he refrained from asking questions. It wasn't difficult – his consciousness was still covered in the fog of silence. Everything cleared up during breakfast.

"Rada managed to find out something important," Boris said in response to Oxana's question. "I think, she'll tell you all about it herself."

"From the seventeenth of August, Kramer will be on vacation by the Black Sea," Rada said quietly. "I managed to find out where exactly he'll be staying."

"And that means we've got a good chance of getting even with him," Denis added. "We just haven't decided yet how exactly we're going to do it. Roman and I wanted to do it all by ourselves. Boris is against that. He wants to have a knightly duel."

"I'm not against it," Boris didn't agree. "I'm for thoroughly thinking it through. We may not have a second chance."

"And how did you find out about this?" Maxim glanced at Rada.

"In a dream," the young woman replied. "I managed to get to one of Kramer's assistants. And the best thing is that he doesn't even remember anything about our conversation."

"I'd love to go swimming in the sea," Oxana said dreamily. "You're going to take me with you, aren't you?"

"Yes, but who are we going to leave the house with?" Roman, who'd been quiet all of this time, asked. There was laughter. Oxana was the only one who wasn't laughing.

"It's not fair," she said in an injured voice. "Couldn't you take me with you, just once?"

"Oxana, we don't yet know ourselves who will go and where they'll be going," Boris said in a conciliatory tone. "We've still got time to think it all over. And if we're going to need your help, you'll go. If not – then you'll stay here; we don't need foolish risks. As for swimming, we'll go to the sea regardless. I promise you that."

Oxana didn't reply, but by her face Maxim gathered that the young woman was left dissatisfied.

Maxim had never been to the Black Sea before. Now, looking at the water colored golden by the setting sun, he could appreciate its beauty.

He came to Gelendzhik with Boris. Roman and Denis, and had been there five days already; Iris joined them a day later. They rented a small house, covered in vine, a couple of kilometers away from the sea. It was very nice there, for the first time Maxim envied those who lived in this town.

"They're lucky," he said in the evening, when everyone had gathered in the main room by the TV. "They can swim and sunbathe whenever they want. And anyway south is south – I don't like cold."

"Well, I don't think anyone likes cold," Boris agreed. "As for the sea, I assure you that the locals go swimming less often than the visitors. I bet many of them haven't been in the sea for several years."

"People don't treasure what they have," Iris added. "When beauty is close by, it quickly becomes boring."

Soon the conversation turned to more serious matters. Denis laid out, on the table, a blueprint drawn on a large piece of paper, then raised the TV volume, just in case.

"The house is being guarded by approximately ten people," he said, pointing with a pencil at the center of the blueprint. "The house is surrounded by a forged fence a little short of three meters tall. The rods on top are pointed, and there's an alarm system installed as well. All access to the estate is controlled by surveillance cameras and, on top of everything, there are a couple of cute huge dogs walking the grounds."

"Rottweiler dogs," Roman specified. "You don't want to run into those."

"The security room is on the first floor, right here..." Denis touched the blueprint again. "There are always at least two guards patrolling outside, the changing of guards occurs at ten pm, at two am and six am. Then at ten am, and so on. The west, south and east borders of the manor abut on the territories of other estates. Entry into the front yard is from the north, right here. The gates are automatic; additional locks are put on them at night. The garden gate is also locked. There are several surveillance cameras installed in the house, including a couple of night vision cameras. About once an hour, without particular order, the guards inspect the territory. Sometimes there is only one, sometimes there are two of them. The remaining time they like to sit on the bench by the entrance. All windows are iron-barred – the balcony door too. The balcony is right over here, with a sea view. On the whole, it's really not that badly organized."

"Kramer is supposed to arrive today, sometime in the evening," Boris added, then glanced at Iris. "He knows your face, so try not to bump into him."

"If he didn't know me," Iris smiled, "I'd have gotten to him without your help."

"And how about the beach?" Maxim suggested. "Since he's coming to the sea, he's definitely going to take a swim, at least once."

"Maxim, the important thing is not only to get Kramer, but to get away once it's done," Denis explained. "Don't forget that Kramer will bring his personal guards, and these are very experienced people. I bet Kramer is going to sunbathe on some private, closed beach, and a couple of divers will accompany him into the sea. On the other hand, he'll feel safe at the guarded villa. That's where we are going to try to get to him."

"All right, but can't you just appear in his room?" Maxim inquired. "All we need is a couple of seconds."

Denis glanced up at Boris, giving him the right to answer the question.

"It's not that simple," Boris said. "First, you forget that Kramer is also a magician. Being in his room, he is de-facto its master. I'm not talking about trivial owning of the place, but about space control. Simply put, Kramer's attention won't allow me to open a portal – we'll discuss this some other time. Second, I don't have any links to this villa, it's unfamiliar to me – so I cannot appear there using this technique. Third, I can't get there by the means of a dream either; you forgot about the guardians – these creatures won't let me access the villa on the ethereal level. So, we'll just have to make our way into the place."

"The best way of getting in is here, from the grounds of the neighboring estate." Denis touched the map with the pencil. "There's an elderly couple living there, at eleven o'clock they are already snoozing. They have a dog, but it's chained and sits on the other side of the house. If we cut through the railing, we could very well make it to the other side. Then we'd have to pass the pool. Here we'll have to crawl and hide behind the bushes – that territory is under video surveillance. We can get up by the bench and proceed along the wall to the balcony. After that it's all child's play."

"And the dogs?" Maxim inquired.

"They'll eat you or me," Denis replied. "But Boris will have no problems."

"I've made a deal with the dogs," Boris explained. "I don't touch them, they don't touch me."

"And seriously speaking?" Maxim looked searchingly at Boris.

"Seriously speaking, they just won't notice me."

Maxim was already about to ask how that can be, but Iris beat him to it.

"Look," she said, looking at Maxim with a grin on her face. "This is a ring." She removed a ring with a small diamond from her finger. "I put the ring on my palm, squeeze my hand together. I open my hand and... where did the ring go?"

Her palm was empty; although, that didn't surprise Maxim.

"In your other hand," he smiled. "It's an old trick."

"Is that so?" Iris grinned. "Keep watching the palm."

Maxim looked at the palm – it was still empty, and then he twitched – something moved on Iris' palm and a moment later Maxim saw the ring.

"All this time it was on my palm and didn't go anywhere," Iris said, looking at Maxim with an ironic smile. "You just didn't see it. That's how Boris will hide from the dogs – they will only see what they'll be allowed to see."

"You'll tell me later how it's done, okay?" Maxim asked and smiled; everyone laughed.

"Someday I'll tell you," Iris agreed. "If I feel like it."

"The dogs won't stop him," Denis said. "And I'll explain how to open the balcony door."

"And then what? What are you going to do once you're inside?" Maxim asked and regretted it immediately – the question, in his opinion, came out as inappropriate.

"Then Kramer and I will have a serious talk," Boris answered quietly. "Then we'll see who's made of what."

A moth was softly beating against the lone illuminated window. This quiet intermittent knocking distracted from work, so the man sitting by the desk got up and lifted down the thick heavy curtain. Then he took out a cigarette, leisurely lighted up and went out on the balcony.

The moon was breaking through the veil of clouds; the gentle breeze barely moved the tree tops. It was stuffy, even the arrived night didn't bring the awaited coolness. The man leaned on the railing and smoked in silence, occasionally flicking the cigarette ashes. Listening closely to the silence of the night, disturbed only by the soft singing of the crickets, he was thinking about tomorrow. He was thinking that even here he's got a lot of work to do, that upon arrival he'll have to, once again, report back to Dags.

A soft humming was heard below; the glass eye of the TV camera was slowly ransacking the night dusk. Having thrown down the cigarette butt, the man went inside the house and carefully closed the balcony door behind him. He stopped by the table and stood there for a little while, deep in thought – he didn't feel like working. He quickly glanced at the clock on the wall, neatly gathered the papers, then walked over to the wall, folded back the corner of the rug and hid the documents in a small secret safe. He walked over to a large luxurious bed, turned on the wall lamp at the head of the bed and turned off the ceiling light. Having undressed, he dragged his feet to the bathroom. Soon there were sounds of splashing water and pleased snorting coming from the bathroom.

Having washed his face, the man, with pleasure, wiped himself with a soft terry towel then critically examined himself in the mirror. He was quite satisfied with what he saw. So, having scratched his chin, he flicked the switch and returned to the bedroom.

A tacky clay mask was hanging on the wall, next to the bed. Its entire appearance indicated the mask being of venerable age. The man touched the mask, softly ran his palm over it and whispered something – as long as it was with him, he had nothing to fear. Then he got into bed, picked up a book in an expensive cover from the side table and opened on the bookmarked page. He yawned deeply and with pleasure – he wanted to sleep. 'Five minutes,' the man thought, carefully reading the lines. He turned over a page, then another, and started, having heard a soft crackle. He looked up at the mask and turned pale.

Before his very eyes the mask got covered with a net of small cracks. Then a bigger crack ran across the mask; a part of the mask broke off and fell down on the bed. The man shrieked.

It became very quiet. Afraid to move, the man strained his ears, listening to the silence that lay now suspended in the room. Finally, he slowly started getting up, his arm stretched out, trying to reach the alarm button...

He didn't manage to push the button. The air suddenly grew thick and dense, there was ringing in his ears. One of the metallic embellishments on the back of the bed – France, eighteenth century – suddenly moved. Having carefully uncurled, the steel tendril skillfully grappled the man around his throat and pulled him towards the bed rail. The man began to wheeze, trying to break free and call for help, his fingers helplessly scratched the steel that had come to life.

"Are you ready?" a quiet and calm voice sounded just nearby, making the desperately fluttering man freeze.

A stranger in a black uniform was standing next to the bed; his face was concealed by a knitted mask. The steel noose eased slightly, its victim could finally gasp for air. Hoarsely breathing, the man lying in the bed was looking terrified at the visiting killer.

"We don't have a lot of time. I asked you – are you ready?" The man standing in front of him knew full well, what terror his words made the shaking victim feel. Slowly, as if he was in no rush whatsoever, the killer pulled the mask off his face. The man in the bed twitched.

"Sly..." The voice of the half-strangled man was weak and hoarse. "It's you... Please, let me go... I'll do anything you want... Don't kill me..."

The murderer folded his arms over his chest, his glance became harder. The bed railing put out another long steel tendril; it smoothly curved and froze before the face of the man that had now grown grey with terror. The tip of the tendril stretched out and turned into a sharp spike.

"Let you go? And what can you offer us?"

"I can offer you everything... Everything... In the safe under the rug... all the papers... There are a lot of valuable things in there... about the Legion... and about you... Take it all... Contact details, names... You'll be pleased... Have mercy..." The man's voice was quavering, his gaze glued to the steel tendril that was rocking before his eyes.

"I'll have to think about that. The code?" The killer's gaze softened, the steel tendril pulled away from the victim's face.

"Thirty two... thirty three... thirty five..."

"Fine, I believe you. But there's one more problem."

"What problem?"

"Dana," the killer said, and the woman's name that escaped his lips made the man scream. The steel tendril around his throat immediately tightened, so the constrained sounds wouldn't reach the ears of the guards on the first floor of the estate. "So, what about Dana?"

"It's not me... it's... Yana, she's the responsible one..." Tears appeared in the eyes of the man, now in despair. He realized, with horror, that this was it – this was the end. There'd be no mercy for him. It shouldn't be this way, it was all horribly wrong...

"But you sent Yana." There were metallic overtones in the killer's voice.

"I... But I was ordered too... Dags ordered me..."

"And now you are lying. Information about the courier reached you only, and you were the one to make the decision. Wanted to gain favor with Dags, deadbeat?"

"Don't... Forgive me... We didn't know Dana would be there... I'll be of use to you, you need me... I know a great many things..."

"I don't need your knowledge; I've come for your life – just your life." The killer pronounced the last words slowly and clearly, giving his victim the opportunity to properly realize the fatal inevitability of what was about to happen. "Your time is up. Smile farewell." The killer's face became tense again; the steel tendril in front of the victim's face curved predatorily.

Blinded with horror the man started twitching desperately. The steel sprout slightly recoiled, then swayed, choosing its target, and with a crunch pierced the man's forehead. The victim's body twitched, curved, then relaxed and went limp. With their mission complete, the steel whips slowly assumed their original position on the bed railing.

The man in the bed was dead. Having made sure of that, the killer slowly walked over to the hidden safe, entered the code and raked out all the papers into the ready black bag, leaving the tight bundles of bank-notes lying on the top shelf untouched. Having scanned everything, he put the mask back on, then walked up to the balcony door, opened it and silently slipped outside. He waited until the slow eye of the TV camera would crawl aside then climbed across the railings and disappeared into the stuffy night air. The crickets were singing all the same, the moon was gleaming of pale yellow, and nothing reminded of the man that had vanished into darkness...

[1] Mayakovsky, V. (1893 – 1930) *Listen!* - a poem
[2] Federal Security Service of Russian Federation i.e. the Secret Service

[3] Svetlomorsk – light sea town (direct translation).
[4] Gus'-gorod – the town of the goose
[5] 1968 Soviet animated film, based on the novel by Astrid Lindgren *Karlsson on the Roof* (tran.)
[6] A very famous quote from a Soviet cult classic movie "The Diamond Arm"

BOOKS

O is a symbol of the world, of oneness and unity. In different cultures it also means the "eye," symbolizing knowledge and insight. We aim to publish books that are accessible, constructive and that challenge accepted opinion, both that of academia and the "moral majority."

Our books are available in all good English language bookstores worldwide. If you don't see the book on the shelves ask the bookstore to order it for you, quoting the ISBN number and title. Alternatively you can order online (all major online retail sites carry our titles) or contact the distributor in the relevant country, listed on the copyright page.

See our website **www.o-books.net** for a full list of over 500 titles, growing by 100 a year.

And tune in to myspiritradio.com for our book review radio show, hosted by June-Elleni Laine, where you can listen to the authors discussing their books.

MySpiritRadio